A Particular Friendship

The Queer Testament Book 4

A Particular Friendship

The Queer Testament Book 4

by
Paul Van Der Spiegel

Perceptions Press

an imprint of
Castle Carrington Publishing
Victoria, BC
Canada

2021

A Particular Friendship
The Queer Testament Book 4

First published in paperback in 2021

Cover Design: © Paul Van Der Spiegel 2021

ISBN: 978-1-990096-53-2 (paperback)
ISBN: 978-1-990096-54-9 (Kindle electronic book)
ISBN: 978-1-990096-55-6 (Smashwords electronic book)

Published in Canada by
Perceptions Press
www.perceptionspress.ca

Perceptions Press

an imprint of
Castle Carrington Publishing
www.castlecarringtonpublishing.ca
Victoria, BC
Canada

Dedication

This book is dedicated to the memory of Bob Summerbell, born October 16th, 1960, who died aged twenty-nine years old.

Bob trained in psychology at the University of British Columbia. In his spare time, he volunteered on telephone helplines supporting the distressed and despairing. Bob became president of the campus LGBT society a few years after his brother, Richard, and then served a term as the student representative on the University Senate.

After graduation, Bob got a job touring the area for the provincially owned automobile insurance company, advocating auto-safety to high school students. As part of his role, he organised events like 'Battle of the Bands' to raise the profile of wearing seatbelts and to highlight the dangers of drinking and driving.

This, and many other instances of Bob inspiring people, came out at his funeral, and it was enough to make one gay friend stand up and protest, 'He wasn't a saint' to make the point that Bob, like any man, could fuck and be fucked. But the throng of people who said that Bob had talked to them at a critical moment and got them back to self-respect was too strong to be resisted.

You never know how many good things someone has done in secret, until their funeral.

Bob Summerbell's name is written on the AIDS Memorial in Vancouver, so that he, and how he died, is not a secret.

Contents

Part One

Angel

Shivering beneath his embroidered vestments, Father Thomas spoke the opening words of the Penitential Rite:

> I confess to Almighty God, and to you, my brothers and sisters, that I have sinned through my own fault, through my thoughts, through my words, through what I've done, through what I've left undone.

The priest struck his chest in supplication, watching as his breath condensed, hearing his voice amidst the murmur of the congregation, words distorted and mechanised by a pre-historic induction loop system, an analogue susurrate seeping from the shadowed corners of the stone-built church.

As the parishioners of St. James' Church, Bussell, emptied their souls of sin and opened their hearts to the grace of God, Tom stole a glance at the former lover sitting in the middle aisle, the man who had been, the man who always would be, the love of his life. Between them, the pillar candle on fire, the illuminated manuscript laid open on the altar, the ecclesiastical mundane eroticised for a moment in time.

The drone of the scattered congregation was swallowed by the domed vault of the Jesuit-built building. Then, silence filled the void, with occasional traffic noise from Greengate puncturing the presence of the Eternal.

Antony was dressed in a long, woollen overcoat, a scarf around his neck. The stubble beard suited him, making him look dignified, more handsome than ever.

The Gospel reading was from Matthew, with Christ being challenged by dogmatists to explain the spousal relationship of a woman who had married seven short-lived brothers.

"Whose wife will she be in heaven?" the Learned had demanded.

'*In the resurrection they neither marry, nor are given in marriage, but are as angels in heaven,*' northern, working-class Jesus had responded, blindsiding his elitist, big-city opponents.

In Jesus' inclusive, diverse, non-binary heaven, Tom could see validation for people like himself, priests who had subordinated their sexuality to the glory of God, gay men and women who had pledged themselves to celibacy to serve God and their fellow human-beings, same-sex attracted followers of Christ, who worked for an earthly organisation that condemned their hearts as sinful, that defined their lovemaking as 'intrinsically disordered.'

Not for the first time, Tom wondered how Jesus had remained unmarried, why Paul of Tarsus had urged the unwed to stay single?

'Lord I am not worthy to receive you,' he said, after the Fraction of the Bread, 'but only say the word and I shall be healed.'

True Faith, Tom reminded himself, was not a leap into an unreasoned certainty; it was a step into a reasoned uncertainty. True Faith was not the assertion of salvation for 'big B' Believers and surety of damnation for everyone else. Instead, it was trust in the timeless source of love, despite being unlovable. It was trust in a ubiquitous force of forgiveness, despite being unforgiveable. True Faith was the courage to face God by those scarred, scourged, stymied by life.

People queued, hands cupped, to receive the blessed body of our Lord. Some knelt at the altar rail, heads bowed, to receive the priest's blessing. Others knelt, hands by their sides, to receive the communion wafer on their tongue.

'The Body of Christ.'

Antony accepted the communion wafer on his tongue.

'Amen,' he said.

After the blessing and final hymn, after another profuse apology for a broken central heating boiler, Tom hurried to the Sacristy with altar-girl, Sophie, holding the Crux Simplex before them.

After she had tidied the altar and brought in the chalice for cleaning, Sophie Arundel waved her goodbye as she pulled her coat around her.

'See you, Father,' she said, disappearing through the doorway and into the belly of Saint James'.

Tom waved, then laid his chasuble and Alb inside the sacristy Credens, the vision of placing a communion wafer on Antony's tongue awakening feelings that had been buried beneath decades of decades of the rosary. The soft knock on the wooden door froze the breath in his chest.

'Father Morton, may I come in?'

'Of course,' Tom said, striding over, reaching out, drawing Antony into a bear hug, exuberance masking his anxiety. 'Good Lord, it's been...'

'Twenty-five years,' Antony said, smiling, holding Tom's hands, 'and you haven't changed a bit.'

Tom laughed out loud.

'I'd like to believe you,' he said, searching for the wedding band on Antony's ring finger. 'You look well. How long are you home for? How's that husband of yours?'

'I'm back to look after my mum.'

'I always think of your mum fondly. She was a second mother to us, back in the day. How is she?'

'She sends her love, Tom. She's…'

Tom was transported back to a tangle of limbs inside a duvet on top of a mattress thrown from its divan, and the embarrassing moment Antony's mum had brought breakfast into her son's bedroom.

'terminally ill.'

'I am *so* sorry,' Tom said, snapping out of his reverie, reaching out for Antony's arm. 'Is there anything I can do?'

'Tell your boss to pull his finger out,' Antony said, pointing to the ceiling.

'Ah, unfortunately that's not how it works.'

'How exactly does it work? I'm all ears, Tom.'

Embarrassed, Tom could say nothing.

'I'm not much of a fan of religion. It has cost me dearly… cost the world dearly.'

'I'm sorry I…'

'If you were to administer the Sacrament of the Sick to my mother, it would mean the world to her.'

Tom caught his breath.

'Yes,' he said, 'of course. Does your mother not have her own parish priest? It must be Father Mulhern if she still lives…'

'If this is too much trouble for you…'

'It isn't too much trouble. When would you like me to come, Antony?'

'Whenever you can—the sooner, the better.'

'Tomorrow midday?'

'Thank you,' Antony said, passing a slip of paper over. 'This is the address. I appreciate you helping us.'

'The same house,' Tom muttered, unbelieving, as he unfolded the note.

For a moment, neither man said anything.

Tom's eyes welled up. He could not help himself, and he wiped his sleeve across his face.

'Sorry,' he said, 'I'm just a little bit overcome, seeing you, again, and such sad, sad news.'

''It is really good to see you,' Antony said. He kissed Tom on the cheek.

'Father Morton,' the voice called from the rectory doorway, 'your supper is ready.'

'Joan!' Tom said, startled. 'This is Antony, Antony Keane, an old and very dear friend of mine. Antony, Joan looks after me during the week. I am the best-fed priest in Lancashire, as I'm sure you can tell by my waistline!'

'I'm pleased to meet you,' Antony said.

'Likewise,' Joan said, unsmiling.

'Midday tomorrow, then, Father Morton.'

'Midday, it is,' Tom said.

After locking and bolting the front entrance of the church, switching all the electric lights off, checking that no candles had been left burning, and re-setting the burglar alarm, Tom turned the long key in the sacristy door that he imagined served as an airlock between the expanse of the spaceship church and the safety of the command module rectory. His in-flight dinner sat waiting for him on the kitchen table—a portion of thick-crusted, carbonised meat pie with shrivelled garden peas.

Tom sighed and dug into his meal with his knife and fork.

'Your friend seems nice,' Joan said, entering the room and fastening her coat, 'a little bit light on his feet though, if you know what I mean.'

'No,' Tom said, chewing, 'I've no idea what you mean.'

'Put your plates in the dishwasher, Father, and I'll see you tomorrow. There's seconds by the oven if you're still hungry.'

'Thanks, Joan,' Tom said, trying not to choke.

The glass front door of the rectory shook on its hinges as Joan made her exit.

The incinerated pie was barely edible. Joan was bound to find it if he put it in the bin. The idea of digging a hole for unwanted food in the graveyard was quickly dismissed.

This town has eyes and ears in every wall, Tom reminded himself.

If he walked to the council bin outside Home Bargains and discarded his wretched dinner there, he knew, somehow, that he would get found out. Offering Joan Bird various housekeeping duties had seemed like a charitable thing to do, given her family's perilous financial position. The money Tom paid her mattered, he knew that. But, by God, she was no Nigella Lawson. Her seamstress skills, on the other hand, had come in very handy.

Light on his feet. What the hell did that mean?

Then, it dawned on him what Joan had been suggesting, and Tom felt stupid, angry, and a little bit scared.

He thought of Lillian, Antony's dying mother, as he picked at the food.

The plan came together. Tom slid the remnants of the fat and gristle pie into an orange Sainsbury carrier bag and left it next to his bike and helmet in the back hallway.

Tomorrow morning, the pigeons in Bussell Park are in for a real treat, he thought. *But whether they will be able to fly again is another matter!*

Father Thomas Morton poured himself a generous bowl of Kellogg's Frosties drenched with silver top milk and switched the television on in the lounge to watch *The Simpsons*.

Unable to concentrate, thinking about his day, thinking about Antony, Tom switched the TV off, traipsed upstairs to the bathroom, climbed out of his clothes and surrendered to his gay biology.

2.

Thomas sat by the side of the overturned car. His little brother was nowhere to be seen. His dad was upside down, talking, but his head was smashed, and his moustache was bloody. Thomas couldn't remember if he had been crying, but Daddy was trying to reassure him. Thomas tried to pull his daddy's head through the window when he stopped talking. He tried pulling him by his hair, but Daddy was asleep and wouldn't move.

He was walking down the road forever, a big road like an empty motorway. The girl was with him, and she was his friend and held his hand and helped him.

'Are you okay?' she asked.

3.

Tom pushed his bike up the gravelled driveway. He threaded the nylon-clad lock through the frame and wheels and secured it to a black cast iron drainpipe next to the bay window. The eaves of the red-brick, Victorian, semi-detached house loomed above him.

He remembered the parties in the backyard, the nights when a group of friends drank beer together, smoked weed, and watched the latest movie releases on VHS. He remembered *that* night, the night he had lost his virginity for the second time, the night that had changed his life forever. Then, he saw the old man looking back at him in the glass of the front door.

How has time passed so quickly, he asked himself, *accelerating like an exponential curve from birth towards death, transforming the mop-topped, skinny teenager into this rotund cleric, this impious imposter counting down the months and years to retirement?*

Tom pressed the white doorbell recessed in the polished stone of the door surround. Antony's form appeared behind the bevelled glass and turned the key with a click.

'Come in, Tom,' he said, pulling the juddering wooden door wide open. 'Bloody thing! Every time it rains, it swells up. We need new doors and windows.'

'Don't you dare put plastic ones in this house,' Tom said, standing on the doormat, 'or I'll personally excommunicate you.'

'My membership is already revoked,' Antony snapped. 'Something to do with the sin of sodomy and not giving-a-God-damn what He, or anyone else, thinks about how I live my life.'

The colour drained from Tom's face.

'That was a poor attempt at humour,' he said. 'I'm sorry. It was wrong of me.'

'No, I'm sorry,' Antony said. 'I didn't mean to bite your head off; it's been a difficult couple of days. Come inside, please. Cup of tea, Vicar?'

'I do understand.'

'Do you?'

'You're right. I don't understand, not fully: but I *am* here for you, and your mum.'

'Weak tea, milk, no sugar, if I remember correctly. Are you going to come in or stand out there all day?'

'Well remembered,' Tom said, stepping past Antony into the carpeted hallway. 'That would be lovely, thank you.'

'I never forget, you know that. You rode from town on that museum piece?' Antony said, gesturing to the bike chained to the drainpipe. 'I'm guessing that monstrosity isn't carbon fibre, probably not even aluminium—more like cast iron.'

Tom stood opposite the wide, dark-wood bookcase recessed beneath the stairway, breathing it in, absorbing the power of the literary treasure trove that he had plundered as a teenager, noting with delight the twin volumes of Florio's translation of Montaigne's *Essays*, the dog-eared '70s original hardback copy of Susan Cooper's *The Grey King* that he had read cover-to-cover over the course of a single weekend, Alan Garner's *The Owl Service,* Bernard Shaw's *Man and Superman,* the volume of Maupassant's short stories, the biography of Frederick the Great of Prussia that had taught him that gay people could be great leaders.

'You know me and cars,' Tom said, unable to take his eyes off Lilian Keane's exquisite book collection. 'Me n' Shadowfax have put some serious miles in together across the years.'

'Best calf muscles in Bussell,' Antony said, as he slammed the door back into its frame. 'That's what I remember. You'd put the riders on the Tour de France to shame.'

'No skinny leg jeans for me.'

Antony chuckled, 'Go through to the sitting room, Tom. I'm sure you remember the way.'

Tom stood for a moment, looking around and about him, lost inside the cavernous hallway, absorbing every detail of the well-remembered house. The wallpaper and decoration had been changed, but everything else—the dark oak stairway, the coving in the ceiling, the ornate carven woodwork, the doorways—were exactly as they had been all those years ago. The warmth of familiarity spread through him, and Tom reminded himself there was no such thing as houses haunted by people, just people haunted by houses.

'Jesus!' Antony said, as he brushed past to turn the handle and open the door for Tom.

'When was the last time you had a shower? I thought it was the manhole overflowing again, but it's you, you filthy beggar. Do priests not have baths these days?'

'Do I smell, really?' Tom said, destroyed. 'I didn't realise. I am *so* sorry. I'll go if you want me to go. I will do.'

'If this is what living on your own does to a man, then heaven preserve me from the single life. Christ, Father Morton, you're humming. Does Sister Joan never tell you that you stink?'

'No, she doesn't.'

'Get yourself upstairs and showered. Scrub yourself clean, man. You'll have to wear the same clothes, unfortunately. There are towels in the airing cupboard. Show me your teeth… For crying out loud, Tom, you should be looking after yourself better than this. You used to have lovely teeth!'

Scolded, embarrassed, Tom climbed the creaking wooden staircase with its runner fastened to the steps with mottled brass rods. He found the black and white tiled bathroom opposite the master bedroom. Then, he locked the door, stripped, and did as he was told, cleansing his body with Clarins for Men bodywash as the heat penetrated his skin.

Fifteen minutes later, Tom turned the flower-painted handle of the white, panelled door from the hallway and stepped into a place reeking of his and Antony's shared history. Inside the sitting room that had been cinema, dance floor, drinking den, drugs den, restaurant, and debating chamber for their group of friends, an oxygen cylinder and face mask now stood at the side of a power lift reclining armchair.

'Feel better?' Antony shouted from inside the kitchen over the noise of an extractor fan.

'Yes, thank you. I left the towel in the basket by the sink.'

'Good man.'

'Which bedroom is Lillian in, Antony?

'Mum is in the room round the corner, off the hallway.'

'The red dining room?'

'That's the one—but it isn't red anymore, and it isn't a dining room either. We have a carer, Mary, who comes in during the week. She's with Mum, now. At weekends, it's just the two of us.'

'That must be tough.'

'It is what it is.'

How long have you been home?' Tom asked, seating himself on the floral settee by the window that looked out into the tiled conservatory.

A pair of spectacles were laid on an open laptop by the coffee table, and Tom felt an overwhelming urge to reach out and touch them.

'Five months. Before then, I was shuttling back and forth from Devon.'

'Five months?' Tom exclaimed.

Antony placed a tray of hot drinks and toasted sandwiches cut into triangles on the coffee table. He lifted the laptop with the glasses still perched on top onto the windowsill.

'It's not been easy,' he said. 'Please, help yourself.'

'Why didn't you…?'

'Just because, Tom. Let's leave it at that.'

'And how is your husband?'

Antony sighed, 'David is living with his new boyfriend, somewhere in Camden. I was traded in for a younger model, a handsome devil who delivered for one of our nut wholesalers, which is ironic given that David is allergic. Naturally, I changed supplier.'

'I am sorry to hear that,' Tom mumbled, as he tucked into a cheese and tomato toastie.

'Shit happens. It's not the first time I've been unceremoniously dumped: years ago, the love of my life ran off with a Palestinian carpenter.'

'It wasn't like that.'

'What *was* it like, Tom? There was no message, no goodbye, just wham-bam, thank you, man, and, then, you and the Big J skip off into the sunset together, holding hands.'

'You must have hated me.'

'I never hated you, Tom. I hated myself.'

'How… why would you hate yourself for something that I'd done?'

'I have a wonderful shop manager in Ottery,' Antony said, ignoring the question. 'She looks after things for me, day-to-day. But it certainly hasn't been the easiest of years. By the way, you do smell better.'

'Good.'

'I said better, not good.'

Tom laughed. 'Are you not eating?' he asked, as he picked up his second sandwich.

'I'm not hungry.'

'Why would you hate yourself, Antony?'

'Would you like to go for a walk, Tom? Two of us not arriving, getting nowhere—like The Beatles song. Mother Mary will be here for another hour or two.'

Tom thought about the finance forecast reports he had to write for the two churches—dull, dreary work he had been putting off for weeks now.

'If you'd rather not, I totally understand,' Antony said.

'I'd love to,' Tom said, 'I'd *really* love to.'

They slammed the door behind them and crunched down the drive. The short walk along the path at the side of the road, down the hill, was a trip down memory lane for both men: two friends, two former lovers, discussing which five-bed executive house on the new estate sitting atop the dingy newsagents that had sold them cigarettes, beer, and vodka when they were underage. The road curved past the explosives works with its health and safety sign celebrating '112 days since our last accident!' Then, the four linear equations were before them—the Leeds-Liverpool Canal, the Blackwater River, the Manchester to Southport trainline, the M6 motorway, intersecting and twisting their way through Hick Bibby Valley like serpents.

The steps from the carpark of The Erie Arms led down to the canal, the stones worn and slippery with wet green moss at the edges, crushed beer cans and chocolate wrappers littering the straggly undergrowth beside them. The cobbled towpath ran beneath the low road bridge, the restricted head-height causing Antony to shuffle his way through the darkness at an angle, winding his way between dank puddles and the path's stone edging. Instinctively, Tom reached for his hand as the two stepped back into sunlight.

'Evening, Father,' the jogger said, as he raced from behind the two men.

'Oh, hello,' Tom said, letting go of Antony's hand, watching as the figure sped away.

'Who was that?'

Tom grimaced, 'I think it was Mike Arundel, Sophie and Danny's dad—they are altar-servers at Saint James.''

'The cat's out of the bag, now, Father Morton,' Antony teased.

'What do you mean by that?'

'We were, you know, holding hands, you and me.'

The canal stretched out before them, hugging the tree-lined valley floor, running parallel to the river and the railway.

'Arundel senior thinks he's an alpha male,' Tom said, as they walked, 'always walking around with his chest puffed out, driving in a four-by-four so that he is a foot higher on the road than everyone else. You know the type.'

'Unfortunately, I do,' Antony said, 'I'm one of them!'

'Ah well, Sophie is the apple of his eye. Young Danny, on the other hand, is a sensitive soul.'

'You need to keep an eye out for him, then.'

'They say it's a small world, but Bussell is a bloody fishbowl,' Tom said. 'You did the right thing leaving. Sometimes it is…just… petty here, small-minded.'

'You left first. You went to that seminary at Ash Burrow. We didn't see you for months, and when you came back you were…'

'I was what?' Tom said, stopping in his tracks.

'Changed,' Antony said, 'and you'd found somebody else. Don't deny it, I could smell him on you.'

Tom shuddered. 'I have comforted the sick and the dying,' he said. 'I have done my best to help people find their own way to God. There is a joy that surpasses this transitory…'

'Good for you, Mother Teresa! And does your invisible best-friend keep your bed warm at night?'

Tom bit his tongue as they walked along the track between the river and the canal, dodging dank puddles with bike tracks imprinted in the soft mud, dodging dog shit, and smashed brown beer bottles.

'God helps me when I need Her the most,' Tom said, as the noise from the motorway grew.

'And what would the venerable Derek Worrell, Archbishop of Preston, have to say about that particular gender heresy?'

Tom turned cold hearing that name, and he was suddenly light-headed, clammy beneath his collar, feeling like he was going to puke on his shoes.

'Are you okay?' Antony asked, reaching out. 'Say something, Tom… you're shitting me up.'

'That man… would happily feed people like us to the crocodiles,' Tom stammered.

'People like us?'

'Yeah, people like us.'

'Reptiles are allergic to Catholics, aren't they? Didn't Saint Paul sit around a barbeque at a beach party with a snake hanging off his arm!'

'He was shipwrecked,' Tom said, his head spinning. 'Crocodiles are amphibians, aren't they?'

'You look terrible,' Antony said. 'What is it?'

Tom shook his head, tears welling up in his eyes.

'Let's keep walking, shall we?' he said.

The two men reached the elevated section of the motorway passing hundreds of feet above their heads. As they did so, the Southport train rattled past, horn blaring, passing under the motorway and then over the two stretches of water.

'Blake's Four Zoas,' Tom said, shouting to be heard over the noise, 'strength, faith, hope, and love. The four-chambered heart. The will to love is being, the will to power is non-being.'

Antony sighed, 'We need to be getting back to the house, Monsignor Morton.'

'I was raped,' Tom said, staring at the cloud-shielded sun, 'at Ash Burrow. I've never told anyone. Not you. Not Pete. Not Michael or Shaun. They don't know. Nobody does, especially my mother. It would break her heart. I'm not sure why I told you now, Antony. I certainly didn't plan to. I am *so* sorry. It's totally inappropriate, especially with everything you have going on in your life.'

'Stop saying you're sorry, Tom.'

'Sorry.'

'I said stop it! What have you got to be sorry for? Do you want to talk about what happened to you?'

The tears were cascading down Tom's face and onto the saturated ground.

'Do you know what song it was that helped me come out to myself?' he asked.

'No, I don't,' Antony said.

'*Blackbird.*'

'The Beatles?'

'Yeah... 'you were only waiting for this moment to be free.''

'It's a great tune.'

'I've really enjoyed our walk,' Tom said, laughing and crying at the same time. 'Perhaps we could do it again, sometime? If you'd like.'

'Even though I told you that you smelled and needed to brush your teeth?'

Tom blew snot into a congealed mass of tissue and dried his eyes on his coat sleeve.

'Yes,' he said. 'Even though you said those mean things to me.'

'Truthful things. It would have been meaner to have said nothing. I'd love to go for a walk with you, again. Who raped you, Tom? Why didn't you confide in us, all those years ago?'

'Have I told you about Shirley's memorial?'

'No, you haven't.'

'We're going to erect it in Bussell Park where it will be surrounded by flowers and bees and children. I think she would have loved that.'

'Yes, she would.'

'We're going to put the truth on the inscription and say bollocks to the threat of litigation. Tell the world that she was murdered, beaten to death by her stalker ex-boyfriend. We've designed it so that it is a heart, four chambers…'

'Stop talking, will you? Come here.' Antony took a step towards him, held out his arms, and Tom fell into him.

All the lost love, all the intimacy he craved, crashed into him as Tom pressed himself into Antony's body and wept, letting go of the shame and the pain.

'I've ruined your posh jacket,' he sobbed, as Antony stroked his head.

'It's okay,' Antony said. 'You can buy me another. I know you're loaded.'

Tom laughed and gulped.

'I was supposed to be comforting you,' he said, 'I'm so sorry.'

'Will you stop saying sorry all the time? The next time you do, I'm going to give you a dead arm! Christ, Tom, what happened at that seminary?'

'Not today, please, another day.'

'You need to let this out. It's obvious that it is poisoning you.'

'I know it is.'

'How did we end up here?' Antony asked.

'We turned left at the pub.'

'You think you're so funny, Mister. You know what I mean.'

'Somehow, somewhere, it all turned to shit,' Tom said, as he straightened himself up and took Antony's hands in his own. 'I screwed it up, didn't I?'

'There you go, again, mini-me Jesus, taking the sin of the world onto your shoulders. And look how it turned out for Him?'

'We can't change what has happened, can we?'

'No, we can't. We can only live for now. So come alive, Tom, come out of that tomb!'

'When we were younger, I used to think of you as the sun… no, really, I did, Antony. You illuminated my life. It was like being bathed in the most glorious warm, yellow radiance. And you are still that light for me, even today.'

Tom took his hands away.

'When we get to the road bridge, I wanna hold your hand—for health and safety reasons, of course. You're too tall, and you might bump your head and fall in the canal. And I wouldn't want that.'

4.

Thomas finished cutting the pictures out of mummy's magazines and began pasting them into a scrapbook: dresses, pictures of food, beaches, snow-capped mountains. Auntie Madeleine was staying at the house and sat on the sofa knitting a patterned scarf. Thomas smoothed the diamond tights from Aunty Annmie and dropped two feet into mummy's high heel shoes.

'Aunty Madeleine?'

'Yes?'

'When will I grow up into a girl?'

'Don't be silly,' Aunty Madeleine said.

5.

'Hello, Lillian,' Tom said, perching himself on the striped armchair at the side of the bed. The curtains were drawn, and through the large bay window came the sound of traffic noise, of cars speeding for the nearby motorway junction.

The woman beneath the white sheets opened her eyes and stared at him, her face and frame ravaged by the disease that was consuming her, but the eyes were fierce and intelligent as she regarded the man before her.

'You're…' the voice rasped through the plastic mask.

She swallowed.

'It's Tom, Lillian, Tom M…'

'bald and fat. I know who you are. Where is Antony?'

'He's coming. He is just putting plates in the dishwasher.'

'Where's Mary?'

'She's gone. She seems like a very nice lady. How are you feeling, today, Lillian?' Tom stammered, cursing himself inwardly as he heard his own incoherent rambling.

Antony came into the room, closed the door behind him, then leaned against the papered wall in front of his mother's bed, arms folded, his face impassive.

Her head propped up on two white pillows, Lillian gazed at both men, examining them in turn until she had made her judgment.

'Thank you for coming,' she said, breaking the silence.

'I owe you so much,' Tom said. 'It is an honour to be with you.'

'You are so…' Lilian said.

The two men held their tongues as the dying woman considered her verdict.

'full of shit. It's infuriating.'

Tom felt like he was a teenager, again, being told off by Lillian for the left-foot lob that beat Pete in the nets and put a Casey through the garage window.

'Antony tells me that you want me to administer the rite of the Sacrament of the Sick,' he said. 'Is that what you want, too?'

'He was going to let me pop my clogs, have me cremated, and then disappear back down south… without anyone knowing that he was here.'

'Mum,' Antony said, 'that isn't fair.'

'Fairs are for children. You are an adult,' Lilian said to her son. 'You,' she said, pointing a bony finger at Tom, 'get on with it.'

'Err, okay. Right… this is an aspergillum,' Tom said, lifting a bronze object with bristles from his backpack. 'I'm going to pour some holy water into the bowl, dip the brush inside, then I'm going to sprinkle you with water to remind you of the gifts of God's love.'

Tom sprinkled the water over Lilian. Then, he stood and did the same to Antony.

'This water reminds us of our baptism, of Jesus's baptism by John in the River Jordan. We remember the forgiveness of sins and the water of life eternal.'

'I would like to make my confession,' Lillian said, 'but not with him here.'

'It's okay, Mum. Call me when you're finished,' Antony said.

He left the room and gently closed the door behind him.

'In the name of the Father, and of the Son, and of the Holy Spirit,' Tom said, making the sign of the cross in the air with his right hand.

'Bless me, Father, it is… fifty-six years since my last confession.'

'Go on.'

'I have sworn. I have lied. I have lusted after men who were not my husband. And I have hated God… for all the injustices He inflicts on us. Does that offend you?'

'No, of course not.'

Lillian laughed, then she coughed.

'I think I have. And I have hated you, Thomas Morton, and the hypocritical organisation you work for… What's the matter, Father, cat got your tongue?'

'I'm listening,' Tom said, stunned and horrified.

'Oh, my God, I am sorry for having offended you. I intend with the help of your grace to do penance and change my life,' Lilian said.

'Amen.'

'Amen.'

'God, the Father of mercy, through the death and resurrection of his Son has reconciled the world to Himself and sent the Holy Spirit amongst us for the forgiveness of sins. Through the ministry of the Church may God give you pardon and peace. I absolve you from your sins in the name of the Father, and of the Son, and of the Holy Spirit. Give thanks to the Lord, for he is good.'

'Is He good?' Lilian demanded. 'Is He really good?'

'His mercy endures forever.'

'When I'm gone, love my son. That's the least you can do.'

'I've loved your son, all my life.' Tom said. 'He is the only man, the only human being, I've ever fallen in love with.'

'Why do this to yourself, dress in black, hide your heart, pretend to be something that you are not?'

'If you had seen what I've seen, heard what I've heard, felt what I've felt, you would understand.'

'One day, you will be close to death, like me. Do not die with regret.'

'I want to thank you for what you did all those years ago, for being so kind to us. You were like our second mum.'

'Antony tried to kill himself, after you left. Did you know?'

'No… he never said,' Tom said, stunned. 'I never knew!'

'I found him. I remember sitting by his bed in hospital, cursing you, cursing God, cursing myself for letting you into our home. I pity you. Get Antony, I'm tired.'

Antony was sitting on the sofa in the living room, glasses on, reading a book.

'We're ready,' Tom said, from the hallway, trying his best to control his emotions.

'Is everything all right?' Antony asked. 'Are you okay?'

'I'm fine,' Tom said. 'It's just been a long day.'

Standing at the foot of Lillian's bed, Tom read from the Bible.

'A Reading from the Letter of Saint John. See what great love the Father has... lavished upon us... that we should be called children of God. For that is what we are. The reason the world does not know us is that it did not know him. Friends, now we are children of God, and what we will be has not yet been made known. But we know that when Christ appears, we shall be like him, for we shall see him as he is. All who have this hope in him purify themselves, just as he is pure. Amen.'

Tom placed the Bible back inside his bag. Then, he walked around the bed and placed his hands in Lillian's head, blessing her.

'Lord God, bless your servant, Lillian, and fill her with new hope and strength.'

From his jacket pocket, Tom brought out a vial of oil, poured some into a finger bowl and dipped his index finger. Then, made the sign of the cross on Lillian's forehead.

'Lord, our God, who watches over your creatures with unfailing care, keep us in the safe embrace of your love. Through this holy anointing may the Lord in his love and mercy help you with the grace of the Holy Spirit. May the Lord who frees you from sin save you and raise you up. Amen.'

'Amen,' Lillian said.

'Thank you, Tom,' Antony said.

'I must go, I'm really sorry... sorry for saying sorry,' Tom said, as he dried the oil from his fingers with a tissue, reaching for his belongings.

'Father Morton,' Lillian croaked, 'when the time comes, will you conduct my funeral?'

'Mum!' Antony gasped.

'Will you do as I ask?'

Tom's body was frozen in time.

'Of course, I will,' he said, head bowed. 'You have my promise.'

6.

Steven Fairfield's birthday party was in the grounds of Bradshaw Hall.

'This is Skip,' Stephen's daddy said to the children, introducing an adult that Thomas had never seen before, 'and you boys do whatever Skip tells you to do.'

Steven had invited all the boys from the reception class at school. And so began the ritual humiliation of kicking a football. After various laughable miskicks, after being relegated to defence, and being pushed over by Peter King, Thomas made for the safety of the rhododendron bushes at the side of the stately home that once belonged to the Bussell's very own local aristocracy.

He saw Skip heading towards him, red-faced, looking angry. Michael O'Keefe ran past Skip holding the plastic gun that Thomas's mum had bought as a present for Steven Fairfield.

'It's broken,' Michael said, panting. 'Steven says you have to buy him another one!'

7.

Tom swung the creaking iron gate open, scrunched his way up the stony path, and knocked on the glass pane of the wooden door.

'Morton!' Pete King said, opening the door, 'How are you? Come in.'

Tom stepped inside, placing the shopping bag filled with snacks, a bottle of white wine, and a four-pack of Newcastle Brown Ale on the floor by the coat stand. The two friends threw their arms around each other.

'Hi, Tom,' Monica King shouted from inside the kitchen. 'I hope you're hungry, Pete's made enough food for the whole town.'

'I'm clempt de'ath,' Tom said.

'Come into the lounge,' Pete said, 'footies on.'

Tom sank into the scuffed, cat-scratched, leather sofa, soaking in the vibe of Pete n' Monnie's bohemian-style, Edwardian terrace. On the wall-mounted fifty-five-inch TV screen, Tottenham Hotspur were playing Liverpool in a game that Pete was streaming from a dubious satellite provider, operating somewhere out of Russia.

'Is it snowing at White Hart Lane?' Tom asked.

'Fuck off,' Pete answered.

Tom laughed.

'Are you not wearing your dog collar tonight, Tom?' Monica asked, as she brought in a bowl of nachos and dips and set them on the coffee table. 'Move your feet, Pete,' she said.

'I'm off duty, Mon,' Tom said. 'How's work?'

'Okay, thank you,' Monica said, crossing her arms. 'It's all new to me, new systems, new people. But everyone is really nice.'

'Oh, oh, ooooh,' Pete gasped, as Roberto Firmino dragged his shot wide.

'Hello, Tom.'

'Now then, Ruthie,' Tom said to Pete and Monica's twelve-year-old daughter as she stood smiling in the doorway. 'How are you?'

'Fine.'

'How's school?'

'Fine.'

'That's all we get. Isn't it, Ruth,' Monica said to her daughter. 'Fine, okay, great.'

Ruth shrugged and smiled.

'Are we biking at the weekend?' Pete asked, stuffing snacks dripping with guacamole and tomato salsa into his mouth, his eyes never leaving the TV screen.

'Yeah, sounds good,' Tom said.

'We'll leave you two lads to it, won't we, Ruth. Do you want a beer, Tom?'

'Please,' Tom said, 'there's a bag in the hallway with some bits n' bobs.'

'Peter?' Monica said, as she turned to go.

'Yes, please… ooooh, so close. What do you reckon? Saturday morning up to Silverdale.'

'Not in your car.'

'Yer big puff.'

'That's called homophobia.'

'It's a good job you're not homosexual then, isn't it?'

'Have you heard from Michael, lately?'

'O' Keefe? Yeah. Him and Ruby are both well. Harrow-on-the-Hill seems to suit them. Hopefully, they'll be back home soon.'

'Thank you,' Tom smiled, as Ruth delivered the two cold beers, 'And Shaun?'

'Yeah, he's good, last I heard.'

'I saw Antony. I didn't know he was back—it came as quite a surprise. He just appeared in church.'

'You mean in a vision? Did he impart any sacred wisdom?'

'No, physically sitting in a pew. Okay, you're messing with me.'

'I didn't realise he was religious, I thought it was just you in our circle of friends who suffer from that particular delusion…'

'Here we go.' Tom said, bracing himself for an onslaught.

'telling people to believe in a figment of some nutcase's imagination.'

'Did you know Antony was back?'

'No, I didn't.'

'His mum is terminally ill.'

'Get in!!!' Pete shouted, as he paraded around the room after Andy Robertson buried the ball in the bottom right corner of Hugo Lloris's net.

'Great goal,' Tom said, as he drank Boddingtons Draught from the can.

'Wise words from a man with two left feet,' Pete said.

'Somewhere out there is a player with two right feet, and together we'd make the world's greatest footballer!'

'You need to find that man.'

'Indeed, I do,' Tom said. 'I said that Antony's mum is terminally ill.'

'Jesus! That's not good.'

'Antony came to St. James' to ask me to administer the Sacrament of the Sick to Lillian. So, I did.'

'I haven't seen Antony in… must be ten years.'

'I haven't seen him in more than twenty.'

'He asked my brother, Brian, to leave his wife and move in with him!'

'Did he?' Tom said, feeling the bottom of his stomach collapse through his legs. 'When?'

'God… a few years back. He said, 'Why have her when you can have me?'

'I didn't know.'

'Awkward!'

'Yeah, it must have been.'

'The times we had in that house,' Pete said, as he flicked off the TV.

'I thought we were watching the game?' Tom said.

'Some things are more important than football, not many, but there are some. So, tell me about Antony. Tell me about his mum.'

8.

The yellow knitted jumper was Thomas's pride and joy. He and Mum had chosen the wool together in Flax Mill. It had taken his mum four months to knit it, stitch by stitch, panel by panel, arm by arm, night after night in front of the TV.

John Cooper was behind Thomas as the school bus slowed down to stop, and the front doors swished open. Thomas stared at the kerb as it whizzed past. Then, he was pushed forward and, just as quickly, he was pulled back. Thomas's heart was racing, and he tried not to sob.

Cooper and his cronies were laughing.

'Nice jumper, Morton,' Cooper said. 'We could see you in the dark wearing that.'

His mum was waiting at the bus stop for him. She took his hand.

'Did your friends like your new jumper?' she asked, as they crossed the road.

'John Cooper tried to push me off the bus,' Thomas said.

He could see the white of his mum's knuckles, and she had gone quiet. He knew that meant she was really cross.

9.

Tom read the gospel according to John.

'When it was almost time for the Jewish Passover, Jesus went up to Jerusalem. In the temple courts, he found people selling cattle, sheep, and doves, and others sitting at tables exchanging money. So, he made a whip out of cords and drove all from the temple courts, both sheep and cattle. He scattered the coins of the money changers and overturned their tables. To those who sold doves he said, "Get these out of here! Stop turning my Father's house into a market!"'

'Jesus was a man of action,' Tom told his congregation, 'a person who would take risks. Jesus did not stop to do a risk assessment, fill the forms in, or consult a firm of speciality solicitors. Instead, he acted out of a deep conviction, the conviction that love is God, that love is central to our lives, that crowding our lives with the busyness of business leaves no room for goodness. Jesus felt fear, just like us, but he did what he knew God wanted him to do.'

After the blessing and dismissal, the Arundel children, Sophie and Danny, led the way from the altar to the church entrance, brother and sister dressed in matching black cassocks and white surplices. Standing on the tiled steps, Tom shook the hands of his parishioners, blessed proffered rosaries and crucifixes on chains, waved goodbye to the choir, thanked visitors for coming.

On his way back to the sacristy, Tom found Mike Arundel waiting by the Lady Altar as his children snuffed out the candles and tidied up.

'Hello, Mike,' Tom said, as he strode past.

'Father Morton,' Mike Arundel replied.

'See you, Father Thomas,' Sophie said, as she hung her cassock on a hanger in the wall cupboard and disappeared into the church.

'How are you finding things at St. Pat's, Danny?' Tom asked. 'I went there myself, a long time ago.'

'Everyone seems really nice. Mister Cooper is strict though.'

'I went to school with your headmaster. He was in the year above me.'

'Yeah.'

'It's a big change, going to high school.'

'Yeah,'

'Do you see your sister around school much?'

'Not much.'

'What subjects do you like best?'

'I like music and drama.'

'What about sports, football and rugby?'

'I don't like football.'

'I didn't like it either at school. I was useless. I like watching it now though.'

'My dad takes me to watch Bussell Athletic.'

'That sounds fun.'

'I've got to go. My dad will be waiting.'

'Hi five, Danny.'

The boy slapped the priest's hand, and then, he was gone.

'Go and sit with your sister in the car,' Tom heard Mike Arundel tell his son.

'Father Morton,' Mike Arundel said, as he stepped into the sacristy, 'keep your hands off my boy.'

'I beg your pardon?' Tom said.

'You heard me.'

There was a loud knock at the front door of the rectory and Tom, still stunned, walked from the sacristy into his home. Opening the door, he found a dishevelled woman with a supermarket carrier bag in her hands.

'Hello, Father Morton. I'm sorry to trouble you. I've had nothing to eat for two days. Can I come in?'

Tom fought the compulsion to tell the stranger to piss off, to tell her that now was not a good time. In fact, it was an incredibly bad time. He bit back his anger. Then, he did what he was supposed to do and invited the woman in.

'Come in, please. Would you like some food?'

'Thank you, Father. I thought you were going to tell me to fuck off there, for a minute.'

'No, not at all. Sorry, I was having a senior moment. The kitchen is this way. Please follow me.'

As his guest took her seat at the table, Tom brought out a slice of Joan Bird's 'Friday fish-day' pie from the fridge.

'I'll warm this up for you. Would you like a tea or a coffee with that? Let me plug that phone in for you.'

'Can I use your bathroom, please? I promise I won't rob nothing.'

'There isn't anything worth stealing, I'm afraid, not unless you like religious books. The bathroom is upstairs, first door on the left.'

Tom warmed the pie in the microwave and put some frozen green beans into boiling water on the stove.

'You're welcome to have a shower while you're here, if you like. There is a lock on the door so you needn't worry about your privacy,' he said, as his visitor returned.

'Are you saying I smell?'

'Gosh no. I would never say that. I was just…'

'I'm messing with you. I'm Rosie.'

'Hi, Rosie,' Tom said, extending his hand, 'I'm Tom.'

'You're a good priest, Father Morton. I can tell. Not like some of the others.'

'That's kind of you. Funnily enough, I've just had a rather unpleasant conversation with a parent who told me in no uncertain terms that I am not allowed to clap hands with his son.'

'The bad apples spoil it…' Rosie said, dissolving into a coughing fit, holding her sleeve to her mouth.

'Are you okay?' Tom asked, concerned. 'Can I get you anything?'

'No, I'm fine,' Rosie said, fishing a fistful of paper napkins from her pocket and wiping her mouth.

'I think your food is ready.'

Tom watched as Rosie devoured the food, finishing her plate in a matter of minutes.

'Would you like a dessert… I've got a Mint Vienetta in the fridge.'

Rosie burst out laughing, 'That's so fucking eighties, fucking Vienetta.'

'It's making a comeback,' Tom said, getting up. 'It's on deal at a pound in Morrisons!'

'You're funny.'

'You want some?'

'Yeah, why not.'

'I reckon Vienetta is humankind's greatest achievement,' Tom said, opening the freezer door. 'Never mind splitting the atom, getting to the moon, or finding cures for terrible diseases, layering ice cream and chocolate together in a frozen dessert is mindboggling!'

Rosie had her fist in her mouth to try to control her laughter.

A knock came from the front door.

'Do you want me to go?' Rosie asked.

'Not on your nelly,' Tom said, putting a bowl and spoon in front of her. 'Get that down you, and I'll be right back.'

'Hello,' Antony said, as Tom opened the door.

'Hello.'

'Is this an inconvenient time? I could come back…'

'No, come in. It's good to see you.'

Tom led Antony into the kitchen.

'Antony, Rosie. Rosie, Antony.'

'Hi,' Antony said, taking off his scarf and hat.

'Hello,' Rosie said, as she ate her ice cream.

'Can I get you a drink?' Tom asked.

'Sure, expresso, two shots, please,' Antony said.

Tom raised his eyebrows and Antony smirked.

Rosie was watching. 'Get a room, you two,' she said.

'It's nothing like that,' Tom said, 'really. Is it Antony?'

'It's nothing like that,' Antony said. 'Really.'

'Yeah, yeah, it doesn't bother me. You look nice together, two older men. Thank you for the food, Father Morton. I'll be on my way.'

'Would you like something to take with you, some water, snacks, erm…'

'Do you have any more of that pie. It was… well, delicious?'

'Of course, I would be more than happy to oblige.'

'Do you have anywhere to sleep tonight, Rosie?' Antony asked.

'I'll try my luck outside the railway station.'

'Wait, please,' Antony said, as he pulled out his wallet. 'Here's fifty. Get yourself a room for tonight.'

'Thank you,' Rosie said. 'You've both been really kind.'

'Don't forget your phone,' Tom said.

'You don't remember me, do you?'

'I'm really sorry, I don't.'

'Bye bye, Thomas Morton.'

After letting Rosie out through the front door of the rectory, Tom slumped into his chair in the kitchen.

'Is it always like this?' Antony asked.

'You shouldn't have given her that cash,' Tom said. 'It's a risk.'

'You shouldn't have given her that pie.'

Tom laughed. Then, he rubbed his face.

'You remember that jogger by the canal, the day we went for a walk.'

'Yes, of course.'

'It *was* who I thought it was, and after mass, today—in a roundabout way—the guy called me a paedophile.'

'For going for a walk with me?'

'No, for hi-fiving his son. He's an altar-server.'

'You need to be careful, no physical contact.'

'What kind of world are we living in?'

'One where adults who have access to children need to abide by the strictest of codes… Come on, Tom, you know the conduct of some of the filth infesting your church. You know the appalling way the investigations were handled, protecting abusive priests, hushing up the damage done to innocents.'

'We're not all like that.'

'No, but that's what protective parents are going to think.'

'Listen, Danny is… I can see myself in him at that age, is what I mean to say.'

'How old is he?'

'Eleven.'

'You need to stay out of this, Tom. It won't end well.'

'I know. I don't need you to tell me that.'

At that moment, Tom wanted a cuddle and a kiss more than anything in the whole world.

Antony put his hand on top of Tom's,

'You know what you need to do to help all the Danny's in this world, don't you Tom?'

'Yes,'

'So, why don't you do it?'

'Because…'

When Antony dragged his chair over and drew him into an embrace, Tom did not resist.

10.

The night before his mum marched into school and demanded to speak to the headmaster was bread and jam night. So, it must have been a Tuesday.

Thomas always thought that jam buttie nights were the best dinner days of the week. It never occurred to him as a child that he and his mum were poor—that homemade clothes, hand-me-down trainers, pack-ups instead of school dinners, a Ferguson black and white TV, not owning a car, no school trips unless they were fully funded, a Tesco bike instead of a Raleigh Chopper, marked him out as different.

Each day of the week had its own dinner: Monday was meat left from Sunday, Tuesday was jam butties, Wednesday was a pie made with meat salvaged from Sunday and Monday, Thursday was spaghetti, Friday was fish fingers, and Saturday was casserole made with frozen minced beef with yoghurt for pudding. Thomas's mum would put food on his plate: a piece of pie, a slice of meat.

She would ask, 'How many pieces would you like?'

Thomas would answer, 'Two,' and his mum would cut what he had in half.

'There,' she would say, 'now you've got two,' and they would laugh at their ritual… a ritual anchored in necessity.

Nana Morton came to stay when his mum had to work late at the ketchup factory. Mum and Nana Morton did not get on. It infuriated Thomas's mum when Nana made comments about his weight or sent him to the pie shop with fifty pence to 'fill him out.'

'You've hollow legs,' his nan would say, as Thomas devoured the treats that she brought with her on the bus from Preston.

His favourites were Jacobs Happy Faces biscuits. He could eat a full pack in one sitting.

Nana Morton told Thomas about his dad, her son, which caused more friction with mum who never talked about her dead husband, or Colin, Thomas's little brother, who had died in the same car accident. Thomas always wondered about the cash stuffed into white envelopes that his mum gave his nana each time she came to visit. He thought it was baby-sitting money, but later learned that his mother was paying back the interest-free loan from Nana Morton that had prevented them from losing the house when his dad died.

Emma Morton, née Pilkington, was devoutly religious, one of six girls from a large Belgian Catholic clan who arrived in England as economic migrants before World War I. As Thomas did his chores each day, usually the washing up after dinner, he was instructed in the essentials of Temse Catholicism, a uniquely female-to-female exegesis passed from mother to daughter, a flame of faith about which Tom was left in no doubt was now his responsibility to keep alive.

Standing with a dishcloth in his hand, Thomas learned that his mother had been three months pregnant on her wedding day, that Grandad Pilks had told his daughter that she did not have to go through with the wedding unless she wanted to, that Grandad Pilks had always known that Thomas's dad was a liar, and that Thomas's mum had gone to confession and confessed her son's conception as a sin.

The knowledge that he was a sin lodged deep inside Thomas's juvenile psyche. The ultimate admonishment from his mother was the line, 'You are just like your dad.' Original Sin became something Thomas perceived as masculine, a weaponised guilt-trigger that would pitch spirituality against sexuality.

Thomas understood, even as a child, that the traumas the woman who was his mother had gone through in her early twenties had left an indelible mark, and that the sacraments of the Roman Catholic Church provided a structure, a framework to manage her daily suffering. He understood that his mum had no-one else to talk to at home, that he had to grow up and be an adult. He also intuited that it would please his mum, the centre of his entire world, if he became a priest.

Emma's youngest sister, Annmie, was only four years older than Thomas, and he and Annmie were more like first cousins. Immersed in a world of ponies, Nancy Drew mysteries, pink clothes, and ballet lessons, Thomas found happiness and security. The Pilkington family structures were fluid, varying from raging arguments to impenetrable solidarity, bonds of love that were volatile but impervious to outsiders. Sometimes, not often, Thomas caught a look, had a sense that his family spotted something inside him that he couldn't see himself, something that made him different.

At the centre of the family were Nana Pilks and Grandad Pilks, who varied between affection and outright hostility to each other. Grandad Pilks had a temper, not in a physical sense, but in terms of his emotional bandwidth. He had a short fuse. He didn't suffer fools gladly. He loathed falsehood. He spoke without thinking, and he passed on his forthright nature to his daughters.

Thomas adored his grandad and loved to watch him work in his car repair garage. He knew that he never wanted to be outside the Pilkington bubble of tempestuous familial love. He would never repay their love with ingratitude. All the same, as Annmie grew, started her periods, bought her first bra, started dating boys, Thomas was filled with a sense of exclusion and jealousy to which he couldn't put a name.

His mum was kind, patient, loving but, every now and then, the smouldering Pilkington fire would burst into flames. Tom had to explain *exactly* what had happened on the school bus when they arrived back home that fateful day, watching as his mother's face blanched in fury.

The next morning, after his mum had been into school and played merry-hell, Thomas Morton and John Cooper found themselves sitting in front of the Headmaster, Mister Blackburn. Thomas had never been in Mister Blackburn's office before. After being instructed to apologise, a scowling Cooper was dismissed and sent back to his classroom.

Young Thomas found himself being observed by Blackburn's piercing blue eyes.

'Would you like a Polo mint?' the headmaster asked.

'Yes, please,' Thomas said.

Nothing else was said, but, for the rest of his time at Saint Cuthbert's Primary School and, indeed, until Mister Blackburn retired, he felt like he had a guardian angel watching his back.

'Your mum's a bloody psycho, you little freak,' Cooper told Thomas that night, as they stood at the bus stop in front of the prefab garages. 'She's as mad as a box of frogs.'

And it appeared that John Cooper, the future Head Teacher of Saint Patrick's RC High School, was not alone in that opinion. Thomas always had the feeling that some teachers did not like him for a reason he could not understand. He always had the feeling that some parents did not like him playing with their children, that they wished he would be friends with someone else.

When he became best friends with Michael O'Keefe, it transformed Thomas's life. Michael was an amazing artist, and his drawings were so much better than everyone else in class. In fact, Michael was wonderful in every way.

And then, Richard Smith became friends with Michael too. Thomas hated hearing that Michael's parents and Richard's parents were friends, that they all went swimming together at Bussell Baths on a Saturday morning. Thomas's mum did not seem to have any friends. She had her own mum and her five sisters, and they were always falling out with each other, then making up again.

Consumed by jealousy, Thomas contrived to break up the friendship between Michael and Richard. He worked on it over a period of weeks, a snide comment here, a disparaging remark there, and, sure enough, the plan worked. Michael was soon back being his best friend and Richard was out of the picture.

For as long as he had Michael, Thomas knew he could survive the terrors of primary school.

11.

Father Tom was responsible for two Catholic parishes: Saint James', Bussell, and Saint Benedict's, Hind Green. Both churches had a micro culture of their own and viewed the other with deep suspicion.

Saint Jimmy's, with its Jesuit heritage and town centre location, attracted 'small c' Catholics, a younger, more family-oriented, progressive congregation.

Five miles away, Saint Benny's was situated in the more affluent area of Hind Green, with an older congregation who had an affinity with conservative Catholic organisations like This Partisan Church. Emma Morton, Tom's mother, and Joan Bird, Tom's part-time housekeeper, were both members of the Saint Benedict's congregation.

The Tuesday night prayer meetings at Hind Green were usually torture for Tom as he attempted to reason with the internet fuelled paranoia of Saint Benny's church council members and their obsession with a Masonic takeover of the Roman Catholic Church led by a Jesuit Pope, aided and abetted by a network of apostate, sodomite priests, and heretic, lesbian nuns with a secret underground headquarters in Rome.

At the Saint Benny's prayer meeting, two weeks after Antony had come back into his life, Tom attempted to steer discussions back to his intended narrative of how the message of Jesus Christ was at the intra, not extra, level, that the forgiveness of sins was an ongoing existential challenge for each human being and not a pre-condition for membership of the club that bore his name. Despite his best attempts, the conversation had collapsed back into exhortations to vet priests for same sex attraction and compulsory dismissal for those homosexual priests responsible for orgies in seminaries, child abuse, and sex trafficking. As parishioners whipped each other up to a crescendo of 'teachers shouldn't be forced to teach the LGBTQ agenda,' and 'we should rid the world of homos,' Tom had closed the meeting down with two acapella verses of *Tantum Ergo*. As they closed their eyes to pray, Tom had suggested that those present should contemplate the two great commandments, a not-too-subtle chastisement that hadn't gone down well with the elderly elders. There were whispers and withering looks, as Tom made good his escape.

On his way back to Saint Jimmy's rectory, Tom had peddled his bike furiously to re-establish a sense of cosmic karma, picking up speed as he flew first past Bussell Infirmary, then the medieval stone pilgrim's cross that stood by the edge of an Iceland supermarket carpark, directing holy travellers to its '3 for £10' deal across frozen lean minced beef, Swedish style meatballs, and 375 grams of diced British lamb. Having Antony around, changed things. Tom felt a sense of purpose that he hadn't realised he had been missing.

Upon his arrival home, Tom parked his bike in the hall and immediately rang his mother to clear the air and prevent any protracted hostilities.

'Hello.'

'Hello, Thomas.'

'That was a mad one.'

'Sexual deviancy is filthy, men lusting after men, women after women.'

'That's hardly very forgiving.'

'We forgive the sinner, not the sin.'

'How is Aunty Madeleine?'

'She's out of hospital now. Annmie picked her up.'

'Good. How are you?'

'I don't agree with your comments on the precious body and blood, neither did Joan Bird.'

'Her pies are offal,' Tom said.

'Are you trying to be funny?'

'Let me ask you a question, Mum, if you had to lay our Faith out, point by point, and then prioritise it, where would transubstantiation come... first, second, seventh?'

'High up.'

'Where?'

'You're trying to be clever.'

'I'll go first... love the Lord thy God with all your heart and soul. Second—we all know which one that is—love your neighbour.'

'You're just like...'

'I'm nothing like him. We both know that.'

'What's in the cat...'

Tom bit his tongue to prevent himself losing his temper.

'I don't want to fall out with you, Mum, but I'm getting sick and tired of that church hall full of old aged Nazis.'

'I saw that school friend of yours the other day in Tesco.'

'Which one?'

'The one near the rugby club.'

'No, which friend?'

'The tall one, he said hello and said he was looking after his mum, that you'd administered the Sacrament of the Sick to her. I hope you didn't mess it up like you did to Missus Hindley, flicking holy water into her hearing aid.'

'I'm going to go. Make sure all the doors are locked. Love you, Mum.'

'I'm going to bed.'

'You do right. Night, night.'

Tom had helped himself to a well-deserved double dram of Jura whiskey whilst he caught up on BBC News on his iPhone. As he scrolled through the latest bad news from across the planet, he thought about what his mum had said and why she had mentioned seeing Antony. He wondered if Joan had been gossiping behind his back, alerting his mother to the dangers of suspicious men who were too light on their feet. One plus one didn't necessarily equal three, but still Tom felt uneasy.

12.

Michael had a Ventolin inhaler because he had asthma. Thomas was delighted when he too got diagnosed with asthma and needed an inhaler. When Michael had a hideous in-growing toenail, Thomas wished him luck at the podiatrists next to the butcher's shop.

Despite having a chronic chest condition, Michael was a fast runner: he just needed to stop every now and again for a quick toot o' the blue. Michael was good at rounders, and Thomas cheered his head off at Sport's Day when his best friend batted the ball into the long grass and earned the team a point. Thomas' attempts were less successful, missing completely and being shooed to first base to make way for someone who had a modicum of hand and eye coordination.

Michael's little sister, Nicola, was two years younger, and Thomas used to hold Nicola's hand on the way from school to the bus stop, skipping and swinging arms, enjoying the company of a girl.

In his class at primary school, Steven Fairfeld, William Scholes, and Eamonn Kelly were the boys that female opinion leaders, Catherine Dales and Ailenn Duff, swooned over. For a reason Thomas could not fully comprehend, Catherine and Aileen held him in the deepest contempt. One Saturday afternoon, Thomas was out on his bike, and he met Aileen carrying a fishing rod and, for once, she was nice to him.

'Will you buy my brother's fishing rod?' Aileen asked.

'Err, no,' a penniless and confused Thomas said, unable to think of anything more horrifying than fishing for pike in a flooded mineshaft.

'I knew you wouldn't,' Aileen spat. 'You're a little queer.'

Years later, Thomas would look back and question why a young girl was walking around a village on her own desperately trying to sell her brother's fishing tackle, and he would forgive Aileen her trespass against him. Years later, Thomas would understand poverty, poverty far worse than the restricted family income he had experienced as a child. As a parish priest, Thomas would come face-to-face with the desperation of families that could not afford to feed themselves, families forced to queue at food banks while others carried their shopping home in gleaming new SUVs.

'Queer,' was the ultimate admonishment on the playground and Thomas knew that he certainly was not a queer, whatever that word meant.

'You queer,' was William Scholes' favourite put down.

The new boy, Daniel Brennan, was a perfect target for Scholes's favourite jibe because he, along with his sister, were Irish *and* adopted. Daniel Brennan brought some relief for Thomas because here was a new target the alpha males, aided and abetted by Catherine and Aileen, could pick apart and destroy.

The times they were-a-changing: Michael had moved to a new house on the other side of town, and he had a new friend called Joshua Whitely, or Josh Whiney as Thomas called him, who lived on the same street. Whiney got to play out in the evenings *and* weekends with Michael… and Thomas hated him for it. On one of his increasingly rare visits to play at Michael's new house, Michael's mum picked up on one of Thomas's catty comments and told him to cut it out or he would not be invited again.

In his last year of primary school, Thomas became an altar boy at St. Cuthbert's, and so did Dan Brennan. Dan turned out to be a good lad, funny and sad in equal measure. Thomas was never able to explain how that mix worked, but it did in Dan. In return for his one and only football book, Tom bribed Will Scholes to leave his new friend alone.

And to be fair to Scholsey, he kept his end of the bargain. Years later, Scholsey would come to Thomas's house to borrow his Joy Division vinyl… but that lay more than half a decade away, and, by that time, Dan would be dead by his own hand.

Dan was into trainers and clothes, and his parents seemed to give him whatever he wanted. Thomas had never really been interested in shoes and clothes before, but Dan's keen eye and knowledge of which sports brands were cool, or not, opened his eyes to a whole new world, a world that Thomas, unfortunately, was unable to access due to his mother's obsession with buying the cheapest and most practical option on display.

And that is why Thomas got himself a paper round, and that is how he fell in love for the first time with an older boy, although he didn't realise it until many years later.

13.

Baptisms for the offspring of the town's Rugby League players were as close to celebrity occasions as Saint James' Church in Bussell got. Sometimes, a photographer from *Lancashire Life* would even turn up. The interesting fact about wealthy weddings, baptisms, and funerals, Tom noted, was that the collection was always smaller than when poorer families had the same events in church. The rich had a talent for moving the collection plate along the pew, or behind them, at such speed that it barely seemed to touch their hands. Rugby balls and collection plates, it was a sight to behold!

As in the days when Tom was an altar server himself, the seven sacraments of the Holy Catholic Church were lucrative for young people prepared to put in a shift at weekends, or during school holidays. Hearing of an unexpected death or an impending nuptial meant loot for the more commercially minded of God's junior faithful. The payment to altar servers was handled by funeral directors in the case of funerals, by the best man in the case of weddings, and by the new parents in the case of baptisms, cutting out the risk of altar servers being short-changed by the more avaricious of the town's population who seemed to assume that churches ran on fresh air, priests ate grass, and altar servers didn't mind giving up their free time because they just happened to be a bit holy.

Sophie and Daniel Arundel played it well, Father Morton noted. They never turned up late, they always were clean and presentable, they looked suitably pious, and, best of all, they kept their faces straight at funerals, never giggled uncontrollably, and they smiled at weddings. Prospective husband and wives, grieving relatives, and euphoric new parents asked for the Arundels specifically, as if the two children were part of a Catholic sacramental package.

Fair play, Tom thought, *milk it while you can.*

Mike Arundel had been frosty for a few weeks after hi-five-gate, but peace seemed to have been restored. Tom knew Antony was right, and he had resolved to steer clear of asking young Danny any questions about life at Saint Pat's school or going anywhere near him physically.

The wedding arranged for that Saturday afternoon was a rugby player from Australia who was marrying a local girl. Tom was shocked to discover that the bride's mother was Catherine Schofield nee Dales. The terror from his primary school greeted Tom like a long-lost friend and introduced him to her husband, mother, father, and a myriad of other family members.

'Have you seen anyone else from school, lately?' Catherine asked.

'I see Pete King fairly regularly,' Tom said. 'Michael is in London, and I did a baptism a few years back. It was Stephen Fairfield's boy, so I bump into people every now and again. How about you?'

'I saw Aileen about ten years ago, but we lost touch. Shame, but it happens.'

'Where is she living?'

'Near Bolton.'

'Right.'

'I expect you've things to be getting on with.'

'I do.'

'It's really good to see you again, and I'm so pleased it is you marrying our daughter.'

'Really?'

'Yeah, really.'

'Thanks'

'And Thomas?'

'Yeah?'

'I never told,' and with that Catherine Schofield nee Dales winked and joined her family.

What the hell? Tom thought, and then he remembered… *Oh Christ, that afternoon at Birch House.*

14.

Beverley Forster flashed Tom as he came up stairs to the bathroom.

The Forsters lived in the semi next door. There were three Forster girls: June, Beverley, and Amanda, plus mum, Denise, with dad, whose name Thomas never knew, away on a gas rig somewhere in the North

Sea, most of the year. Sometimes, when his mum was working late, Thomas would be sent next door for his tea, then he would watch TV with the Forsters until his mum got back from Bradley.

Beverley was a year older than Thomas, and she was the first girl that he saw naked. Beverley was wrapped in a bath towel, waiting as he climbed the stairs to the toilet. She held the towel by the corners and showed him her hairless body.

Thomas was rooted to the third stair from the top as he gazed at the girl that he had known most of his life, unsure what the hell was going on. Beverley casually wrapped the towel round herself and shut the bedroom door.

He did not tell his mother.

Emma Morton warned her son about the public toilets next to the playing fields at Birch House. Emma warned Thomas about the wicked men who lay in wait for daft, unsuspecting boys. Thomas would make money on Saturday and Sunday mornings getting returns on the glass bottles that the big lads had left on the playing fields, five pence per bottle. Sometimes, Thomas would walk past the open door to the brick-built toilets on his way back from the off license on the high street, catch a draft of the fetid air within, and wonder who on earth would want to go in there in the first place?

Birch House was a magnet for the local children with its adventure playground, riding stables, and two full-sized football pitches. Thomas went with Dan Brennan to make the numbers up at a footie game with some older boys.

'Do you like Echo and the Bunnymen?' dark hair, dark eyes demanded.

'Err, yeah,' Thomas said, not having a clue who Echo and the Bunnymen were.

'What's yer name?'

'Thomas.'

'Is that yer first name or last name.'

'First.'

'Right. Yer name's Tom now.'

'My mum hates it when people shorten my name.'

'Do you want to play or not?'

Dark hair, dark eyes looked after Tom that night, telling the younger lad he was a good footie player, bigging him up before the others. Dan went home early, but Tom stayed. Somehow, Tom ended up in the public toilets with dark hair, dark eyes who showed Tom his penis and asked if he wanted to touch it. Tom had only ever seen one willy and that was his. His new friend's willy was huge in comparison. He could not take his eyes off the monster cock but shook his head anyway.

'Maybe when you're older,' dark hair, dark eyes said.

The two boys came out of the public toilet entrance just as Catherine Dales was walking across the cobbles from the stables with a riding hat and whip in her hands. Fortunately, Catherine had gone to Hind Green High after Saint Cuthbert's, rather than following the Church school route through secondary education, and Tom was spared any immediate malicious gossip.

Tom would see dark hair, dark eyes in a packed pub in town about six years later. He was with a group of lads and girls and blanked Tom completely. Which was a shame, because now he *was* older, and Tom knew every line, every verse of every song on *Crocodiles*.

He did not tell his mother.

15.

The funeral service for Lillian Keane was to be held at Saint James' with the cremation taking place at the council crematorium on Winwick Road. It was a Wednesday and chucking it down with rain, so, reluctantly, Tom accepted a lift with the funeral directors to the house.

Trains, planes, buses, he was okay with; but cars, even limos, brought back the familiar feelings of panic and lack of control. The dream he had had all his life—of his dad and brother's deaths—Tom was not sure whether it was factually true or just a distorted amalgam of five decades of repressed feelings. Who was the girl in his dream, the girl keeping him company on that eerie empty motorway? Whatever the complexities of the psychological trauma inflicted at a young age, whatever the intricacies of a grief that had never truly healed, Tom was pressing an imaginary brake pedal with his foot, wincing at every turn the black Daimler made as it threaded its way down the winding, tree-lined streets.

Lilian's body rested in a coffin set on a stand in the middle of the sitting room. Tom put on his best Father Morton persona, comforted Antony as best he could, shook the hands of cousins, uncles, aunties, second cousins, and then, taking his cue from the Head Funeral Director, he began the antiphon.

'"I am the resurrection and the life," the Lord says. She that believes in me, though she is dead, yet shall she live. Whoever lives and believes in me shall never die. Grant us, with all who have died in the hope of resurrection, to have our consummation and bliss in your eternal and everlasting glory, and with the blessed Virgin Mary and all your saints, receive the crown of life, which you have promised to all who share in the victory of your Son Jesus Christ.'

I'm just an actor, Tom thought, *playing a part. So, play that part well, Morton.*

Tom sprinkled the wooden casket with holy water.

'In the waters of baptism, our sister Lilian died with Christ,' he intoned, 'and she will rise with him to new life. As a father has pity on his own children, so God is merciful to those who love goodness. He knows where we are made. He knows we are the dust of stars and supernovas. The days of men and women are like grass: we flourish as a flower in the field, but as soon as the cold wind comes, we are gone. But the goodness of the Lord endures for ever and ever. Grant eternal rest to Lilian, O Lord, and let light perpetual shine upon her. Amen.'

He tried to kill himself after you left.

The gloved, suited, shiny-shoed Head Funeral Director indicated towards the coffin, and Antony and three relatives lifted the coffin onto their shoulders and carried it from the house, placing it gently in the back of the hearse.

The family and friends of Lillian Keane were gathered, holding umbrellas, and shivering in the cold as the funeral cortege arrived at the church.

Once inside the building, Father Morton, now dressed in the white robes that signified hope and ascension, addressed the mourners.

'Almighty God and Father, it is our certain faith that your Son, who died on the Cross, was raised from the dead, the first-fruits of all who have fallen asleep. Grant that through this mystery your servant, Lilian, who has gone to her rest in Christ, may share in the joy of his resurrection. We ask this through our Lord Jesus Christ, your Son, who lives and reigns with you and the Holy Spirit, one God, for ever and ever. Amen.'

After the Liturgy of the Word, Responsorial Psalm, readings from the Book of Wisdom and the Book of Revelations, Tom announced the words of Jesus.

'A reading of the Gospel according to Matthew,' he said.

'Glory to you, Lord,' the congregation responded.

'Jesus saw the crowds, and he went up a mountain and sat down. The disciples came to him, and he began to instruct them. "Blessed are the poor in spirit, for theirs is the kingdom of heaven. Blessed are those who mourn, for they will be comforted. Blessed are the meek, for they will inherit the earth. Blessed are those who hunger and thirst for righteousness, for they will be filled. Blessed are the merciful, for they will be shown mercy. Blessed are the pure in heart, for they will see God. Blessed are the peacemakers, for they will be called children of God. Blessed are those who are persecuted because of righteousness, for theirs is the kingdom of heaven. And blessed are you when people insult you, persecute you, and falsely say all kinds of evil against you because... because of me. Rejoice and be glad, because great is your reward in heaven... for in the same way they persecuted the prophets who were before you." This... is the Gospel of the Lord.'

Antony was watching him.

Love my son.

The Prayers of the Faithful, the Liturgy of the Eucharist, Holy Communion all followed as Tom switched into priest-autopilot. And then, it was time for the Commendation of the box inside the box, the empty cage that no longer held a force of personality inside it to animate its actions, to tell stories, laugh, cry, lie, scold, hold, to give birth to more life.

'To you, O Lord,' Tom prayed, 'we commend the soul of Lilian, your servant. In the sight of this world, she is dead; but in your sight, she *will* live for ever. Forgive the sins she committed through human weakness and in your goodness, grant her everlasting peace.'

Is he good?

The coffin sat atop of a polished metal stand. Tom held the aspergillum aloft. Then, walking a circuit, he sprinkled holy water over the casket.

A thurible with red-hot charcoal inside was hanging by its chain from a brass frame at the side of the altar. Tom lifted the top half of the thurible and used a spoon to carefully add powder from the incense boat. The incense crackled into life and began to spit and smoke. He closed the lid and, taking the thurible by the chain, he swung it towards the earthly remains of Antony's mother.

'Into your hands, Father of mercies, we commend our sister in the sure and certain hope that, together with all those who have died in Christ, she will rise with him on the last day. We give you thanks for the blessings that you bestowed upon Lillian in her lifetime. These wonderful blessings are sure signs of your infinite goodness. Father turn toward us and listen to our prayers: open the gates of paradise to your servant and help those of us who remain to comfort one another with assurances of faith until we meet at the end of time and are with you for ever. And may almighty God bless all of us gathered here today, may he keep us safe in the knowledge that we are all dearly loved.'

As the congregation sang the hymn, *The Lord is My Shepherd,* Tom watched as Antony left his seat to speak to the Head Funeral Director.

The coffin was carried outside, and the congregation began to disperse and make their way to cars parked on the main road. Tom spoke to Missus Hopwell, one of the church wardens, to ensure the building was going to be locked in his absence. Then, he disrobed in the sacristy, put his vestments inside a case, and hurried outside.

'Need a lift, Father?'

'I thought you'd gone.'

'I waited for you,' Antony said. 'You did us proud, Tom, although, I think you might have deviated somewhat from the official authorised version? Can I have a hug?'

He was outside the church, on the street, in full view of everyone.

'Of course,' Tom said. Holding Antony close, he added, 'I'm so sorry for your loss.'

'Can you say it?' Antony whispered.

'Say what?'

'You know what. You can't can you?'

'I don't…'

'We'd better go.'

Tom watched as Antony strode across the paved square. He felt a tightness in his chest and reached into his pocket for the salbutamol inhaler that he carried everywhere—just in case. Two sprays later and his lungs were reset.

He hurried after Antony.

16.

Tom was on his way to church when Stephen Fairfield and his fair-haired neighbour climbed over the fence from the special school.

'Moron,' Fairfield said, 'where are you off to now, you fuckin' bender?'

It was two against one, but Tom had had to pass up on watching the new live action Spiderman on TV to do his duty at seven-thirty evening mass and he was properly riled up.

'Fuck off, Fairy,' he said.

The pain exploded inside Tom's mouth, and he felt his head move backwards with the force of the blow. But he did not cry. He took the punch and stood his ground. And then, something very weird happened. Stephen Fairfield started to look uneasy and gave him a compliment.

'You took that well, Morton. You're not crying. Where are you off to?

'Church.'

'Are you?'

'Yeah.'

'See you at the bus stop in the morning.'

'Yeah.'

Father Spence was lighting candles on the altar when Tom arrived clutching his face.

'No Dan tonight?' Father Spence asked, his voice echoing inside the empty church.

Father Spence had been the parish priest at St Cuthbert's for as long as Tom could remember and, thanks to biblical narratives like the Passion Play read out on Palm Sunday, as far as Tom was concerned Father Spence's voice *was* the voice of Jesus.

Tom shook his head, the pain in his jaw throbbing.

'Ah well, it is Friday, I suppose. What happened to your face?'

Tom started to fill up, and he wiped his eyes with his coat sleeve.

'What happened?'

'Stephen Fairfield called me, then he punched me in the face.'

The old priest's face showed that he understood fully.

Then, Father Spence asked the question that changed the course of Tom's life.

'Thomas,' the voice of Jesus asked, 'have you thought about what you'd like to do when you are older? I could take you to visit the seminary at Ash Burrow if you would like.'

17.

'No, Joan,' Tom said, 'he is not staying over. I am looking after a friend of mine, making him some dinner, comforting him while he deals with the grief of losing his mother to a horrible wasting disease. I would do the same for any of my family, friends, and parishioners.'

'Father Thomas,' Joan said, arranging the plates inside the Welsh dresser, 'you would be alone in this house with a… homosexual.'

'You don't know…'

'It isn't right! My Joe says…'

If he heard the phrase 'my Joe says' one more time, Tom had decided he was going to run out of the room screaming. Why the hell would he ever want to take advice from a wife-beating, alcoholic, deadbeat, who sat at home in an armchair in front of the tele whilst his wife worked all hours that God sent to keep him in egg n' chips and super-strength cider?

'He's sick of the sexual corruption in the Catholic Church, that there is a homosexual cabal secretly selecting other gays to go into the seminaries. The cardinals are gays, and they elect the Pope, and they choose the bishops who are in league with the Trappists and the Jesuits. We could end up with married priests, woman priests, openly homosexual priests, even lesbian priests!'

'Joan, would it be so bad if priests could get married?'

'Priests getting married isn't going to help! Good Lord, Father, I was on the website and This Partisan Church says that up to sixty percent of Catholic priests are homosexual. Can you believe that? This Partisan Church says that most of the priests molesting little boys… are gay. We've got to pull this gay network out by its roots, close the seminaries until they are certified gay free!'

'Listen to me, Joan Bird,' Tom growled, 'there is a Grand Canyon-sized gulf separating same-sex attracted people and the perverts who abuse children and adults. One is consensual and the other is criminal.'

'There'll be gay masses next, those horrible rainbow flags hanging from the churches, the abomination of desolation in plain sight.'

'You're right, there *will* be a mass said where gay people will be warmly welcomed, and it will be here in Saint James. I'm going to throw the church doors open during Pride week.'

'It's filth, Father, filth… and I want no part of it. I'm sorry, I can't work here anymore.'

'Joan, you don't have to go. Please reconsider. I'd like you to stay.'

'Wait 'til Bishop Worrell hears about this.'

Joan Bird bustled from the kitchen, grabbing her handbag, and slamming the rectory door behind her.

No more dog shit pies, Tom thought, gleefully.

Then, the realisation hit just how much trouble he was going to be in with the Diocese, the Scripture Stazi at Hind Green, and with his own mother. And then, there was the matter of the Bishop.

18.

Tom and Dan built their own base on Tatty Cragg—the turn of the century slag heap that had become overgrown with conifers and grasses.

Back in the early 1980s, Tatty Cragg was a surrogate adventure playground for Tom, Dan, and the other local children. There were rope swings, bunny jumps for BMX bikes, and a long, grey, scree slope that was perfect for sliding down on top of a curved sheet of metal that had been stolen from the back of a motor workshop.

There were bases all over the Cragg, claimed by various gangs, and almost all these semi-permanent camps had their own supply of pornography stashed away in a secret hiding place. Where the 'nac mags' came from, no-one was quite sure, but they were traded for with alcohol and cigarettes.

Tom learned to express the correct sentiments when presented with pictures of naked women in various sexually explicit poses, and so did Dan. But the boys preferred their own company, and often escaped to their base hidden away at the back of Tatty Cragg.

The area behind the imposing black hill was riddled with old mine workings, filled-in air shafts, abandoned industrial buildings, and the old mineral railway that ran towards the town centre. For a time, it was paradise.

Then, Eamonn Kelly from primary school, started showing up with his friend, Eddie, and they were sniffing glue and petrol.

Tom was happy enough to have a quick toot on a Baby Regal, but solvents were not his bag. Dan, on the other hand, was introduced to sniffing glue by Kell n' Eds.

Back at their base beneath the conifer trees, Dan was acting weird. He pressed his mouth to Tom's and put his tongue in. Taken aback, Tom scrambled for safety and ran home. Dan stopped being an altar boy and started sitting with other people on the top deck of the school bus. After weeks of misery, Tom decided to call at Dan's house to see if he would play out.

'He's not in,' Dan's younger sister, Rosemary, said, eyeing Tom with a knowing look.

'Where is he?'

'With his friends.'

That was that. The two boys would pass each other in the busy corridors of St Pat's and not a word was spoken between them. Meanwhile, Eamonn and Eddie became the local scag heads, ultimately graduating from weed to heroin.

A year or so later, Tom learned that Daniel Brennan's adoptive parents had split up, and the house was being sold.

Dan took his own life, aged sixteen, just after taking his GCSE examinations. The story was that he tidied his room, left a note on the bed, and told his dad he was going out for a walk. His body was found by the police hanging from a tree at the top of Tatty Cragg.

Thirty years after Dan died, the ancient spoil heap ignited and burst into flames, an industrial eye-sore transformed into a fire-demon, looming above the new housing estate that had been built across the road. The solution taken by the emergency services was to level Tatty Cragg and to transport the flammable remains to a location devoid of four-bedroom executive detached houses, hot tubs, and trampolines.

But that was in the future. The reality for teenage Tom was a funeral, a funeral for a boy with whom he had served at funerals, two young lads in their church frocks, looking sombre, looking like butter wouldn't melt in their angelic mouths... until they pocketed the money in the small brown envelope, and then, laughing together, they were walking and running their way back home, life triumphing over the ceremony of death.

Tom took the easy option and did not attend Dan's funeral, a decision he regretted for the rest of his life.

That intoxicated kiss became a memory that smouldered in the deep recesses of Tom's mind for decades, until it too suddenly burst into life and threatened to engulf all that surrounded it.

19.

Tom showed Antony a copy of the book that had arrived in the post.

'God in Our Hearts,' Antony said, reading the cover. 'It looks innocuous enough.'

'Watch out for the teeth beneath the fur,' Tom said. 'This is the teaching material from the Diocese that describes being gay as "objectively disordered."'

'Love the sinner. Hate the sin?'

'And this garbage gets to be taught in Sunday Schools, Primary Schools, and Secondary Schools.'

'I bet they'll love this at Saint Benedict's.'

'I've got a meeting with Jeff Knight, the guy who leads the Jam Club...'

'Jam?'

'Jesus and Me,'

'Yeah, right,' Antony scoffed.

'There's nothing wrong with the name. It's about what they do in the half an hour that Jeff and his wife, Lyn, have them in the church hall. You want to see some of the pictures those kids draw of Jesus on the cross... Mel Gibson would wince!'

'You need to be careful, Tom, this sounds like...'

'They've both been DBS checked.'

'Abuse isn't just physical and sexual.'

'Yeah, I know.'

'So, this book is about white, straight, nuclear families, a mummy and a daddy, good kids who go to church, pray hard, work hard, and get into hetero heaven?'

'There's black families in there, too.'

'Lucky them. What about here at Jimmy's.'

'We'll carry on regardless.'

Antony had finished his breakfast. 'Do you think people know about you?' he asked.

'Know what?' Tom asked, sipping his coffee.

'And there, in those two words, lies the entirety of your problem, Tom.'

'What problem?'

'Jesus! You should listen to yourself. It frustrates the *hell* out of me. I'm going to go. I can't listen to any more of this shit. One day, you'll grow a pair.'

'It's not as easy as that,' Tom shouted as Antony closed the front door of the rectory behind him.

20.

Father Spence was on holiday. Every year, Father Spence and Father Worthington went on holiday together to Austria, to go climbing in the mountains. Father Worthington was a lovely, tall, smiley man, who still had jet black hair, unlike Father Spence, who was shorter and whose hair was a slicked-back silver helmet. Father Worthington was a teacher at Ash Burrow seminary as well as being chaplain at St Pat's Sixth Form college.

Father Molloy was the parish priest at St. Bernadette's, Crow Wood, and he looked after Father Spences' churches when he was on holiday, and vice versa. Father Molly, as Tom and Dan had taken to calling him, was built like a brick shithouse, a big man who rarely communicated, but who was a dab hand at Benediction, singing the verses in Latin instead of just reading them out like Father Spence did.

With no Dan, now that he had given up being an altar boy, Tom was stuck with Twang, or Mark Stringfellow to give the lad his full name. Twang was a tough kid from the council estate near the baked beans factory. He fought like a kangaroo in street fights, bouncing and outboxing his opponents. Twang was a year younger than Tom, half Tom's height, and he continually asked him for a fight on the way home from church. But to be fair to Twang, he had never punched Tom in the face like Fairy had.

'Why do you want to fight me?' Tom asked, as the boys put on their cassocks.

'I know I can beat you.'

'My mum knows your mum.'

'So?'

The monstrance was a beautiful object, a metal sun with the body of Christ at its centre, and as Molly held it aloft during the exposition,

Tom felt a mystical connection with this beautiful, solar Roman ritual, a sense of belonging among the sacramental structures and penitential rites of the Holy Catholic Church. A boy with no dad, no inherited football team, had found his male role models in Jesus, the Saints, and the priests of the universal church.

Deus, qui nobis sub sacramento mirabili, passionis tuae memoriam reliquisti: tribue, quaesumus, ita nos corporis et sanguinis tui sacra mysteria venerari, ut redemptionis tuae fructum in nobis iugiter sentiamus. Qui vivis et regnas in saecula saeculorum.

The words meant nothing to Tom in a literal sense, but as a rich stream of consciousness, spoken or sung, they were hypnotic, comforting, other-worldly.

And then, Twang nearly burned St. Cuthbert's to the ground.

Two charcoal bricks burned inside the thurible. All Twang had to do was walk across the carpeted altar, pick the thurible up by its chain and carry it across to Father Molly, then lift the lid and stand there and do nowt. Tom would bring the incense boat. Molly would take a few spoons of powder, drop it in, and then take the thurible from Twang, a few shakes of the incense shaker, and all Twang then needed to do was carry the smoking thurible back to its metal stand.

Unfortunately, short-arse Twang tripped over the hem of his cassock while carrying the thurible and dispensed the burning contents over the green carpet before falling on top of it himself.

Tom sprinted over, pulled the boy up, checked he wasn't on fire, and then, using the thurible base and lid, he captured the renegade burning coals.

'You okay?' Tom asked Twang, who was now on the verge of tears. 'No burns?'

The boy shook his head.

Father Molly was on his hands and knees with a dustpan and brush, sweeping up the incense from Father Spence's new altar carpet, which was now looking less than pristine.

Father Molly was nothing if not resilient, and as Tom reminded himself in later years, there ain't much that two verses of Tommy Aquinas's *Down in Adoration Falling* sung in Latin can't mend. Led by Molly's energetic baritone, the traumatised congregation gave it their all, raising the rafters in an accentual attempt at group therapy,

Tantum ergo Sacramentum
Veneremur cernui:
Et antiquum documentum
Novo cedat ritui:
Praestet fides supplementum
Sensuum defectui.

Genitori, Genitoque
Laus et jubilatio,
Salus, honor, virtus quoque
Sit et benedictio:
Procedenti ab utroque
Compar sit laudatio.

'I'll fucking kill you if you tell anyone at school,' Twang said, on the way home.

'I'm not going to say anything to anyone,' Tom said.

'Not even your mum?'

'Not even my mum. But there was a church full of people back there, Mark.'

'They're just gibbers.'

'Fair enough.'

'See you.'

'See you, Mark.'

Twang became a major talking point, a few years later, when it was reported that he got a hard on in the boy's showers in the Saint Pat's sport's hall after a game of rugby. To damp down a story that was spreading like wildfire, Twang offered to fight anyone who called him a puff outside the school gates. The threat of violence persuaded all but the unwary into silence. And, as everybody knew, puffs were soft. Twang was cock of his year, so how could he be a puff?

21.

'Father Morton?' Danny Arundel said, after his sister had scarpered out the door of the sacristy.

'Yes, Dan,' Tom said, as he filled in the attendance record sheet with a black pen.

'I have a friend.'

'That's good,' Tom said, his back turned.

'My friend asked me if being…'

'Being what?'

'If being gay is sinful.'

Tom noted that Danny had muffled the 'g' in the word gay, as if saying it out loud in a church was an offence to the other three letter 'g' word. Tom put his pen down and faced the boy.

'And does your friend know that they are gay?' he asked.

Dan stared at the floor.

'Yes,' he said.

'Boy or girl?'

'Boy.'

'God created your friend, so God loves your friend.'

'How can he know that?'

'Do you trust what I say?'

'Yes. But what if… when they find out… my friend's parents throw him out, and his other friends stop being friends with him?'

'The people that really love your friend will love them as they really are. It might just take some time.'

Danny nodded his head.

'Are they teaching you 'God in Our Hearts,' in your RS lessons at school?'

'In our year group assemblies, but not in RS.'

'Is your headmaster leading these assemblies?'

'How did you know?'

'Just a wild guess. Dan, I'm going to tell you something that I hope you'll keep to yourself.'

'What is it?'

'I… well… I don't like Mister Cooper. In fact, I can't stand the sight of him. And I definitely don't like that dreadful book 'God in Our Hearts,' so you tell your friend to be true to their self. Yeah?'

Danny smiled.

'Have you ever thought about what you'd like to do when you are older?' Tom asked.

'Yes,' Danny said.

'What would you like to be?'

'A doctor.'

'That's a great job, making sick people well. You'll be a fantastic doctor. Now, get out of here before your dad comes looking and Dan...'

'Yeah.'

If your friend ever needs to chat, I'm always here.'

22.

Skip and ASL became the father figures that Tom had never had. On Friday nights, Scout meetings were held in the church hall. Skip was a policeman and two of his lads were scouts. ASL was an accountant, and his five young children were in cubs and brownies.

The uniform, the rituals, all appealed to Tom, as did the sense of belonging to a tribe. There were camps away at Tawd Vale, and Tom loved everything about those days and nights: leaky tents, mud, bad food, tricks like hiding foul things in people's sleeping bags, sitting in the van when it was raining so hard all the activities were called off, beating all the other packs in West Lancashire in an orienteering competition because Declan McGuiness was a fast runner and could work a compass.

Tom's mum sewed the badges he earned onto his green Scout shirt—each badge had a specific place it needed to go. Tom and his mum were thrilled when he was named as one of the Assistant Patrol Leaders.

The day that Skip announced that he was leaving left an indelible mark on Tom. He wanted to cry, openly weep in the church hall, but that was impossible. Skip had two sons there, and it wasn't as if he'd died or anything. He was just... leaving Scouts, and Tom had responsibilities as an APL.

But this felt like grief.

'You okay, TM?' Skip asked, as he shook Tom's hand.

'Yeah, thank you,' Tom said.

ASL took over as Skip, but, to Tom, he was still ASL.

Tom saw ASL's cock when the troop was doing a seven-mile sponsored charity walk around the back of the reservoirs. ASL had stopped to take a piss in the bushes, and Tom hung back and waited with him. Tom thought of ASL's tiny blonde wife and winced, wondering how the mechanics of sex made it possible to fit ASL's penis inside her vagina?

ASL's significant manhood was imprinted on his memory, but Tom didn't think about the why, or what that signified.

23.

'Father Mallon,' Tom said, opening the door. 'Come in.'

'Father Morton,' the priest replied, stony-faced, as he stepped into the rectory porch.

'We can use my study,' Tom said.

'That would be grand.'

Tom smiled, nodded his head, and decided not to offer the loathsome sycophant in front of him a drink.

'That eye of yours, the scratches on your face, what happened?'

'I got punched,' Tom said, matter of fact.

'At a football match?'

'No nothing like that. I was putting the bins out, the security light didn't come on, and somebody attacked me.'

'Good Lord. And what did the police say?'

'They've given me a victim reference number, but without witnesses, CCTV, or me being able to identify my assailant, unfortunately, the chances of catching the perpetrator are slim.'

'These are difficult times that we live in, Father Morton.'

'Indeed, Father Mallon. Now, how can…'

'And what of the graffiti that was daubed across the church doors?'

'It was nothing.'

'"Rev M is a kiddie fiddler," is not nothing, Father. I'm sure you'll agree that the attack on you and the vandalism of a church with these allegations written on the door in white paint is, in fact, something.'

'Like I said, Father Mallon, I'm waiting to hear back from the police.'

'Bishop Worrell has had some complaints, Father, strongly worded correspondence from concerned Catholics that you are not embracing the spirit of the "God in Our Hearts" programme, and that you are "vague" on aspects of Church policy where there is no room for ambiguity.'

'And these complaints came from where and from whom?'

'You were trained at Ash Burrow. Were you not?'

'I was.'

'And are you one of those who mourned its closure?'

'Ash Burrow was where I spent a significant part of my life, to tear that beautiful old building down and build a housing estate in the grounds is a travesty.'

'The Church needs to balance its books and, besides, we had overcapacity in our priest training colleges, and...'

'And Bishop Worrell hates the place.'

'He does not hate the place.'

'How well do you know Derek Worrell, Father Mallon?' Tom asked.

The priest sitting opposite him said nothing.

'Then, I see we've both had a similar experience, because "primate" is the right word for Derek, isn't it? The physical and sexual mastery of other males. Derek likes to humiliate people. I wonder what happened to Derek as a boy to turn him into what he became.'

'That's *His Excellency*, Bishop Worrell, to you, Father Morton.'

'The day I call Derek Worrell "His Excellency," is the day I've had a lobotomy.'

'Your parish priest was Father Spence, was it not?'

'It was.'

'And your Spiritual Director at Ash Burrow was Father Worthington?'

'Father Eden was my Spiritual Director at Ash Burrow for the first three years. I knew Father Worthington as St Pat's Sixth Form Chaplain.'

'Fathers Spence and Worthington had a reputation as, and here I quote, "a pair of queens who enjoyed the café bars of Vienna."'

'I can only tell you that they were true priests, followers of Jesus, and two of the kindest and most loving men that I've ever met.'

'Would it surprise you to learn that Father Spence died from an AIDS related illness?'

'Father Spence valued his privacy,' Tom said, struggling to control his temper, 'and I never pried.'

'So, in summary, you were recruited and trained by two known homosexuals, one of which, possibly both, died from a sexually transmitted disease. Father, a question...'

'There is a lot of assumption, generalisation, and ignorance in those words, Father...'

'Father Morton, if I may… a simple question, are you same-sex attracted?'

'I would remind you, Father Mallon, that I took a vow of celibacy when I was ordained. Everything else is none of your business.'

'This isn't a formal investigation, Father Morton… yet. So, of course, you have your rights. But I would advise you…'

'Time is pressing, Father. And as much as I enjoy your company, I have a sermon to write about The Greatest Love. Perhaps you have some advice and tips for me?'

'One of the initiatives that Bishop Worrell…'

'The sadistic, rapist prick, Bishop Worrell…'

'His Excellency, Bishop Worrell, is very keen on giving his hard-working priests, priests like you, Father Morton, the opportunity to reflect on their vocation. Maybe we could ask someone else to run your parishes for a while, say two or three years, so that you can… recharge your batteries.'

'That is a kind and generous offer. But really, there is no need. I thrive working on the front line, with the sick, the old, the infirm, as Our Lord did.'

'In which case, I would advise that familiarising yourself with the key parts of the Diocesan plan and ensuring that your parishes are compliant should be top of mind. There are godly priests who I know would relish the opportunity to raise standards in this *Jesuit* house. And if congregation numbers were to fall, we would, of course, have to be financially prudent. How would St. James' look as a nightclub, a restaurant, a gym, or a block of trendy apartments?'

'You have my word, Father,' Tom spat, 'that I will *always* act in line with the will of God.'

'Try acting in line with the will of the Church leadership. Let your superiors worry about God. Oh, and Father Morton…?'

'Yes?'

'This queer Mass that I hear you and your boyfriend have organised… if that event went ahead without the permission of the Bishop, then your actions would constitute grounds for dismissal: no home, no salary, no car, no pension. Is that understood?'

'You wouldn't dare!'

'Yes, we would. Perhaps I could send you a complimentary set of "God in Our Hearts" teaching materials for you to be familiarising yourself with?'

'Aye,' Tom said, 'that would be grand. And thank you, Father, for your time and your generosity.'

24.

The paper round was building Tom's leg muscles as he biked up and down the hideous hill to Mere Head. Behind Mere Head was the reservoir and the convent, and behind these was the old medieval road from Bussell to Preston with its stone pilgrim's crosses. Tom worked each weekday morning and evening after school and earned five pounds, fifty pence per week. It was a fortune. Each week he could afford a new cassette by his favourite band, or he could save up for six weeks and buy a decent pair of fashion trainers like the ones Dan Brennan had.

Tom had decided to up his game and take on a Saturday and Sunday round too, and the opportunity arose when sixteen-year-old Paul Meyer decided to pack in his weekend round.

'Sounds like a German name to me,' was what Tom's Grandad Pilks said, when Tom blurted out his admiration and esteem for Paul after two weeks of training.

Paul was thorough, showing Tom which letter boxes to use, how to avoid the dogs at the farms, and his top tip was to send each household a personalised Christmas card each December, to maximise seasonal tips. Paul was tall, slim, blond, and Tom didn't even mind it when Paul farted, and the wind blew the smell into his face.

In the newspaper-shop, the owner's daughter, Chloe, was flirting with the boys, feeling their muscles as they lifted the paper bags. Chloe laughed as she felt Tom's feeble arms. Paul was too tall, and he had his parka on, so Chloe couldn't get near him, which Tom was glad about.

He was his Paul, if only for a short time.

Paul finished, and Tom only saw him fleetingly through the window of the St. Pat's school bus as Paul stood waiting for a bus into Bussell town centre.

Paul was dead-gorgeous, and he was also dead-right about personalised Christmas cards from 'Tom, your paperboy.' Tom raked in forty quid in his first season.

It was like winning the national lottery.

25.

Tom pedalled from the town centre uphill to Mere Head, then freewheeled into Blackwater valley, following the line of the gurgling river born on the West Pennine Moors. From the Hind Green roundabout, it was half a mile of flat to the red-walled Dyeworks that was built across the flow of the stream the Ancient Britons had named the Dub Glais. The stretch up to the reservoirs and the visitor centre was a short climb, so Tom stayed in low gears. Turning right into the carpark, he locked the frame and wheels against the lichen covered wooden fence at the side of the toilet block and the new touchscreen parking-payment machine.

Antony arrived by car, his SUV jolting from side to side as it navigated the stone-strewn carpark and its deep, pitted puddles. He waved when he saw Tom waiting for him, backpack at his feet, a bike helmet tied to the straps.

Tom wondered if Antony would understand the decision he had made.

Pragmatism or cowardice—you couldn't put a cigarette paper between the two concepts, he thought.

The two men embraced and started across the stony path around the reservoir, the sunlight sparkling like diamonds across the surface of the drinking water destined for the homes and businesses of Liverpool. They met a dogwalker with an inquisitive collie as the path turned from gravel to a dirt track, but otherwise, they had the rocks, woods, moors, and the squelching mud of the drowned valley to themselves.

'Why couldn't I pick you up at the vicarage?' Antony asked, opening a wooden gate and holding it so Tom could pass through. 'Surely that is easier than riding your bike all the way here, going for a long walk, and then riding your bike all the way back into town?'

'I don't like being in cars.'

Antony let the gate swing shut behind him.

'I'm a safe driver, you know.'

'It's not you and your driving. Honest.'

'Don't say it's about your dad. We both know that's bollocks.'

'What do you mean?' Tom asked, feeling hurt and annoyed.

'It's a lack of trust, an obsession with control. If you are embarrassed of me coming to see you, just say,' Antony said.

'I'm not embarrassed of you, and I never will be.'

'In that case, we take the front wheel off your bike, stick it in the back of the beast, and I'll run you home. Deal?'

'Promise you'll drive slow?'

'I promise, Grandpa.'

The path shifted uphill to avoid a rocky promontory overlooking the water. Antony stumbled and Tom reached out to steady him.

'So, what actually... happened the night you were attacked?' Antony said, catching his breath.

'Whoever it was, was waiting. I didn't see them, but they came lumbering out of the darkness and punched me in the face and stomach, then ran off.'

'Did you see anything, hear anything?'

'I've been hit before—hit hard—but these punches were laboured swings that happened to have the element of surprise. My assailant had been drinking. I could smell the booze on him.'

'Which narrows it down to...?'

'Half the town, unfortunately.'

'You've been queer bashed, Reverend,' Antony said. 'How does that make you feel?'

'Rather angry,' Tom said.

'Rather angry? You should be bloody furious!'

'I'm raging about the graffiti daubed across the church entrance. I had to scrape the paint off, sand it, reseal the wood. Those doors are two-hundred years old. It's senseless vandalism.'

'So, you weren't angry about a slanderous message accusing you of being a predator altar boy rapist: you were annoyed with *where* they'd written it?'

'Of course, I'm angry about that,' Tom said. 'I'd never hurt a child, ever.'

'Every time they try to link being gay with abusing children, it has to be challenged,' Antony said. 'It *cannot* be accepted, tolerated, or ignored. It's your job to call it out, Tom. Don't just remove the evidence and hope that nobody sees it.'

'It is not as easy as that,' Tom said. 'The Bishop is being lauded as a true Catholic, a man standing up to the homomafia in Rome, a pious priest attacking the Luciferian, left-wing, homo-heresy championed by "the man who is currently the Pope,"—a fake Pope, a Jesuit Pope, possessed by an anti-white, anti-capitalist, anti-one-true-God, sodomite devil. Derek Worrell is spinning a narrative about gay priests, and I am a gay priest, Antony. That odious man is saying that no one is born gay. They choose it. Did you choose to be gay, Antony? I'm damn sure I didn't. As much as I loathe him for what he subjected me to, as much as I despise everything he stands for, I have responsibilities—for my parishioners, to ensure St. James' is there for future generations.'

A barbed wire fence separated walkers from nearby grazing sheep, embossed metal signs instructed dog-owners to keep their domesticated wolves on a lead, wooden warning notices announced that anyone caught lighting a fire or having a barbeque would be liable to prosecution.

'Did you fall in love with Pete's brother?'

Antony sighed. 'I did, for a time. I've always liked Brian.'

'Oh.'

'Why don't you go to the police and tell them about what that man Worrell did to you?' Antony asked. 'Or are you going to turn the other cheek to this fiend in priest's clothing.'

'Bishop Derek is the hard man of conservative Catholicism. He is a powerful man. Who would believe a man like me, after all these years? Who would believe a pinko priest over a man tipped to be a cardinal by the time he is fifty-five?'

'I believe you,' Antony said, as he stopped to take in the view of the reservoir as it followed the natural curve of the valley then disappeared behind a line of trees. 'I believe you, and others would too, because you are a truthful man.'

He sighed and reached for Tom's hand.

'It's so beautiful here. There's none of the ugliness of towns, none of the vile belligerence of people trying to hurt other people, none of the banality of evil disguised as rite and reason.'

'They're man-made lakes,' Tom said, 'but you're right, it is beautiful here.'

'Your man-made God,' Antony asked, 'is he still beautiful?'

'I used to deliver papers to some of the farms off the main road when I was a lad. I looked to these reservoirs, to the hills that fed them, and I wondered what was on the other side.'

'Yorkshire,' Antony said, 'bloody Yorkshire, that's what's on the other side!'

Tom laughed, 'I was trying to make a serious theological point in answer to your challenge.'

Antony put his arm around Tom.

'You have to choose a side. You know that don't you? Your Church is tearing itself into two: on one side, a traditionalist hierarchy that does not accept queer lifestyles, and never will; and, on the other, an embryonic organisation that puts love at the centre of its teachings and practice, regardless of sexuality and gender. The Church of England is going through the same thing. But the Catholic Church has the biggest opportunity and the biggest danger, because so many of its priests are gay... men and women like you, who hide their love away, disguising who they are within the trappings of organised religion.'

'If only it was that simple.'

'It *is* that simple, Tom. You have to come out. The Church needs to come out.'

'These things take time and patience. The Church is two-thousand years old. It's...'

'Your congregation isn't going to wait forever. And I'm not going to wait forever.'

Antony pulled Tom into an embrace and, as the sun warmed their faces and the breeze whipped their clothes, they kissed.

'Incredible,' Tom breathed, his eyes closed.

'What is?' Antony said, smiling.

'That visceral connection. It's just not there for me with women, only men.'

'It's called "choosing to be gay,"' Antony teased.

'Forgive me,' Tom said, pulling away, still holding Antony's hand.

'For what?'

'I've cancelled the mass at Saint James. I'm so sorry.'

'The celebration of queer lives mass?'

Tom nodded.

'You're fucking kidding me, right?' Antony said, taking his hand away. 'You cancelled it, after I got all the local LGBTQ groups involved?'

'I had to.'

'Why, Tom?'

'They threatened to close my church... to sack me.'

'Your Church threatened to close your church? And you believed them?'

'You don't know these people.'

'How did they find out?'

'Does it matter?'

'You're a big scaredy cat, Thomas Morton,' Antony said, tears forming in his eyes. 'More fool me for giving you another chance. You'll never change, will you?'

'I'm sorry.'

'Stop fucking saying that you're sorry all the fucking time. Do you have any idea of the damage that things like this do to young gay people, to gay elders who are still in the closet?'

Tom said nothing.

'I feel really let down, *really* let down. You can make your own way home, Mister. And I don't ever want to see you, again.'

Antony strode off, heading back down the path in the direction of the carpark.

Tom sank to his knees.

'Eternal Father,' he prayed, watching as Antony disappeared behind a dry-stone wall. 'Please, please, tell me what to do. Help me to choose the right path. I don't know what to do. In the name of your son, Jesus Christ, Our Lord. Amen.'

And Tom cried bitter tears of loss and regret, as the grief of separation consumed him physically, spiritually, and mentally.

26.

Tom was home from school and the house was locked. Panic set in, and a dim memory of his mum mentioning a doctor's appointment came to mind. Tom raced down the road, down the cut past the Rec, past the butchers, the vets, over the zebra crossing, past the chippy, the pub, and into the entrance of the surgery housed in the austere row of houses.

He heard his mum's voice coming from Doctor Taylor's room and he pushed open the door.

'Mum,' he gasped, 'you're here.'

Doctor Taylor looked embarrassed, and his mum's face drained of colour.

From the surgery to the chemist and all the way back home, Tom got both barrels from his mother.

Tom took the tongue-lashing, telling his mum how sorry he was, acting penitent, but all the while he gloried in her attention.

All that mattered was that he wasn't on his own.

All that mattered was he wasn't locked out, on the outside looking in.

All that mattered was authority was not absent.

27.

After 6 o'clock Confession at Saint Benny's—an hour listening to the self-declared sins of Hind Green's middle-class congregation—Tom locked up the front door of the 1970s church constructed on top of the remains of the original Saint Benedict's, switched his bike lights on, and began the long climb home. He was just past the West Coast Mainline train bridge when the heavens opened.

Arriving home, soaked to the skin, Tom peeled off his wet biking gear and threw it in the washing machine. His priest's clothing was carefully wrapped in the lined backpack: Tom straightened the jacket and trousers and hung them on hangers from the picture rail in the hallway. The dark grey shirt, minus its clerical collar, was screwed up into a ball and deposited with the saturated jacket, leggings, and underwear.

Tom showered with the temperature set at maximum to shake the cold from his bones. He was on the ledge mentally. He knew it. Below was the swirling void, the comforting numbness.

He dressed in jeans and a smart shirt, put on his winter coat and shoes and, leaving the sanctuary of San Tiago behind him, Tom turned up his collar, opened-up his umbrella, then merged with the human horde rushing between bars, restaurants, and taxis on that wet weekend in Bussell.

Pete King's 50th birthday celebration was being held at the Bowling Club, which was a five-minute walk around the shopping centre, past the Technical College, past the park gates, then down an avenue of pre-war semis.

Inside the Bowling Club, the music was pulsing, the buffet was out, guests had arrived, and Tom spotted Michael O'Keefe at the bar with Pete.

Tom hugged Michael.

'Now then,' he said, 'it's good to see you.'

'It's been too long,' Michael replied.

'Put the man down, Morton. Do you want a drink?' Pete asked.

'I should be getting one for you. Happy birthday, Pete. I've got a present for you.'

'If it's a bible, you can stick it up your arse,' Pete said, shouting over chanted verses of *I Will Survive* echoing from Monica King's side of the family, who were all camped out at the dessert end of the buffet table.

'I said, *"What* do you want to drink?"'

Michael was creased up, laughing.

'Guinness.'

'Pint?'

'Is the Pope Catholic?'

Tom noticed that it was Shaun Burke DJing in the corner of the room, a laptop and an amp set on a table between a set of flashing disco lights. With the cold stout in his hand, Tom raised his glass to salute his friend, who was doing a sterling job at the decks, playing the classics for aunties and uncles, grannies and grandpas. Shaun smiled and waved back.

'You missed Antony,' Michael said, 'He was here earlier, but he said he couldn't stop.'

'That's a shame,' Tom said.

'His mum died, and he's been settling her affairs. Once the house is sold, he's moving back down to Cornwall.'

'Devon,' Pete corrected.

'Devon,' Michael said.

'I didn't realise the house was up for sale,' Tom said.

'We had some fun there,' Michael sighed, 'back in t'day.'

'We did,' Tom said, 'did Antony…?'

'So, where's my present then?' Pete asked, interrupting. 'It's a book, isn't it?'

'Kind of,' Tom said, supping his drink.

'Remember what I said, Reverend Morton. You're going to have a very sore bottom if this is a religious treatise.'

'It's definitely a Bible,' Michael said. 'He got me one for my fiftieth last September, the bastard.'

'Shaun got one, too,' Tom said, 'so we'll make it a clean sweep!'

'Doesn't feel too heavy,' Pete said, tearing off the wrapping paper, 'Shit, the official programme for the European Cup Winners' Final 1966, Liverpool versus Borussia Dortmund, Hampden Park. We lost 2-1, but who cares, where did you get this, mate?'

'I got it online.'

'Nice one,' Pete said, throwing his arms around Tom, 'I take everything back that I said about you before you arrived.'

Pete disappeared to show his wife and daughter his new treasure.

'Very thoughtful,' Michael said, as Shaun came over to join them.

'Hello, Tommy,' Shaun said, as the friends embraced.

'Is it nice to be back home?' Tom asked.

'Nah,' Shaun said, shaking his head. 'Coming back always reminds me of why I left.'

'Is Monica's dad, here?' Tom asked, looking around, concerned in case Pete's father-in-law, a man with a pathological hatred of priests, was around.

'Haven't seen him,' Michael said.

'How come you never moved away, Tom?' Shaun asked. 'There must be a nice seaside parish somewhere, rather than one ten minutes down the road from where you grew up?'

'I asked for Saint James.'

'Jesus,' Michael said.

'Why would you do that?' Shaun asked.

Tom shrugged.

'What's your view on them shutting Bussell Town Hall as part of the local government shake up?' Michael asked.

'Why should we be ruled from Manchester?' Tom said. 'Local people should make local decisions.'

'There's a hundred thousand people in this town,' Michael said. 'There are some streets in London with those numbers, and they don't have a Town Hall, a mayor, all the costs of administration.'

'I'd never want to live in London.'

'You should spread your wings, mate,' Shaun said, 'see a bit of the world before it's too late and you're sitting dribbling in front of the TV in some priest retirement home. You are the one person I know who went through Catholic education and still believes in God, the Virgin Mary, and Baby Jesus. I don't remember much of that nonsense, but I do remember that "harden not your hearts" line from the Bible. *If*—and it's a big if—we all arrive on a train together in eternity, it is not going to matter whether you are in the front carriage or the last? We'll all step onto the platform at the same time. *Unless* you are the guy who refuses to get up from his seat because the real heaven doesn't match with your idea of what it should look like.'

'What are you saying?' Tom asked, sensing an ambush.

'A change is as good as a rest,' Michael said. 'Getting out of your comfort zone might do you some good. You know what I mean?'

'No, not really.'

Michael and Shaun were both silent for a moment as the music played and people pushed past them to queue at the bar.

'What do you mean?'

'Don't lose love, Tom,' Michael said. 'If you lose that, then what kind of priest would you be?

'Look, we're your friends,' Shaun said, 'and we just want you and Antony to be happy.'

Tom was stunned, unable to say anything.

'You think that me and Shaun didn't know?' Michael asked. 'We were in the room next door when the two of you were going at it hammer and tongues all those years ago.'

'You don't know anything. I have responsibilities, I have...'

'Look, Tom, we've always known,' Shaun said.

'I'm not... what you think. I...'

'And the cock crew for the third time,' Michael said.

'It would be easier for us to say nothing,' Shaun said, 'to soft soak yer, to let you miss out on a real chance at happiness. But what kind of friend would do that?'

Tom put his empty on the bar.

'I've got three masses tomorrow,' he said. 'So, I'm going to call it a night. Always a pleasure, boys, never a chore.'

'We love you, man,' Michael said. 'Remember that.'

'Say goodbye to Peter,' Tom said, 'and I'll see you next time you're home.'

Tom walked home across town in the rain, feeling the gentle push on his shoulder blades, the nudge to let go and fall forever.

28.

The school bus crashed into the Manchester to Southport railway bridge, taking half of the top deck off. The driver and conductor would later defend the decision to take a 14-foot bus under a 12-foot bridge by suggesting the screaming children panicked and confused them.

It seemed to happen in slow motion for Tom, a nightmare that morphed into reality. Everyone knew only single deck buses came down this road, no adult would be so stupid as to take a double-decker down the road into Hick Bibby Valley. Children streamed down the stairs from the top deck, crowding the front and middle doors as the looming stone tunnel drew ever closer.

The impact was surreal, a movie in real life. Debris cascading down the stairs, the bus stopped in its tracks by the unyielding Victorian architecture, crying children with splinters of glass in their hair, the driver leaning against his colleague in tears.

Tom realised that he was clutching Michael's hand.

'Are you okay?' Michael asked.

29.

Tom picked at the food his mother had made for him.

'It was the happiest day of my life,' Emma Morton, said, as she brought the buttered bread to the dining room table. 'Nine pound six ounces you were.

The nurse said, 'I bet he'll be playing for Bussell Rugby when he's older!''

'I was never much good at rugby.'

'No, but you were good at lots of other things.'

What about Colin, Tom thought. *What about Dad?*

'The second happiest day of my life was the day you were ordained.'

Tom stared at his ham and cheese salad.

'I'm glad the Church is finally confronting the gay priest problem, aren't you? All those little boys and girls molested by homosexuals.'

'They say Cardinal Newman was gay, Mother.'

'They're wrong,' Emma said, flinging her fork down. 'He definitely wasn't.'

'He is buried with his lover.'

'Gays are *not* created in the image of God, Thomas.'

'Abuse by priests has nothing to do with whether they are heterosexual or homosexual. It has everything to do with whether they are rapist bastards or not.'

'I will not hear language like that at this table, not from you, not from a man of the cloth.'

Would you still love me, Mother, if you knew who I am. I grew inside your womb. Would you reject me, your own flesh and blood?

The thought of maternal rejection, of being cast out from the female clan that stretched back through time and space was a thought too hideous for Tom to contemplate, even after five decades of life, even after the death of his grandmothers.

'When was dad in prison, Mum?'

''71 to '72. Your nana Morton never told your grandad that he was there. She told him he was on a residential sales course. She said if your grandad had found out the truth, he would have never spoken to your dad again.'

The dining room was lined with bookcases, shelves upon shelves of Catholic histories, lives of the Saints, insights into theology from American and Canadian priests, books on Communion, Sacred Mysteries, books about the Popes, books by the Popes.

Fuckin' pointless, Tom thought. *You and I both know that Colin was conceived while dad was inside. What happened, Mum? Did you fall in love, or did something terrible happen to you? You're a Catholic, so you bore the child, but did you love him? And what did Dad say?*

Tom could still remember little curly haired Colin and love welled up inside of him for his brother, a joy followed all-too-soon by an all-pervading sense of despair at the negation of life's possibility.

This room, this house, cluttered with books that you use to insulate yourself from hurt and life's cruel fuckery, these framed pictures of your priest son are all a sham, Mother. But I'm not brave enough, not vicious enough to tear it all down. So, we lie to each other. And it is killing us, sending us both to hell.

'What was the third happiest day in your life?' Tom asked.

'Don't be cheeky,' Emma Morton said. 'Eat your tea. And buck your ideas up. You haven't smiled once since you got here.'

'I love you, Mum, always remember that.'

'I love you too. Now eat your food, otherwise it's a waste of money.'

30.

The blows rained down on Tom's head as he fought off the woman who had given him birth. He ran down the path at the side of the house, but she was fast and easily caught him. She was crying now, the blows losing their strength, the curses losing their sting.

'I can lift it up,' Tom said, 'Mum, stop, please.'

Tom ran into the backyard and prised open the grid with the rake handle. Green strands hung from the metal and the stink of the drain was in his face as he put his hand inside.

The thought of rats, snakes and squishy bugs lurking in the curved pipe filled him with terror as he groped in the slime for the feel of metal. And then, he felt it.

Holding the dripping brown mass before his silent mother, Tom ran to the outside tap and washed the set of keys clean.

'Give them to me,' she said. 'Go in and wash your hands.'

Afterwards, she hugged him as they sat on the kitchen step.

'I love you so much.'

'Love you too,' Tom said.

'I'm sorry for losing my temper. But you must try not to be so clumsy all the time.'

'I'm sorry,' Tom said.

He knew that, somehow, in some way, he was helping to heal whatever trauma his mother had endured that day. After dinner, he rode to the Spar shop at the traffic lights on his bike and bought his mum some flowers.

'These are to say sorry,' he said, as he presented the spray of carnations and chrysanthemums that had cost him half a week's paper-round wages. But they weren't to say sorry, they were to say something else. His mum cried as she accepted the gift from her twelve-year old son.

'Have I told you which day was the happiest day of my life?' she said, hugging him.

'You have,' Tom said, with his arms around her waist.

And he promised God, there and then, that he would never bring pain to the woman who was his whole world.

31.

The envelope on the coir doormat had 'Father Thomas Morton' written in black ink on the front.

Antony's letter began by thanking Tom for leading his mother's funeral service, and for his support and friendship in the weeks that had followed. The handwritten page informed Tom that Antony had settled his mother's estate, that he would be returning to Devon to look after his restaurant and delicatessen business, and that, if Tom were to find himself in the southwest, there would always be a warm welcome and a pot of tea waiting for him.

'Having reflected on the latest pronouncement from the Congregation of the Doctrine of the Faith,' Antony wrote, 'I could not, would not, ever be part of an organisation that believes being gay is morally disordered and intrinsically evil. And I wonder how you can stomach this duplicity, Tom? Claiming that you are working to change the system from within is moral cowardice—we both know this to be true. We are all children of God: LGBTQIA and heterosexual cisgender people alike. The Roman Catholic Church says that it cannot in good conscience bless same sex unions because it cannot bless sin, a statement of monumental hypocrisy given that most of its priests are gay.'

'I can appreciate the isolation and trepidation of the individual priest trapped in this institutionally homophobic organisation, this medieval, authoritarian dinosaur,' Antony wrote, in his penultimate paragraph, 'but when a servant of Christ, however powerless they feel themselves to be, welcomes homosexuality *and* faith, they contest the dangerous assumption that these two are somehow mutually exclusive.'

'I will always be your friend,' the letter finished, 'and I will always love you. Now and forever, Antony.'

Tom ripped the letter up and threw it in the bin.

And then he picked the torn paper from between the satsuma peelings and cold tea bags, pieced it together on the kitchen work surface, and wept.

32.

Michael helped Tom choose a new pair of jeans from Stolen from Ivor, then they got the 635 bus back to Michael's house. There, in Michael's bedroom, they listened to music, Michael educating Tom on new sounds, new artists, and classic vinyl. Tom stayed over at Michael's house that night, sleeping on the floor at the side of Michael's bed, sharing a blast of Michael's deodorant in the morning.

Michael was going on the Saint Pat's school ski trip to the French Alps, which Tom couldn't go on. It was Grandma's birthday the same week, he told his friend, otherwise he would have come too.

Tom hated the thought of his best friend going without him, but there was nothing he could do about it.

In school, Tom had worked out how to flick two pence pieces in the vending machine slot, so they bounced off the magnets either side of the mechanism, which allowed him to claim a ten pence drink. He also started selling his mum's home-made bread sandwiches, which he had grown to hate, but the boys in his class, for some strange reason, seemed to love. Tom used the money to buy chips and gravy from the school canteen.

In Home Economics classes, Tom was told he made great pastry. In Mathematics, he knew that he was struggling. In English, they were reading *Lord of the Flies*. In Art, he was making progress, Science was okay. History was great—prehistoric human sacrifices. French was boring, Technical Drawing was dull. Sport was a misery, and Religion was something he was good at. Religion was taught by an Indian teacher, called Reg Reynolds, who insisted that the early Christians were all communists.

Saint Pat's was built on the site of a former monastery, and a headless monk was rumoured to roam the basement near the art department. Tom sat next to Shaun Burke in art. Shaun was picked on by one of the tough kids and had had chewing gum mashed into his hair, which then had to be cut out by one of the ladies in the school office, leaving him temporarily with a monk's haircut. Shaun was anxious in social settings, stuttering and fidgeting. He was good at drawing, but not as good as Michael.

Tom tried on his mother's underwear and clothes sometimes when he got home from school. The feeling he got from dressing up in his mum's clothing was electric and discovering the feminine inside himself felt like a step into the unknown.

Tom's new friend, Shirley, was in his form group, and she was hilarious. Sometimes, when Michael was playing badminton in the Sports Hall, Tom would hang out with Shirley and her friends, revelling in their company and playing chasing games around the school.

And then, Michael met Robert Dowson at Badminton club. Robert was good-looking, extremely intelligent, and he used sarcasm like a scalpel. Michael, and Shaun too, had started following Robert around as part of a gang that seemed to hang on his every word. Naturally, Tom hated him, and it did not take long for Robert to notice this.

As much as Tom loved spending time with Shirley, he didn't want to spend all his time with her, and even she seemed to have a soft spot for evil genius Dowson because he could play the piano.

When Robert referred to Michael, one day, as 'Gormless O'Keefe' in Tom's earshot, the rest of the Dowson fan club sniggered. Tom wanted to kill him on the spot for insulting his best friend, a boy who was clearly wonderful in every way. Michael himself didn't respond to Robert's barbed comment. He didn't defend himself: He just took it and Tom wondered how anyone could stay friends with someone who was just plain mean, nasty, and vindictive.

Gradually, Michael drifted away from him, preferring the cool club with Rob, the Spider King, at the centre of the web. The school ski trip made things even worse as they all had a shared experience that Tom did not have. Tom had to go through a process of grieving until he had reached a point where he could meet Michael in the school corridors and exchange pleasantries without wanting to run away to the toilets for a quiet sob in a cubicle for ten minutes.

The person who helped Tom through this difficult period of adjustment with their kindness, compassion, and good sense was Father Spence.

33.

Tom flew down the road to nowhere, a 1960s construction project that had been intended to act as the connection between a dual carriageway into Bussell town centre and the M6 motorway. The money had run out, and the four-lane highway had never been built. These days the road ended at a mini-roundabout and a slip-road into a garden centre.

Buses, cars, trucks accelerated past the furiously pedalling prelate, a continuum speeding towards the motorway junction. The wind rushed around Tom as the bike gathered momentum, hurtling towards the red iron railings suspended above the void, the tarmacked abyss with its screaming demons that had so terrified him as a child. The brake levers were spongy in his palms.

Tom pushed his 'acquired-capability-for-lethal-self-harm' as hard as he could, pedalling with all his might before his courage could become corroded by doubt and fear. The momentum was delicious, the air caressed his face, and death was an adventure. The give-way junction was before him, the railings over the Styx were before him. From the corner of his eye, he saw the green car exit from the southbound slip-road. He saw the driver watch blank-faced as two independent variables intersected. He felt the Ballardian sexual release of collision, the ragdoll-roll over the smooth painted roof of the estate car, the sudden impact on the pitted road. He heard the screeching tires and horns sounding, car doors slamming, shouting, the blue-light ambulance ride to the infirmary.

The next day, he was home, battered, bruised, brain-scanned, clutching a transcript of his interview with the police, but minus his beloved bike and still very much in the land of the living.

Tom was in the sacristy, spaced-out on heavy duty painkillers, as the Arundel siblings were getting dressed for mass. Danny Arundel found something that Tom had accidentally left out on the table.

'Father Morton?' Danny said, shaking the contents.

'Yeah, Dan,' Tom said, from his position in a grey parallel universe of misery.

'What does lamivudine do?'

Part Two

Protection

34

The week that Father Ronan stayed at his house was a week like no other. The school had sent letters home to parents and carers asking if anyone had a spare bedroom for the New Life School Ministry Team. Tom and his mum hit the jackpot when they learned the top priest himself was going to be staying at their house for four nights.

New Life's mission was to make Jesus known in Catholic secondary schools by leading assemblies, taking religious studies lessons, hanging around the refectory while lunch was being served, and getting to know pupils at break times.

For a week, Tom didn't have to catch the school bus, and he had a lift with Father Ronan in his beat-up Austin Allegro. The twenty minutes on the journey there, and the twenty minutes on the journey back at the end of the school day, were an opportunity to spend time with Father Ronan one-to-one, and Tom loved the man for his kindness and generosity.

The fifteen strong team of priests, nuns, and young people, armed only with acoustic guitars and the love of Jesus, blitzed the school with a gospel of joy and positivity. It was a time of great energy and celebration, and Tom was swept along by the good vibe Christianity that seemed so different to that of Father Spence and St Cuthbert's.

Tom made it known that Father Ronan was a guest at his house, and he enjoyed the bubble of celebrity that gave him throughout the school with pupils and teachers alike.

The week culminated with a mass in the school hall, and Tom was virtually in tears as he watched 'his' Father Ronan lead the celebration of the Eucharist.

As Father Ronan was saying his goodbyes that Friday night, his mother slightly spoiled things by asking Father Ronan when the board and breakfast money would be paid. The apologetic priest assured Tom's mum that the payment would be made through the school the next week, and then he was gone.

Tom had slept on the floor in his mother's room while Ronan had stayed in Tom's room. On the bed in his room, Tom found a thank you card and a present: a painted plaster statuette of Saint Francis of Assisi blessing his animal friends.

Cheap, mass-produced religious tat it might have been, but Frankie and the Bunnies became one of Thomas Morton's most treasured possessions—because Father Ronan had given it to him.

35.

Oh shit, Tom thought, as Monica's priest-hating dad, Joe Gallagher, opened the front door of the King household.

The two men stared at each other as the rain sploshed onto Tom's shaven head.

'Hiya Joe,' Tom said, 'is Pete in?'

'Didn't expect to see me, did you, Father Morton?' Joe said, in his tobacco-deepened, scouse accent.

'No,' Tom squeaked, 'I wasn't. How are things, Joe?'

'You can come in if you want. Monica and Peter won't be long.'

'Thanks,' Tom said, as he stepped into a hallway full of Joe's decorating equipment: paint pots, brushes, rollers, dust covers, step ladders.

'Do you want a drink?' Joe said, disappearing into the kitchen. 'I was just about to make myself one.'

'Tea, please, white, no sugar.'

'Get that wet coat off your back and sit in the parlour,' Joe shouted above the noise of the kettle boiling.

Tom hung his jacket over the dark-stained balustrade. Then, sinking into the scarred leather sofa, Tom breathed in deep and exhaled, letting go of his ego, readying himself for the inevitable ontological onslaught from Monica's damaged dad.

Joe carried the pair of steaming mugs in, setting them on top of blue floral coasters on the coffee table.

'How's the wrist?' Tom asked.

'Better,' Joe said, sitting down in Pete's favourite armchair, wincing as his bottom sank into the cushion.

'Good, because I know Pete and Mon were worried about you.'

Joe slurped his drink.

'Sometimes I cut, and I don't know when to stop. I missed the tendons, just. You can't do much painting and decorating if you've got no tendons, Father Morton, can you?'

'We've known each other a long time, Joe. Call me Tom, please.'

'What's up with your shoulder, Father Morton?' Joe asked.

'What do you mean?'

'What did you do?'

'I fell off my bike.'

'Whereabouts?'

'Salt Lane.'

'Which end of Salt Lane?'

'Raven Wood.'

'The roundabout?'

'Yes,' Tom said, avoiding eye contact.

'It's a busy roundabout that, Tom, a *dangerous* junction, lots of accidents. Did a car hit you?'

'Yes, it did.'

Tom knew that Joe could smell bullshit, that Joe sensed the despair hidden beneath the trappings of faith. Of all the people in the world he could have done to avoid after an unsuccessful, bollocks-up of a suicide attempt, it was Joe Gallagher.

'Do you really want to die, Tom? Does death obsess your every waking moment? Or was this a lovestruck spur of the moment act of self-negation?'

You old bastard, Tom thought. *You see me, and I see you.*

All the emergency hospital admissions, all the mental health problems, all the pain and suffering, all the hatred that Joe had for Catholic priests led back to one inescapable conclusion. The problem was that no-one, not Joe's family, not even Joe himself, had ever thought about pulling the poison tree out by its roots.

An eye for a fucking eye, Tom decided.

'How old were you, Joe?' he asked.

Joe's face blanched and his moustache twitched.

'What do you mean?'

'You know exactly what I mean.'

'You mean how old was I when that devil raped me for the first time?'

Tom remembered his own ordeal as an adult, the sense of powerlessness, the shame, and the overwhelming feeling of worthlessness. For that to happen to a child was unforgiveable. He felt the shiver run down his back.

'Yes, how old were you when that devil raped you for the first time?' he said.

'I was seven years-old.'

'Fuck! I'm so sorry,' Tom said, wiping a tear from his eye.

'I believe that you are sorry. But that's not good enough, is it? Not good enough at all. Because it is still going on. And priests, like you, are complicit in the cover up because you say nothing. And the evil men and women get away with it.'

'But what can I do? I'm just one man.'

Joe got up from his chair and stood by the window.

'I told my mother about what happened, and she sent me to apologise to the priest for making up stories. Can you believe that? My own mother sided with the all-powerful Catholic Church. I told Monica's mother about what happened to me before we got married—I had too. Now, she's dead. No-one else knows. But I see that you and I share something. I wouldn't wish that on my worst enemy. How old were you, Tom?'

'I was in my twenties.'

'Another priest?'

'Yes. And now, he's high up, and I'm just a foot-soldier.'

'Why did you let Antony walk away? Are you a fool or something?'

'How did you know about me and Antony?' Tom gasped.

'I saw you two at Monica's wedding. I knew back then, but I didn't say anything. There's a reckoning coming for you, lad, and its' been coming a while. Freedom comes with a high price. First thing you need to do is look after yourself, because you look like shit. Second, don't tell our Monica, or Peter, about this conversation, or I'll fuckin' do yer. Third, when you get the chance, and you will, nail the bastard.'

'They are attacking gay priests as a smokescreen to protect themselves.'

'Of course, they fuckin' are. Jesus! I'll tell you this, Tom Morton, I've lost track of how many times I've tried to kill myself. The guilt, the self-hatred, the self-loathing, the dirtiness I've felt all my life because of what was done to me as a boy. That wasn't done by a gay priest. That was done by a ravening wolf dressed in priest's clothing.'

'I'm going to go,' Tom said, standing up and finding that his legs had gone wobbly, feeling like he was going to retch.

'Tom?'

'Yeah, Joe?'

'Thank you for listening to me. And Tom…'

'Yeah, Joe?' Tom said, the mother of all headaches forming against his right temple.

'If you ever need to talk…'

'It won't be to you, Joe,' Tom said, 'no offence.'

'None taken. Tom?'

'Yeah, Joe. What is it?' Tom asked, as he retrieved his coat from the bottom of the stairs and staggered for the front door.

'Grow a pair, for fuck's sake. Either kill yourself and be done with it, or bring the temple down on their heads, like Samson.'

'I think Samson died… as the building collapsed,' Tom said, his fingers trying to open the stiff Yale lock.

'Father Morton!' Joe demanded.

'Yeah, Joe,' Tom said, as he lurched from the doorway, stepping down onto the metal grill that served as a boot scraper.

'Fuck off, yer priest cunt.'

36.

Tom knelt as he pulled up the weeds in the flower beds, the fingers in his gardening gloves were worn through and the chocolate-cake soil was packed underneath his fingernails. The sun beat down on his uncovered head and neck, and the sweat ran down his back. He sat on his bottom on the grass and drank a mouthful of warm, dilute orange cordial from the glass resting on the paving stone. From the rectory garden at St. Cuthbert's, he could see the beacon on the other side of Hick Bibby valley, and across to Burrow Moor.

Father Spence, dressed as always in priestly black, was finishing up the edging around the lawn with a pair of long handled shears.

'Are you ready for the new school year, Thomas?' he asked.

'Mum makes my school pants,' Tom said. 'The thing is, they are a different shade of brown than my blazer and I get called cack pants and bum boy.'

'Who by?' Father Spence asked.

'Just boys at school.'

'Can you empty the grass cuttings in the compost bin, please?'

'Yes, Father,' Tom said.

He lifted the basket and carried it against his chest down the bumpy path, down the sloping hill to the red-brick wall that bordered the rectory gardens. On the other side of the wall was a field of corn that sometimes had a deer or two passing through it. On the other side of the field was the Hermitage, the stone ruin that had once been a place of solitude and prayer.

'How are thing between you and your friend, Michael?' Father Spence asked, as Tom returned from dumping the cuttings.

'He's friends with Robby Dowson now.'

'Is he? How does that make you feel?'

'Upset,' Tom said, as he picked up the hand trowel and stabbed the soil.

'Don't dig up the anemone bulbs. Just the dandelions, daisies, and any grass that's growing. Leave everything else,' Father Spence said.

'Okay,' Tom said, watching as Father cut a perfect line in the lawn, parallel and equidistant to the path, a man as precise in his gardening as he was in performing the Sacraments of the Holy Roman Church.

'Are you still delivering newspapers on that death-trap bicycle of yours?' Father asked, as he clipped and snipped.

'Yeah, both pedals have fallen off now. It's just a frame with wheels and no brakes.'

'That sounds incredibly dangerous, Thomas,' Father Spence said.

'I nearly got run over free-wheeling from a cul-de-sac into the main road. I couldn't use my trainers to stop.'

'You'll be burning lots of shoe leather doing that.'

'I see Mister Blackburn sometimes, our old headmaster from primary school, sitting in his car as I go down Bolton Old Road.'

Father Spence stopped what he was doing and looked up at Tom.

'What does he do?'

'Nothing, he just sits in his car.'

'Does he ever wave?'

'No.'

'You'll tell me if you see him again, won't you? It's nothing to worry about. It's just that he's a little forgetful these days. People with his kind of illness need looking after at home.'

'Yes,' Tom said, trying to make sense of what Father Spence had asked him to do.

After they had tidied up the garden and put the gardening tools away in the shed, and after Tom had washed his hands in the old Belfast sink in the kitchen, he sat eating an egg and cress sandwich and drinking milk at the metal table set on stone flags by the back door.

'What do you think of this, Tom?' Father Spence asked, as he wheeled a bicycle through the garden gate.

'I think it's a BMX, Father.'

'Somebody abandoned it in the church carpark a few months ago and never came back for it.'

'Can I try it?'

'Go ahead.'

Tom rode through the gate and into the gravelled church carpark, riding in circles, doing figures of eight, then skidding to a sudden, satisfactory halt when he jammed both brakes on together.

'How is it?'

'Amazing. Really amazing.'

'Do you want to look after it for me, Tom?'

'What if the real owner comes back?'

'We'll give them another week or two. After that, I think we can consider that it is yours, don't you? And I owe you four pounds for all your hard work today, make sure it goes in your pocket and you don't lose it on the way home. If your mum has any questions on where you got that bicycle, just ask her to ring me.'

'I will.'

'And Tom?'

'Bring your old bike here. We can fix it up one day and use it as a spare. Is that a fair deal?'

'Deal,' Tom said, stretching out his hand, 'Thank you, Father.'

'You are very welcome.'

'Father?' Tom asked, 'is Father Worthington coming for his tea, today?'

'Yes, he is. How did you know?'

'You put flowers in the vase in the kitchen. You always do that when Father Worthington comes for his tea.'

37.

Tom placed the pill beneath his tongue, then he drank the water and swallowed.

'*Give us this day our daily meds,* he thought ruefully, placing the glass in the sink.

The morning's visit from St. James' parishioner, Dawn Arundel, had been brief. Tom was devastated to learn that Dawn's husband, Mike, had left her and moved in with a woman he had met at work. Tom comforted Dawn as best as he could, while inside cursing the man who had cast aside his wife and abandoned his two children.

'Sophie seems to be putting a brave face on it, but Danny seems very withdrawn,' Dawn had told him.

Tom had promised to keep an eye on both children.

Family break-ups were a difficult area for Tom as a priest. After all, what practical experience could he, a man with no companion and no children, offer? The best he could do was offer to pray for the family, a suggestion that sounded hollow even to Tom. Of course, he was on the side of the wronged wife and the two children, but how much could he really know of a relationship and what went on behind closed doors?

The day was before him as he packed waterproofs and his prayer books: home visits to the sick, midday mass at St. Benny's, St. James' Primary School assembly, and a governor's meeting, a criss-crossing of the local area to be navigated astride the second-hand mountain bike that he had bought after the motorway junction 'accident.'

Father Thomas's first trip out on his not-so-new bike had been to the Sainsbury's Local in Hind Green. The four-pack of Stella Artois, deep pan ham and pineapple pizza, and a 70cl bottle of Jameson's were sitting in the bagging area of the self-scanning till as Tom waited for someone to confirm he was over 25. He had turned around to see a short queue of Saint Benedict's faithful gathering behind him. Tom smiled as the parishioners stared at the contents of his groceries, half-wishing— as the store assistant typed seemingly random numbers into the machine to approve his purchases—that he had also bought a pack of condoms, lube, and this month's edition of *Gay Times*.

Tom knelt on the tiled floor of the rectory, taking care not to put too much weight on the knee he had scuffed in his failed suicide attempt.

'Father God,' he prayed, 'please forgive me my many sins, and forgive me because I have had enough of this life, and I want to die. Look after my mother when I'm gone.'

Tom thought of the chosen place, and suddenly he felt guilty for the inconvenience he would cause to travellers and commuters, and for the impact his death would have on the train driver. But there was no way round it, death by hanging would traumatise anyone who found his body, and an overdose could go wrong and leave him incapacitated but still alive.

The decision had been made, and Tom felt an immense sense of peace.

38.

Confirmation evening classes at the convent included listening to tracks chosen by a priest and a nun. Father Beard had selected *I am a Rock,* by Simon and Garfunkel—two folky geezers who Tom hadn't heard of before and had no intention of ever listening to again. The pint-sized priest, with pale skin and wispy facial hair, closed his eyes and lip synced as Tom and his fourteen-year-old classmates looked on and sniggered. The nun's choice was a bit more rock n' roll, *Pride in the Name of Love* by U2, which Tom thought was a half-decent tune. Still, it was a bit embarrassing having to sit quietly while a plain clothes sister with a skinhead tapped out Larry Mullen Junior's drum intro on a table with metal legs.

'Shall we listen to that one, again?' Sister Bonita asked.

Everyone nodded.

Grandad Pilks was lined up to be Tom's sponsor for Confirmation, press-ganged into it by Tom's mum and nana. Confirmation, as one of the 'Big Seven,' was a vital step for young Catholics in the affirmation of their faith. The sponsor's role seemed a bit vague to Tom and involved little more than putting a hand on the candidate's shoulder as they knelt before the altar. So far so good. The bombshell for Grandad Pilks was discovering that the ceremony conflicted with 'Thursday night lad's night.' Dependable and creative Knight of Saint Columba that he was, Grandad Pilks squared the circle and invited his grandson to play snooker at 'the club,' straight after the Confirmation service.

Playing snooker with his grandad was a real coming of age event, the problem was Tom had never played snooker in his life, and the huge table, the heavy cue, and the unbearable pressure of being judged by a roomful of northern, male, old age pensioners led him to declare early and decide that he would sit at a small table, drink his coke, eat his cheese and onion crisps, and 'just watch.' And so, it began.

Grandad Pilk's pals started ribbing him, suggesting he had a ton of money hidden away in the Abbey National Building Society. Tom's grandad took it in good humour, especially as he won game after game, picking up the money from the side bets.

Then, the Extraordinary League of Catholic Gentlemen, Tylesbury branch, turned their attention to Pilk's young grandson.

'What saint's name did yer choose, young Thomas, for yer Confirmation?'

'Saint Francis of Assisi.'

'What did you choose him for?'

'Wasn't he queer?'

'Could you not have chosen someone English?'

Tom was bewildered, and he looked to his grandad for back up.

'What did you choose him for, our Thomas?' Grandad asked.

'Father Ronan gave me a statue of him.'

'Father who?'

'He hooked up with other gay boys, called himself 'Mother,' recruited cross-dressing women and was friends with Muslims.'

'Who was? Father Ronan?'

'No, Francis of Assisi. His parents wanted him to get married. So, he did one, ran off, and hid in a cave with his 'particular friend,' if you know what I mean.'

On their way home in the tow truck, Grandad asked Tom if he wanted to come and play snooker at the club again.

Tom nodded his head, and Grandad burst out laughing.

39.

'Ask that Paki,' Grandad said, as he lay in the hospital bed surrounded by his family.

'You can't say things like that, Dad,' Tom's mum, Emma, said.

'I can say what I like, can't I, Thomas?' Grandad said.

'You can't say things like that, Dad,' Aunt Annmie said. 'It's not nice.'

Tom went over to the male nurse, apologised for his grandfather's racist language, and asked if they could have a bedpan.

'How are you, Mister Pilkington?' the nurse asked Grandad.

'Fair, I'd say,' Grandad said.

The nurse smiled and passed over the grey disposable bedpan.

'He's all right, him,' Grandad said, after the nurse had moved on. 'If me and my mates had seen the state this country would get into with all these arse bandits and immigrants, we'd have never gone to war. We wouldn't have bothered. Politicians start the wars, and they sent us to sort it out. Do you still believe in God and Heaven, Tom?'

Tom saw fear in the eyes of a dying man, existential dread, and it made him think of Colonel Kurtz in Joseph Conrad's *Heart of Darkness*. This man, his grandfather, had been a rock throughout his life, unmoveable, so sure, and now here he was, trembling as he faced either potential non-existence or a one-to-one with his maker.

'Of course, I do,' Tom said, taking his grandad's hand. 'Without God, nothing could exist, and God is love.'

'Where's that dog?'

'There's no dog in here, Dad,' Tom's mum said.

'Can you get me some cash out of that cashpoint in the bathroom?'

'There's no cashpoint in here, Dad,' Aunt Annmie said.

'Those men I killed, those German boys, am I still a good man?'

'Of course, you are,' Aunt Annmie said.

'You did what you had to,' Tom's mum said.

'I was asking Thomas: he's a priest.'

'You are a good man,' Tom said.

He could see Grandad did not believe him. There was nothing he could do but pray for the soul of Joshua William Pilkington.

Tom decided he would wait until after his grandad was dead before he killed himself. That made him think about Dan Brennan hanging by his neck from a tree growing on the side of a spoil-heap.

40.

The Saint Pat's High School leavers disco was held at Dean Wood Country Club. No alcohol was allowed, but Shaun Burke had managed to smuggle in a hip flask with some vodka that he'd pinched from his mum and dad's drinks cabinet. Tom joined the others in a quick toot, grimacing as the neat alcohol hit the back of his throat.

Tom was dancing with Shirley and her friends as Dan Brennan came across to speak to him. Tom hadn't spoken to Dan for years, not since that day on Tatty Cragg.

'Do you want to dance with me?' Dan asked, having to speak loudly over the chorus of *Just Can't Get Enough*.

Tom shook his head.

'Go and dance with him,' Shirley said, shouting into his ear.

Tom shook his head.

Shirley took his arm and led him away. Tom saw Shaun give him the thumbs up as he and Shirley went outside into the carpark.

'Tom,' Shirley said, as they stood shivering next to the kitchen bins, 'dance with Daniel Brennan. You'd make a really nice couple.'

'What do you mean?' Tom asked.

'I know, Tom. I've watched you.'

'Know what?'

'Tom, it's obvious.'

'What is?'

'You like boys.'

'No, you've got that wrong.'

Peter King and the first-team football lads were spilling out of the front door, and they saw Tom with Shirley.

'Get in, Morton!' Pete shouted, and the laughter and catcalling began.

'Piss off, Shirley,' Tom said, and he stalked back inside.

Michael O'Keefe was standing in the reception area talking to Shaun.

'Where's your friend, Michael?' Tom sneered. 'Don't tell me Dowson's ditched you!'

'You're a bastard, Tom,' Shaun said.

'You *are* a bastard, Tom,' Michael said. 'Your mum told me after I fucked her.'

Tom didn't know whether to laugh or to punch his friend in the face. The belly laugh rolled out of his stomach, and then, he couldn't stop.

'Dowson's fucked-off with the spotty mates he's going to Weston College with,' Shaun said, watching as Tom and Michael hugged.

'Told you he was a wanker,' Tom said. 'No one loves you like we love you, Michael.'

'Fucking high-achievers,' Shaun said. 'Who wants to be one of them?'

'Not me,' Michael said.

'You want to come back to ours, Michael?' Shaun asked, 'Tom's staying over. We've got booze, smokes, and one of my brother's special videos.'

'I'll have to ring my mum, but yeah, sounds good.'

'Your bird's getting off with Dan Brennan,' Shaun said, as they boarded one of the four executive coaches that the school had booked for the occasion.

Through the tinted window, Tom could see Shirley and Dan huddled together, talking outside the Country Club entrance.

'She's not my bird,' Tom said, as he threw himself into a tiger patterned seat.

With a swish of compressed air, the coach door closed, and the 49-seater began to navigate the carpark heading towards the exit.

'What's she doing with him, then?' Shaun asked, sitting next to Tom.

'Shit-stirring,' Tom said.

41.

Tom left the hotel and got a taxi into the city centre.

'I want to go to a gay bar. Do you know any?' Tom asked the Asian taxi driver.

'No, I don't know any,' the man shouted. 'Where do you want to go? Tell me a street.'

'I don't know,' Tom said. 'I don't know this city. Surely you know where the gay bars are.'

The man ranted under his breath.

Tom didn't care. He'd had a couple of pints in the hotel bar and had insulated himself from the feelings of other people. All he wanted was some company for the last time before he topped himself.

The taxi driver was getting more and more stressed, asking Tom where he wanted to go.

'I don't know,' Tom said. 'It's your city, just take me to a gay bar.'

The rainbow painted on the railway bridge was a good sign.

'Stop here,' Tom said.

Tom paid his taxi fare. Out on the busy street, he decided that an establishment called 'Queens' was as good a place as any to start. The bar was empty, so Tom sat on a stool and ordered himself a bottle of Budweiser. One of the bar's few customers came over and sat next to Tom, a young man who smiled at him. Tom bought him a drink and they kissed. And then, he was gone, and Tom was on his own again.

Across the road, a pub with a rainbow flag hanging above the door had a queue forming outside, so Tom decided to try his luck in another place. He joined the throng, aware that as a dull, bald, older man, he stood out in the long line of vibrant, young, queer people.

'This is a gay bar,' the bouncer smirked, as Tom reached the front. Shouldn't you be somewhere else?'

'I know what it is,' Tom said.

Inside, it was madness. Drunken couples were arguing, there was beer all over the floor, the music was too loud. Tom made his exit without even buying a drink.

Tom decided to call it a night and to walk back to his budget hotel. He was crossing the painted iron bridge over the river when he saw a man standing on a ledge above the water.

'Hello, mate,' Tom said. 'Is everything okay?' He could see the man was crying, tears cascading down his face. 'What's your name?'

'Fuck off.'

'Fuck off, eh? That's a nice name,' Tom said.

'Piss off. Leave me alone.'

'I'm here to listen if you want me to.'

'I'm going to kill myself.'

'Has something happened today?

'Yes,' the man nodded.

'Why don't you climb down and tell me about it, and if you still feel the same way afterwards, then fair enough.'

Tom held out his hand. The man grabbed it and stepped down.

'Cold out, isn't it,' Tom said, 'and I reckon it would be freezing in that water. Now, tell me about your day.'

The man sat on his bottom on the stone paving, his back to the wall, hands over his face, weeping.

'What's your name?' Tom asked, as the suicidal man sat down beside the suicidal man.

'Dave. Dave Stoughton.'

'Hi Dave. I'm Tom. Have you had much to drink tonight?'

'I told him I'd do it.'

'Men are such bastards.'

'Why? have you had experience?'

'I have.'

'You don't look gay,' Dave said, wiping his tears with the back of his hand. 'You look like my fuckin' dad.'

'How are gay people supposed to look?' Tom asked.

'I'm HIV positive. I've just found out. I'm devastated.'

'I'm HIV positive too. Have been for twenty years.'

'Really?'

'Yeah, really. Did your boyfriend dump you?'

Dave nodded.

'Because of the test results?'

'Yeah.'

'More fool him, eh? For letting a good one go.'

'Are you a counsellor or something, or just some nosey bastard, hanging round bridges looking for jumpers?'

'I'm a priest, a Catholic priest. My name is Tom.' Tom held out his hand.

'Jesus, a Catholic priest with HIV. Just wait 'til I tell my mum.'

'You may be surprised how many gay priests there are in the Church of Rome.'

'I don't think, I would,' Dave laughed. 'Is it a good job?'

'"I am a Rock,"' Tom said. 'You ever heard that song?'

'No, I don't think so.'

'*I touch no one, no one touches me.* It's a Catholic priest anthem.'

'Jesus, I thought I had it bad,' Dave said, standing up.

'Will you be okay, getting home?' Tom asked.

'Why? Do you want to come home with me?'

'No,' Tom laughed. 'I just want to make sure that you'll be all right.'

Dave hugged Tom, 'I'll be fine. Thank you.'

'Get yourself sorted. Yeah?' Tom said. 'This isn't the end, it's the beginning.'

Tom watched Dave stop and wave before he disappeared around the side of a pool and snooker bar. Tom stared at the black river for a moment. Then, he set off towards the railway station and his shitty hotel room.

42.

Tom was sitting with his mum, half-way down the church, as the sacristy bell rang, and Father Spence stepped out alone. Now, aged seventeen and on his way to being a man, Tom had packed-in altar serving, but it was not good enough that his slapdash, flaky-arse successors had let the increasingly frail Father Spence down, especially at Sunday Mass.

Tom stood up, genuflected at the side of the pew, walked into the sacristy, and put on a black cassock and white surplice and joined Father Spence at the altar.

The dream team, back together, he thought.

Father Spence's last sermon at St. Cuthbert's Church was on 'The Disciple whom Jesus Loved.' This was a sermon that stuck with Tom for years afterwards, almost as if it were an address meant for him alone. Tom learned that the phrase 'the disciple whom Jesus loved,' was used six times in John's gospel, but nowhere else in the New Testament. This un-named disciple lay stretched out beside Jesus during the Last Supper, and it was he who asked, 'Which of us is going to betray you?' Then, during the crucifixion, Jesus tells his mother, 'Here is your son,' and to the beloved disciple he says, 'Here is your mother.' When Mary Magdalene discovers the empty tomb, Peter and the beloved disciple rush to check it out, but it is the beloved disciple who has his Inov-8 running shoes on and gets there first. In the last chapter of John, the beloved disciple is present at the stupendous catch of fish. When Jesus indicates how Peter will die, an understandably perturbed Peter says, 'And what about this lad, then?' referring to the beloved disciple. Jesus answers, 'If I want him to remain here until I come back, what's that to you? Get on with it, Pete.'

'John the Evangelist,' Father Spence told his congregation, 'based his entire gospel on the testimony of the disciple whom Jesus loved.'

In the fullness of time, Father Thomas Morton would recognise the debt he owed to Father Spence, to John the Evangelist, and to the un-named disciple whom Jesus loved. Tom would encounter po-faced Christians who would attempt to pigeon-hole John's gospel as a 'Jesus Poem,' rather than a factual account, perhaps fearful of the message hardcoded in unique stories like the transformation of water into wine at the Wedding in Cana. For Tom, the lines 'In the beginning was the word, and the word was with God, and the word was God,' were some of the most beautiful lines written in any language. And, perhaps, the light that was full of grace and truth was a queer light: gay, bi, lesbian and trans.

Father Spence left St. Cuthbert's for the last time, sometime during the week that followed that earthquake sermon. The note from the Bishop read out at Mass the next Sunday by a stand-in priest, explained that due to ill-health, Father Spence had 'gone to live with his sisters.' There were no goodbyes, there was no tearful leaving mass, no presents and cards presented by a grateful congregation for twenty-five years of hard work, and Tom never got to say goodbye and thank you face-to-face to the man who had truly been his Father figure.

Father Spence died three months later, a gay Catholic priest with AIDS, a man whose death was swept under the carpet by the organisation for which he had worked so tirelessly.

43.

'Depravity.'

'Contrary to natural law.'

'A sexual act closed to the gift of life.'

'Gay is not okay.'

'Where is Dad?'

'Perverts.'

'The Lavender Mafia.'

'*Extra Ecclesiam Nulla Salus.*'

Just another thoroughly depressing prayer meeting at Saint Benny's, Tom reflected, as his parishioners mingled over tea and biscuits, anoraked pensioners with woolly hats praising the love of God with one breath and condemning sinners to eternal torment with the other.

Emma Morton, Tom's mother, was deep in conversation with Joan Bird, and Tom decided he would leave the Lancashire Catholic Conservatives to their favoured pastimes of Pope Francis baitin' n' Gay Priest hatin.'

'Father, can I have a word?' Tom heard, as he reached the bottom of the wooden steps.

Joan the Raptor was following close behind him.

'Hello, Joan,' Tom said. 'How are you?'

'I'm well. Father Morton, I heard that your friend has gone back home. Your mother told me.'

Tom studied the woman.

'He has,' he said.

'Antony, was it?'

'Yes.'

'That must have been hard for you?'

Tom felt his eyes filling up, and he fought the cracks forming in his emotional dam.

'Yes, it was,' he said, through gritted teeth.

'I have to make an apology to you.'

Tom felt a sudden swing in his emotions and an urge to burst out laughing at the thought that Joan might apologise for her terrible cooking.

'Go on,' he said.

There was thunder on the staircase as a party of five parishioners descended.

'Good night, Joan. Good night, Father.'

Tom smiled, wishing them 'safe home' while he waited for the staircase to clear so he could hear whatever minor misdemeanour Joan believed that she was responsible for: crinkling a newspaper too loudly, stepping on a spider, not paying for a carrier bag in Tesco.

'Joan, you can always keep this for Confession on Saturday evenings,' Tom said, as Joan fiddled with her wedding ring.

'No, I've got to get this off my chest.'

'Fine,' Tom said, 'lets' have it then, Joan. We've known each other long enough and I am a priest, after all. My mother is upstairs, and, if I'm mean, you can always tell her, and she'll give me a clip around the ear!'

There was more nervous twisting of the wedding ring.

'I told my husband about... you and Antony, and I'm afraid he put two and two together and made five.'

'What are you telling me?'

'My husband beat you up outside the church.'

Tom's blood froze.

'Joan, did he write those words on the church door?'

Joan nodded, holding the handles of her handbag in both hands, the bag positioned in front of her chest as if she were in danger of being punched in the stomach by a man of God.

Tom was enraged, but also aware that Joan was making a form of apology.

'Do you have any idea what it feels like to have that kind of accusation made against you, Joan, by someone who then does not have the courage to provide any kind of evidence?'

Joan shook her head, tears forming in her eyes.

'Do you have any idea of what it is like to be attacked, kicked, and punched in the dark?'

Joan said nothing.

Tom was getting the kinaesthetic ping-back that told him he needed to tread carefully, despite his righteous anger.

'Joan, I appreciate you letting me know. It must have taken a lot of courage for you to tell me.'

'Are you going to go to the police?'

'Do you want me to?'

'No.'

'Right then. I won't say anything, but if Mister Bird puts a single feather wrong, then you tell me, and I'll have a word with the golden eagles. Yeah?'

Joan nodded.

'For your act of contrition, I would like two fruit pies and a steak and kidney, please, Missus Bird. And should you ever change your mind and want to come back, your old job is always there.'

'You're very kind, Father,' Joan Bird said, 'I'd be happy to take care of you, again.'

'And Joan,' Tom said, 'don't think for a second that you have to endure any kind of physical intimidation. I can always help. I'll leave that with you.'

'Your mother must be very proud of you,' Joan said.

Tom found himself on the verge of tears again.

'You know my mother. If she knew who I really am, what I really am, then how proud of me would she be then, Joan? Could she ever show her face in here?'

'Your mother loves you.'

'My mother loves her own edited version of me. Anything that contradicts that image is deleted inside her mind.'

'I shall pray for you both.'

'Pray hard, Joan, because, right now, I need those prayers more than ever.'

44.

Saint Pat's Sixth Form Roman Catholic College was a mile down the road from the high school. For Tom, Michael, and Shaun the freedom to wear their own clothes instead of the cursed brown uniform, the freedom to come and go as they pleased outside of lessons, and a pub either side of the college was a dream come true. Summer days lying in the beer garden of the Old Engine with a cold bottle of dog after two hours of Economics and Modern History was a revelation.

The three friends became a gang of four with the transformation of football and cricket jock Pete King into bearded, long-haired, Jim Morrison lookalike, Pete.

Shaun was the musical pioneer, discoverer of good vibe tunes, and the chief purchaser of illegal substances for the gang: smokes, speed, e's, trips, the occasion line of coke... but nothing *too* stupid. Michael was the film critic, art expert, clothing connoisseur, and indie music supremo. Pete was social secretary, inspirer of good nights out, and official Sunday morning cooked breakfast maker. Tom was in love with all three of them.

Despite being officially underage, they never had a problem getting served in pubs, and when Shaun passed his driving test and bought a car, it was easier than ever to access drugs and clubs.

Tom played hard, worked hard. Miss Worthington was his European History 1648 to 1788 A Level teacher. Miss Worthington was Father Worthington's sister, which just showed what a small world it was, especially in Bussell. Father Worthington was based at Ash Burrow seminary, but also served as St. Pat's sixth form college chaplain. Father Worthington was drop dead gorgeous, early forties, tall, jet-black hair, and built like an athlete. After a few months, Tom built up the courage to stop the chaplain in the corridor one day, introduce himself, and ask about Father Spence.

'Come with me, Tom,' Father Worthington said. 'Let's have a coffee in the refectory.'

'The famous Tom Morton, in the flesh,' Father Worthington said, sipping a machine vend Americano.

'The famous Father Worthington, in the flesh,' Tom said, sipping a white tea with one sugar. 'How is Father Spence, we all miss him?'

Father Worthington said nothing for a while as he contemplated the young man sitting in front of him.

'Can we talk in confidence, Tom?'

'Of course.'

'Everything I say to you stays with you and does not go back to your friends, family, or anyone at St. Cuthbert's? Especially your mum.'

'Of course.'

'All right then, here's the truth. Laurence has AIDs, Tom.'

'Oh, my God! How did he catch that?' Tom exclaimed.

'It's difficult to know where we contracted HIV, but we did.'

'We?'

'Laurence is my life partner, Tom. He has been for the last twenty or so years. He was my spiritual director at Ash Burrow, my mentor, my friend, and then my lover.'

Tom was stunned, unable to comprehend what he was hearing.

'All this time, Father Spence was a puff.'

'We prefer the word "gay."'

Tom wanted to run away, to escape from what he was hearing. The perfect parish priest who he had known and loved, the voice of Jesus, was being transformed into a dirty homo.

'But you are priests,' Tom snarled. 'You're not supposed to do that kind of thing. Does Miss Worthington know?'

'You asked me about Father Spence, Tom, and I told you the truth.'

Tom felt like his insides had been ripped out. He walked away, leaving the priest on his own at the table. At smoker's corner, he cadged a fag and lit up, feeling the hit in his synapses. The terrible shadow was on the rise, and it needed defeating. That afternoon, Tom caught a bus into town with Michael, and they drank whiskey in a decrepit town centre bar until neither of them could see straight. Tom got a bus home, ate his tea with his mother, and, somehow, she never twigged that her son was hopelessly intoxicated.

Gay Jesus! What the fuck? What the fuck, man?

And so began the race for oblivion, the hunger for sensation, the compulsion for consumerism, anything to be one foot in front of that thing, that gay gremlin that Father Worthington had unleashed and set upon him in the college refectory.

45.

The plan was that this would be the last bike ride and Tom's goodbye with his friend, Pete.

They rode their bikes to Snow Hill. Tom tried riding the twisting path with the killer gradient but had to give up half-way, leaning on his handlebars at the side of the path to catch his breath.

'I thought you lived in the saddle,' Pete said, as he sailed past.

Tom shook his fist, cursing his friend and his four-grand, 6.8 kilo, Optimum Compaction Low Void, carbon fibre wet dream. He pushed his own aluminium steed to the top of the very steep hill.

Pete was waiting at the base of the stone tower that stood sentinel over the valley. The monument to a long-dead local philanthropist, the column gave a 360-degree view across Lancashire, West Yorkshire, North Yorkshire, Cumbria, Derbyshire, Cheshire, and the distant Welsh hills. As Tom gulped orange barley water from a plastic bottle and gorged on a bag of jelly sweets, Pete regaled him with the story of their primary school classmate Eamonn Kelly's sex-tourism exploits in Amsterdam in the company of his ex-junkie, now cleaned-up pal, Eddie Wolfenstone. Kells was partial to being pissed on and had paid extra on this latest trip to have a sex worker shit on his chest. Eds was partial to older women and had managed to find a sex worker in her 70s. Then, the two men flew back into Manchester Airport, back to their wives and families, sharing stories of a relaxing golf weekend in Groningen.

'You shouldn't be telling me this,' Tom said. 'I'm a priest, I'm sensitive to sin.'

Pete scoffed, 'Bollocks, Morton, I know you love a good gossip.'

'I remember meeting Eamonn's wife at your fortieth birthday bash, I thought she was lovely. What the hell is she doing with that loathsome creep?'

'He's an award-winning local businessman, Tom. He does lots of good work for charity.'

'Tax deductible charity work, I imagine. I never liked him.'

'As we forgive those who trespass against us, Father,' Pete said.

They followed the stony path along the ridge, weaving in and around groups of walkers, taking it slow as they slipped past plodding ponies, stopping to admire a gushing stream as it cascaded down a rock face, and then they took the muddy path onto the heath.

Over mud and mire, they pedalled, past staring sheep, past cone-shaped cairns until they were riding higher than the hills. On the roof of the world, they came to the Pilgrims Cross, the ancient stone monument that had marked the way across the West Pennine Moors for thousands of years.

'How's work?' Tom gasped between mouthfuls of warm drink as the two men rested beside the carved stone cube.

'It's okay. I help where I can. I get people the support they need. Most of the time, it's not enough, but what can you do?' Pete said.

'I envy you.'

'Really, a priest envies a social worker?'

'At least you can do something material. What can I do?'

'Tom, no offence, but you're turning into Marvin the Paranoid Android.'

'Funny,' Tom muttered.

'Jesus, you really *are* down.'

'Piss off.'

'No really, Tom, tell me, how are you feeling?'

'Like… there's no hope.'

'Tom, I need to ask, are you feeling suicidal?'

'What makes you ask that?'

'Have you had suicidal thoughts?'

'Piss off.'

'Have you?'

'Yes, I have.'

'Have you thought about how you'd do it?'

'Yes, I have.'

'Tell me, how would you do it?'

'Jump in front of a train.'

'Where?'

'In town.'

'What's happened to make you feel like this?'

Tom laughed, bitterly. 'This is ironical,' he said.

'I don't think "ironical" is a word,' Pete said, 'but tell me anyway, why is this ironical?'

'I talked a guy off a bridge the other week.'

'Well done you.'

'Yeah, well done me.'

'How is your work?'

'I don't know.'

'Do you still believe in God?'

'Of course, I do. I'm just not sure I believe in the Church.'

'Fair enough, neither do I.'

'We'd better get going before we get cold.'

'Nah, man, we're going to talk this out.'

'Whatever.'

'Have you been to a doctor and explained how you are feeling? It's amazing what they can do these days. There are all kinds of drugs that can help. It's about finding the right combination for you.'

'I'm already rattling. More drugs won't help.'

'Yes, they will. Mon is on antidepressants. She has been for years. There's no shame in admitting when you are unwell.'

'I keep thinking about Shirley and Dan.'

'That ain't going to do you any good. There was nothing any of us could have done, Tom. Don't torture yourself with that.'

'Shirley died in slow motion.'

'That's how stalkers work. She complained to the police, and they told her to stop wasting their time.'

The tears were flowing, and Tom couldn't stop them.

Pete held his sobbing friend to his chest.

'That God of yours is a fucking bastard,' he said.

'Don't say that,' Tom said. 'You'll get us both struck by lightning.'

'Easier than throwing yourself under a train.'

'Thanks, Pete!' Tom said.

'Will you promise me that you'll go to the doctors?'

'I will.'

'Tom, your life is your decision. As a humanist, I respect your right to decide. But if you kill yourself before England wins the Euros this year, I'll never forgive you.'

'What the fuck is a humanist?' Tom asked. 'Prove to me that Humanism exists so that I too may believe. Let me see its wounds and put my hand in its side.'

'That's more like it,' Pete said. 'That's the total prick we all know and love.'

46.

Father Dean Wesham was the new parish priest at St. Cuthbert's. Father Dean was young, super-slim, super-organised, vegan, and as camp as Christmas. Father Dean took no shit when it came to the charade of baptism in exchange for a place at St. Cuthbert's Catholic Primary, the local church school rated as 'outstanding' by Ofsted, the Office for Standards in Education. Father Dean zealously put parents through the full baptism training process, then shoehorned up to two baptisms into each Sunday Mass.

Emma Morton thought turbo-charged, no-nonsense Father Dean was amazing, and teenage Tom was soon sick of hearing about this mega-motivated, modernising living saint.

Thomas Morton's view was that Father Dean did not sound like Jesus at all, the re-ordered altar looked like a tacky Methodist rip off, and cancelling Benediction sung in Latin was inherently suspicious and an insult to Catholic tradition.

Father Dean was *so* gay. And young Tom hated that.

The great thing about the Catholic God was that he could be put back in the God box when faith became momentarily inconvenient, an event that was happening with increasing frequency for Tom, who had discovered that he really liked drugs: whizz and ecstasy, in particular. Dancing too. Tom loved the feeling of being adrift in a sea of sweat-soaked, drugged up, loved up ravers, lost in waves of trance induced euphoria, the dirty bass reverberating through his diaphragm. Aided and abetted by Shaun's new set of wheels, the four friends were getting to know the best clubs in the northwest of England, or so they thought.

Shaun had geared them up for a night out at Shelleys in Manchester, a club that he'd heard rave reviews about on the 808 State Radio Show. Shaun pulled over in his car to ask people standing in the queue outside the legendary Hacienda on Whitworth Street West if they knew where Shelley's was?

'Yeah, mate,' came the response, 'it's in Stoke on Trent.'

Poor Shaun never lived that episode down, and 'it's in Stoke on Trent' became the go-to line to tease him.

The other constant in Tom's life was *Moonlighting,* which was, without doubt, the best show on TV. The ups and downs of David and Maddie's relationship kept Tom enthralled for four years.

Tom was asked out by a girl he knew from his history class at Saint Pat's High School. He persuaded her to go with him to see the new Bruce Willis movie *Blind Date* at the Ritzy Picture House in Bussell. It was *such* a great film, and Tom assumed that his date had enjoyed it as much as he had. He was flabbergasted to find out from her best friend that she considered it the most boring date she had ever been on.

Tom considered himself to be a nice man, a gentleman, and if he did not come onto girls then that was because his mother had brought him up to be respectful of women. If some girls thought that nice was boring, then that was their problem, not his.

And it wasn't Christian to get it on with a girl in a cinema either. Yep, there was God, again, allowed out of his god box to agree with Tom and then shut back in again.

Sunday mornings had become a bit of an endurance test. Tom often arrived home after an all-nighter, without having slept a wink, either coming down or still buzzing. Going to 10:30 a.m. mass at St Cuthbert's with his mother, who never asked a question or suspected anything, was like being in an alternate reality. The only slight paranoia Tom had was with Father Dean, who seemed to have a built-in bullshit detector and who always looked knowingly at Tom's red eyes and dilated pupils.

47.

'The door isn't locked. You can get up and go anytime you want. Your mum is waiting for you in the car. Is that okay?' Tom said.

The boy nodded.

'Your mum said those lads smashed your phone, Danny,'

'Yes.'

The boy was close to tears.

Danny was sitting in the window seat in the rectory vestibule, visible through the window, his mother waiting outside, parked in front of the church doors. It was a bullshit protection mechanic, but Tom was paranoid about accusations of child sex abuse, and if he was going to talk to children on his own, he had to take sensible precautions.

'Do you want to tell me what happened?'

'They called me gay. They said my phone was gay.'

'And are you… gay, Danny?'

Danny nodded his head, tears falling down his cheeks.

Christ, Tom thought, *he's just turned twelve. Why was I so late in understanding myself? How am I going to respond to this boy coming out to me? If I respond negatively, it could hurt and harm him for the rest of his life. If I respond positively, I could get into trouble with his mum, his dad, with the Church.*

Tom handed Danny a clean handkerchief.

'How do you feel about being gay, Danny?'

'Frightened.'

All the doubts in Tom's mind were dispelled in that instant.

'Don't be frightened. There are people around you who love you and being gay is no different than being right-handed or left-handed. It's just how God knitted you perfectly inside the womb.'

'What about Mum… and Sophie?'

'Would you like me to be there when you tell your mum?'

'Yes, please, Father Morton.'

'And your dad?'

'I don't care about him.'

'He needs to know, Danny. But you should tell your mum and sister, first.'

'It's really scary.'

'Dan, would you like a hug?'

'Yeah.'

And so, Tom gave Danny Arundel a big hug, making sure that Danny's mum could see them through the glass.

'I had a friend,' Tom said, 'and he was called Daniel, just like you. He tried to tell me that he was gay, and I didn't want to listen. I didn't want anything to do with him because I didn't want anything to do with me... if that makes sense.'

'Not really.'

'I was a rubbish friend, and I'll regret what I did, what I didn't do, for the rest of my life.'

'I bet you were a good friend really.'

'What model was your iPhone?' Tom asked.

'An 8,' Danny said.

'Wow, very posh. I found this phone in the church, and it has been unclaimed for six months, and you are very welcome to have it. It's a 7 plus, not as good as yours, but it will get you back in business. I've done the factory reset. You just need to swap the SIM card over. I can help if you like. Does silver work for you? You don't have to take it if you don't want.'

'Thank you.'

'If you ever need to talk to anyone, you can talk to me, in confidence, and it will not go any further, just like in confession. Shall we get your mum, now? Tell her your news. She loves you very much.

'Yeah, I know.'

'Father Morton?'

'Yeah.'

'Would you speak to Mister Cooper, for me.'

'Your headmaster?'

Danny nodded.

'You want to tell your headmaster that you're gay?'

'Yes.'

'Wouldn't you rather your dad or your mum did that?

'Would you do it, please? He will listen to you.'

'I'm not sure…'

'Please?'

'Yeah, Dan,' Tom sighed, 'I'll speak to Mister Cooper for you.'

48.

'I hear your mate has topped himself,' John Cooper sneered on the bus to college.

'You're a fuckin' wanker,' Tom said.

Cooper squared up to Tom. Tall, stocky Pete King got off his seat and placed himself between the two antagonists standing in the aisle. The bus took the sharp left down Harbour Road and the chassis tilted on its suspension, pushing the three teenagers together.

Tom threw a soft punch that landed on Coopers' jaw.

Mayhem broke out as other lads, girls too, started wading in, taking the opportunity to kick the shit out of Cooper and his two pimply mates.

Just before the road to nowhere, the driver stopped the bus and threw everyone off. It was either going to be a long walk home or a long walk to college. Cooper and his pals had done one, bags on their shoulders, making a quick exit in the direction from which the bus had come.

A huge cheer broke out amongst the group of students at the side of the stationary bus.

Shirley was there, and she hugged an emotional Tom. Shirley was everyone's mum, everyone's confidante, and they were both crying as the bus driver radioed Bussell Bus HQ to report a mass riot on his vehicle.

Pete had his arm around Monica Gallagher, Shirley's best friend.

'Are you coming to Dan's funeral?' Shirley asked.

'I don't think I can,' Tom said. 'I'm busy.'

49.

'Headmaster,' Tom said, extending his hand.

'Father Morton,' John Cooper said, holding the door open, 'always a pleasure. Follow me, please. We need to get you signed in.'

Tom followed John Cooper through the main entrance of a building that he purposefully hadn't set foot inside for thirty-four years. The

1960's winding marble stairs up to the first and second floors were the same as he remembered, beyond that the serious fire of the early 2000s had meant all the narrow wood floored corridors of his childhood had been replaced with wide modern easy-clean linoleum that made the new Saint Pat's look more like a hospital than an education establishment.

With his photo ID and name badge tucked inside a plastic lanyard, Tom followed John Cooper past an unsmiling, female Executive Assistant who was sitting at a desk behind a monitor, tapping furiously on a keyboard. Cooper's austere office was bereft of pictures, photographs, and personal items.

'Can I get you a drink?' Cooper asked, sitting down.

'No, thank you,' Tom said. 'How is Lisa?'

There was a moment of strained silence.

'We're getting divorced,' Cooper said, staring at the wall.

'I am sorry to hear that,' Tom said. 'This must be a difficult time for you, Lisa, and the children.'

'Are you sure I can't get you anything?'

Tom shook his head, 'I'm trying to limit my caffeine intake, doctor's orders.'

'Very wise. I drink too much of the stuff myself. Now, let's get to the point, Father Morton, if we can. I've seen a copy of the letter from Missus Arundel. I've also received an email from Daniel's dad. It is never easy when two parents are at war and fighting over their children. The school often gets caught in the middle. I do have to say, however, that it is *very* unusual for a parish priest to become involved.'

'I'm a family friend.'

'That is not how the father sees it. He has made some strong accusations, Father Morton, *very* strong accusations. I just hope that he does not see fit to send these to the Bishop's office. Goodness knows what could happen then.'

Tom stared at the man in the black leather chair, the man enjoying his moment of power.

'I think this is about Daniel's wellbeing… that all of us should put him first.'

'We are a welcoming school at Saint Patricks. No doubt you've seen our inclusion policy and our mission and values statement. Wellbeing is top of our agenda, alongside knowing Jesus and academic progress. You know Jesus, don't you, Father?'

'This school has the best exam results in the area,' Tom said. 'You must be proud of your students and their achievements.'

'We practice tolerance toward our same-sex attracted pupils,' John Cooper said, leaning forward across his desk, 'however, we are a faith-led school under the umbrella of the Diocese of Preston. As a priest, I'm sure you know that the Bible is clear that homosexuality is a sin.'

'Where does it say that?'

'Paul says it, Leviticus, Genesis, Judges. The list goes on. What we cannot tolerate is the assertive promotion of a homosexual sub-culture. *If* Daniel Arundel stays with us, and *if* he continues to insist that he is gay, something his father says is an idea planted in his head by his mother and his parish priest, then he needs to understand that we will not accept elements of a fashionable lifestyle being thrust in the faces of other pupils and staff.'

'Fashionable lifestyle? You're kidding me.'

'I have to ask whether it would be better for Daniel, and his parents, if they were to consider taking him to another school more aligned with... alternative lifestyles. It is nothing personal. We all like Daniel, but it is about what is best for Saint Patrick's Roman Catholic High School, and its pupils—now, and in the years to come. Shall I show you out, Father Morton?' Headmaster Cooper said, getting up from his chair and gesturing to the door.

'The one or the ninety-nine?' Tom asked.

'It's the ninety-nine,' the headmaster said. 'That's reality.'

'And what about knowing Jesus?'

'It's been great to catch up,' Cooper said, cheerily, as he led Tom back to the reception area. 'I'm meeting with the Diocesan team and Bishop Worrell in the next few weeks, and I'll be sure to mention that you popped by. We always enjoy contact with the local clergy, here at St Patricks. Don't be a stranger, Tom, you're always welcome. There'll always be a coffee here with your name on it.'

'One last thing,' Tom said, as Headmaster Cooper pressed to open the sliding front entrance doors. 'Your PA is very pretty, John. It could be expensive if Lisa finds out. And it could be embarrassing if parents and governors find out that you have been violating the sanctity of marriage.'

John Cooper was silent, crimson with rage.

'It's practically written across the two of you,' Tom said. 'Now, if I find out that young Danny has been pinched, punched, or if he gets as much as a scratch on his new phone, I could get careless with what I say and to whom. Look after that boy, John,' Tom said, his heart pounding as he turned his back on his feared childhood adversary.

50.

'Half the college was there. Everyone was crying,' Shaun said, taking a swig from his diet Pepsi bottle. 'It is fucking weird to think he's dead. I mean his consciousness has been exterminated, wiped from existence. How does somebody get to the place, at seventeen, where they want to kill themselves?'

The college canteen was full of students getting their lunch, and the queue at the tills stretched back up the stairs to the corridor. Tom and Shaun were perched on the end of a table of six. The four other students sitting with them were engrossed in their own conversation and were ignoring the two interlopers.

'I hate that public display of grief bullshit,' Tom said, playing with the loose change on his wooden tray. 'None of those arseholes actually knew him. They turn up for his funeral, first time they've been in church for ten years, have a bit of a cry, then go back to normality. And they're the decent people, and I'm the bad guy.'

'How come you didn't go, Tom? I thought you were a friend of his from way back.'

'I was busy.'

'That's cold, man.'

'People are moping around, acting like Dan Brennan was Jim Morrison or Ian Curtis or some shit like that. It's just fuckin' sick.'

'You're the one that's sick. Jesus, Tom, where's your empathy?'

'Fuck off, Shaun.'

'I beg your pardon?' Shaun said.

'You heard me.'

'Whatever, man, but don't think you're getting in my car again.'

'I have to be pissed, or high, ideally both, to get in your car. You're a fucking terrible driver.'

Tom watched as Shaun, who never fell out with anyone, shoved his tray into the racking and stormed out of the canteen.

'What?' Tom said to the other four occupants of his table. 'Show's over, you fuckin' geeks.'

Tom decided to sack-off his lessons for the rest of the day and persuaded Pete to catch the bus with him into town, and the two of them got rat-arsed with the crew of a dustbin lorry in the Mason's Arms. The lads from the lorry turned out to be a hoot, and Tom was able to score some coke from a sun-bronzed, handsome refuse worker with a crew cut.

'I thought you were out on a date with the girl from your economics class, tonight?' Pete asked after the Bussell Council Refuse Collectors had jumped back in their wagon and hit the road.

'I am.'

'Look at the state of yer.'

'We're just going out for a drink.'

'You need to get home, get showered, have something to eat. You're pissed, high, and you look like shit. Do you really give a damn about this girl?'

'It'll be reet.'

'You are a terrible man, Thomas Morton. One more for the road?'

'It'd be rude to say no.'

'Is that a yes?'

'It's a double negative, so yes, it's a yes,' Tom said, staring through a pint glass.

'That's not always true,' Pete said, jabbing the table with his finger. 'The phrase, 'they don't have none,' appears to be a double negative and, therefore, a positive, but is in fact a positive on a negative, and therefore a negative.'

'In that case,' Tom said, 'I'll have a double Jamesons, please.'

Pete considered Tom's request. 'That's a positive on a double positive,' he said, after weighing up the linguistic perambulations.

'And two bags of crisps,' Tom added, 'I don't give a fuck what flavour.'

51.

Tom spotted Rosie as he stepped onto the raised section of the railway bridge. She was wrapped up in a sleeping blanket with a paper cup half full of change in front of her.

'Hi Rosie,' Tom said, as he knelt beside her. 'How are you?'

'Father Morton,' Rosie said, 'I've been waiting.'

'I remembered,' Tom said. 'It came to me, eventually... Rosemary Brennan.'

'I saw you up here, recognised who you were, saw you looking at the track with that look on your face: desperation, abandonment, isolation, entrapment. I've seen it before, on my brother's face, in the weeks before he hung himself.'

Tom sat next to his long-dead friend's sister as people hurried to-and-fro from the station to the station car park.

'I'm sorry,' he said, 'I should have recognised you when you came that day to the rectory.'

'Why would you? Our lives went in opposite...' Rosie barked into her hands, the convulsions racking her body.'

'You need that cough looking at,' Tom said. 'It's a stinker. Can I...'

'No. You can't. Stop talking... listen. Our lives went in opposite directions. Back into care, then into a hostel for troubled girls, and believe me, you don't want to know what happens to girls with mental health issues and emotional trauma who fall through the cracks in the system.'

'I am sorry.'

'I hated you for years, holding you responsible for Dan's death, my protector. Then, I spotted you here, and I wanted you to die, like he did. I followed you back to your fancy church. And then, I met you and your boyfriend.'

'Antony isn't my boyfriend. Anyway, he's gone now.'

'I know that Dan would want you to be happy.'

'I came here to find you, to see if I could help.'

'You look better.'

'I'm on medication to help stabilise my moods. I don't get so low, down so fast. I only wish I'd done something earlier. I did some silly things: I messed things up with Antony, I... tried to kill myself and make it look like an accident, but all I got was a grazed arm.'

'Thank you,' Rosie said, as a passer-by dropped coins into her paper cup.

'Your brother kissed me once, Rosie, and I didn't know how to handle it.'

'It looks to me like you still don't know how to handle it. I think you need to be who you are and not who you think other people expect you to be. Dan left you a letter, but my mother ripped it up. I read it before she destroyed it. Do you want to know what it said?'

'Yes, I do.'

'He said that he loved you and wanted you to be happy.'

'Oh Jesus.'

'Where are the queer elders, Tom? Where are the role models for boys like you and Dan? Who is there to help young gay men and women stop self-harming, to listen to them with empathy so they don't end up feeling worthless and hanging themselves from a tree? Who is going to take a stand against the bigots inside and outside of the Church? Who is there for the lesbian, gay, bisexual and trans Catholics, both young and old?'

'You don't understand. I can't do that.'

'You can. You owe it to my brother. Your sins are forgiven, Thomas. Grow your own legs, stand up, carry your mat, present yourself to the authorities. Follow Christ, and don't fear the toxic Christians who wear the badge of religion but don't walk the walk of love.'

'Rosie, it hasn't been prayer, or divine grace, that has helped me through this difficult time. It is happy pills courtesy of the National Health Service.'

'That's utter shite, false priest, and you know it. God did it. Remember my brother's love and friendship and do what's right. Now, piss off, you're making me mad, and the regulars are avoiding me since you showed up.'

'Can I help you, Rosie? Is there anything you need?'

'Have you been listening to a word I said? Fuck off.'

Tom stood up, brushed off his trousers.

'I will come and see you again.'

'Don't bother, unless you have something to tell me. Now, do one, Thomas Morton, or I'll start screaming for help.'

52.

They arrived at the ground floor, the bell pinged, and the ancient elevator doors rattled open.

Tom was sitting on the grimy carpeted floor, grinning inanely, pissed out of his head on grapefruit Mad Dog 20-20. Pete was retching aniseed Aftershock into a Waitrose carrier bag. The elderly couple who had called the lift down wrinkled their noses and allowed the doors to judder to a close.

Back on the eleventh, the game of strip poker organised by Master of Ceremonies, Shaun, had boys and girls in varying stages of undress. Michael sat, blurry eyed, on one of the beds with his arm around a blonde-haired girl called Hils. Hils' red-headed best friend, Lisa, sat scowling beside them. The word on the street was that the two teachers, nominated to keep an eye on the students that night, had been seen getting wankered in the hotel bar and had then headed up to the bedrooms together holding hands. That night, the decaying budget hotel on Russell Square was under occupation by a small army of Lancastrian college students enjoying the freedom of being far away from their mums and dads.

The annual field trip to London was the only and best reason to study Geography A Level at Saint Pats College of Further Education. It was Tom's first time in the Big Smoke, and he was determined to milk it for every ounce of experience. Unfortunately, Mad Dog had lived up to its brand promise and overindulgence had rendered him incapable of anything other than gremlin-like facial expressions and random hooting noises.

Shaun had joined the threesome on the bed and now had his arm around redhead Lisa who continued to stare at Tom like he was a piece of shit, which was very perturbing for Tom, who had always thought that he got on okay with Lisa.

'Fuck this,' Pete was telling him. 'Let's head off into town, find some trouble. I'm not sitting watching this shit. Come on, man.'

'Mmm,' Tom agreed.

The two boys soon discovered that there was little to do near Russell Square, but a short cab ride got them to the ULU bar on the nearby university campus. The bar was buzzing, full of fabulous students who looked the part, and Tom and Pete realised they looked like country bumpkins in comparison.

They got talking to two friendly gay lads, who invited them back to their place to 'make cookies.'

'I've got a girlfriend,' Pete said, 'but he hasn't,' pointing to Tom.

Somehow, they managed to score some LSD from an American back-packer and a dentistry student from Bristol.

The next thing Tom knew was he was lying on some grass next to Pete in a baroque churchyard, looking up as blue and yellow clouds skidded across the night-time sky. Then, a woman in heels and a short skirt jumped over a hedge and started rummaging in the shrubbery.

'I've lost my purse,' the woman said upon noticing the two reclining teenagers. Then she dived back over the bushes.

'Did that just happen?' Pete asked.

'Yeah,' Tom said, laughing, 'it really happened, man.'

'Thank God, you saw it too.'

'That statue is stretching though, which is quite intriguing.'

'You know that Lisa fancies you, don't you?'

'Lisa, as in Shaun's Lisa?'

'She doesn't even like Shaun. She likes you, apparently.'

'Jesus. I haven't even spoken to her. How can she fancy me?'

'Tom?'

'Yeah?'

'Have you got that ladies' purse?'

The two friends started laughing, and they couldn't stop.

53.

'Vocation burn out,' Dean Wesham said, as they walked the walled garden, 'you're not the first and, unfortunately, you won't be the last. The routine of masses, confession, baptisms... everything that is so precious about the Church loses its luminescence and becomes dulled. Take some time out, Tom. God knows you deserve it!'

'Are you well?' Tom asked, as they passed beneath the stone arch into the Japanese garden. He stretched his hand forward to touch Dean's arm.

'I feel great,' Dean said, taking Tom's hand and squeezing it, 'and don't try to change the subject, Tom, we are talking about you.'

Their reflections shimmered beneath the wooden footbridge. Around the edges of the pool, orange shapes flittered between the water lilies.

'I'm taking my combination medication. I'm exercising. I'm eating well, and, of course, no sex.'

'Apparently, there will be no funerals for gay people in the Catholic Church,' Tom said.

'In which case, there won't be many priests having funerals,' Dean replied.

'I wonder what my mother would say if she knew that her favourite priest, her son's spiritual director, was his lover, once upon a time.'

'She once told me that the bones of sexual deviants litter the floor of Hell.'

'Can you imagine what would have happened if she'd found out?'

'I think if your mother had suspected, even for a minute, that I was her son's lover, then I would have been murdered in my bed, stabbed with knitting needles. I'd have ended up looking like Pinhead in *Hellraiser*.'

'There are reasons why she is the way she is.'

'Conservative Catholics have a point, Tom. We priests should be able to resist temptation.'

'I respected your decision to be celibate all those years ago, Dean, even though it hurt like hell. I understand that there are spiritual benefits to chastity, but to demand that every priest, gay or straight, should give up their right to a loving relationship... how can that be right?

'We gay priests do what we have always done, doff our cap to Rome, to the Bishop, and then get on with helping the poor, the needy, and all those scorned and marginalised by society. That's our job.'

'I know I've said it before, but let me say it again...'

'No, Tom, don't.'

'I will regret for the rest of my life that I was careless and that it was me who infected you. You trusted me, and I let you down.'

'You shouldn't. We've discussed this,' Dean said.

'I beg God for forgiveness every day,' Tom said.

'It so beautiful here in these gardens.'

'Now, you're the one changing the subject.'

'We're so lucky to have Bradshaw Hall on our doorstep, aren't we?'

'Apart from the fact that the Bradshaw family used income from slave plantations to build the house and gardens? The slaves weren't lucky, were they? It's thanks to brutality and murder that we have this place.'

'We need to recognise the past in the present, here in Bussell. We should always acknowledge the truth, look it square in the face, unflinching.'

'But what is truth?' Tom asked. 'Surely it is in the eye of the beholder.'

'I believe someone else asked that question, a long time ago. The truth is that I understand what people with HIV are going through, because I am HIV positive myself.'

'People don't know that you have... that disease.'

'It has a name, Tom. It is called Human Immunodeficiency Virus. My parishioners don't know that I have it… but they will soon.'

'Dean, be careful. That's a dangerous road.'

'There are no easy roads, Tom. You have the chance of happiness with the love of your life—no, don't interrupt, let me finish—you have that chance, and I beg you to grasp it. You have my love and my blessing. I have my own path to follow, and as Jesus looked after the sick, the forgotten, the destitute, so shall I. And I hope that you will let me have your blessing. Come on, let's walk among the borders. I love to see the colours of the flowers and trees as summer turns to autumn.'

'The Church will crucify you if you tell.'

Dean sighed. 'In which case, I will be in good company, won't I? And Tom, if you ever feel down, so down that you want to hurt yourself, you must be humble enough to ask for help. There is no shame in that.'

54.

Tom and Michael worked in the bar at the Station Hotel. Weekends were mayhem, but the place was shut by eleven, which gave them time to get changed, get picked up by Shaun and Pete, and go clubbing 'til the early hours.

There was a 'no girlfriends at weekends' rule, proposed by Tom, and agreed with by all the guys. Michael saw his girlfriend, Hils, during the week after college. Tom got on with Hils. She was a nice girl, and she had made the effort to get to know Michael's friends. Tom got on with Monica, Pete's girlfriend, and future wife. Tom got on with Shaun's new girlfriend, Sarah, who was dark-haired, pretty, stick thin, with an appetite for drugs and alcohol that made Shaun look like a model of temperance.

When the other lads were with their girlfriends, Tom would hang around with Shirley, who always made him giggle and feel better. Shirley had blossomed into a beautiful woman, and she got more than her fair share of attention when they went out in Bussell together for a drink. Tom found himself ready to step in when horrible men started letching over her in busy pubs. But Shirley told him to stop being stupid and over-protective.

Tom told Shirley about the technician who had come up to talk to him in the IT suite at college.

'I was just sitting there, and he came up to me and started asking me what work I was doing, did I like my courses, and he started saying he liked my T-shirt and…'

'Oh, my God, he fancies you,' Shirley said. 'That's amazing. He's really hot. I think he's married. How did you feel? What did you do?'

The truth was that Tom had felt fucking amazing. He felt special, turned on, giddy, and he'd gone from zero to major crush in six seconds. The truth was that Tom had invented a reason to go to see Mister Lab Tech at the next break to return a pencil that he hadn't dropped. The truth was that after he had handed over the pencil, Tom felt incredibly guilty, stupid, and he had promised himself that he would avoid the gorgeous, brown-haired, brown-eyed, man-god for the rest of his time at St Pat's college.

'I just ignored him, Shirley.'

'But why?'

'You know why. I don't like boys.'

'Yeah, right,' Shirley said, 'and I'm Blessed Saint Theresa. I know why you won't come out, Tom.'

'And why is that?'

'Because you're terrified of your mother, and you're terrified of admitting to yourself that you are gay.'

'Wrong on both counts,' Tom said. 'I won't be coming out because I am *not* gay.'

55.

Tom and his mother ate their tea together in the cramped dining room filled with bookcases filled with religious books filled with religious words.

'What have you given up for Lent, Mum?' Tom asked, as he sliced the cold ham with his knife.

'Chocolate and sweets,' Emma Morton said.

'You don't eat chocolate and sweets,' Tom laughed.

'I like a treat every now and again.'

'I'm coming to the realisation that I can make a difference as a priest,' Tom said, breaking the silence that followed.

'That's good,' Emma Morton said, swallowing. 'It's only taken you thirty years to figure that out. You've had a face like a slapped bottom these last few months. You need to pull yourself together.'

'I'm thinking about how I recommit to the oppressed and the marginalised.'

'Just remember that Jesus said, 'Your sins are forgiven. Go and sin no more,' not, 'Your sins are forgiven. Go and do as you like.''

'If I were to challenge aspects of the Church's social policy, would you be ashamed of me.'

Emma put her knife and fork side by side on the green and white plate and looked at her son.

'Jesus challenged the doctrine of the religious. As long as you are living your life in accordance with the Bible, then that's good enough for me.'

'I've always wondered if the prodigal son fled his family to avoid being trapped by their expectations of him, by society's expectations of him,' Tom said. 'Maybe the prodigal son had his reasons for getting out of his father's house.'

'He came back though, didn't he?' Emma said. 'And he committed to living by the rules of his father's house.'

'But he would always be the prodigal.'

'Yes, he would. But he would be the prodigal who realised there was something bigger than himself and that subordinating his will to God's will was the purpose of his life.'

His mother took away the dishes and began clattering around in the kitchen, putting dirty pots in the washing up bowl, opening the oven door, taking cutlery out of the drawer, and putting it on the marble surfaces.

'I'll help you wash up,' Tom said.

'I've made you a sponge pudding with jam. Do you want custard or fresh cream?'

'Custard please, Mum.'

'Do you remember Father Spence going on holiday each year with Father Worthington?' Emma called from the kitchen.

'Of course, I do,' Tom said.

'That was nice, wasn't it?'

'It was.'

'They were such gentlemen.'

'They were good and decent men.'

'Some of these priests these days—not Catholic ones, I'm talking about Baptists and Methodists and such like—all you hear about from them is gay rights, asylum seeker rights, women's rights. It drowns

God's message of forgiveness of sins in buzz words. I've no time for people like them, rubbing other people's faces in it.'

There was his mother's message, hidden in parables and stories. It was the furthest either of them had come to confronting the truth of his sexual orientation. But it didn't go far enough for Tom, not now. It meant more hiding, more falsehood disguised as climbing trips to Austria. And there was the specific threat, the risk that an overtly gay identity would sunder his relationship with the mother who drove him crazy but who he loved beyond measure.

The sponge pudding and custard arrived steaming hot in a bowl with a spoon wedged inside.

'There, your favourite.'

'Thanks, Mum. Is there enough for seconds?'

'Oh yes,' she said, beaming with pleasure.

'The father saw the prodigal from a long way off and came running. didn't he?' Tom asked, as he spooned the delicious dessert into his mouth.'

'He did,' his mother said, with suspicion in her voice.

'And the father told the sulky brother to welcome his sibling back?'

'He did.'

'The father wanted everyone to be friends together, didn't he? Not falling out and sitting in separate rooms.'

'He did.'

'That's the God that I believe in, Mum. That was great. Thank you.'

'Don't do anything stupid, promise me.'

'I won't do anything stupid. I promise.'

56.

The Basin was Bussell's go-to nightclub. A converted mill across two floors with zero health and safety, foul toilets, sticky carpets, an age policy of pre-school to pensioner. The only entry requirement was the five pounds admission fee. The job description for the meathead door-staff seemed to entail getting off with underage girls, dealing drugs, and punching the living daylights out of pimply eighteen-year-olds with one too many tequilas inside of them.

The reason why The Basin was so popular despite being such a calamitous shithole was it was the *only* nightclub in Bussell apart from Mounts, a heavy metal gaff and, therefore, certain death for indie kids and ravers. The music was decent on Wednesday nights, an eclectic mix of '60s, grunge, dance, guitar-based, with a sprinkle of punk and Irish folk tunes thrown in for good measure. If it sent the dance floor into a frenzy, the DJ played it again, and again. Requests were made by writing the name of the song and the band on a pad next to the DJ's booth. The rumour was that the DJ would wipe his arse with the request pad because no request that Tom and his mates made ever got played.

As well as booze, the Basin did a roaring trade selling chips and burgers to pissed teenagers. The kitchen with its Mordoresque deep fat fryers was situated next to the fire escape on the second floor. When the club got too humid, too smoky, the staff would open the fire door, and the clientele would gather on the metal gantry that hung ten feet above the Leeds-Liverpool canal.

Tom, Michael, Pete, and Shaun had some wicked nights out in The Basin, dancing, getting drunk, getting high, meeting people, flirting, and it was there that they met Anya and her friends, who were students at Bussell College, in the centre of town. Anya was great crack, pretty, tiny, of Indian heritage. She loved her music. She could drink more Newcastle Brown than Tom could. Anya was fiercely intelligent but, for a reason Tom could not comprehend, she wanted to be his girlfriend.

Tom loved having girl friends; Shirley for example, who was practically his sister. What Tom did not want under any circumstances was a *girlfriend*. The reason was obvious, wasn't it? Eighteen was far too young to settle down. Now was the time to party with the friends he adored. Already, the lads were slipping, little by little, into the morass of serious relationships, and Tom sensed this golden age of debauchery had a best before date that was rapidly approaching.

But Anya was determined. She might have been small in stature, but, by Christ, she was relentless. Integer-by-integer, she extracted Tom's home telephone number and pinned him down to a date, time, and location where they could meet, just the two of them. Michael, Shaun, and Pete were delighted that their friend had finally made a move on a girl they approved of… at least now any suspicions could be allayed.

Tom was distraught. He thought the world of Anya, loved sitting next to her in The Basin, necking cheap booze, chatting, and laughing, dancing to *Ever Fallen in Love* by The Buzzcocks, and he knew, from past experience, exactly what the feedback would be from a date in the real world—'the most boring date I've ever been on.'

So, he stood her up.

Anya and her friend were on the phone, giving him hell, which Tom knew he deserved. Tom knew that he owed Anya an explanation, so the next time he saw her in The Basin, he went over, apologised, and told her the real reason that he couldn't date her—he was going to be a Catholic priest.

57.

Tom was summoned for a face-to-face meeting with Bishop Worrell's enforcer, Father Mallon. He took the West Coast mainline train from Bussell to Preston, then walked to the Diocesan offices that were housed in a red brick building adjacent to the Cathedral.

Tom was escorted to the third floor to find Mallon and an unsmiling male assistant waiting for him inside a white-walled meeting room. Papers, pens, and foolscap document folders were laid out in front of them. It was a trap, but, other than turning around and walking out, Tom didn't see that he had many options.

'Sit down, Father Morton, please,' Mallon said. Father Mallon introduced his personal secretary, and Tom promptly forgot weasel-man's name. Mallon explained that Bishop Worrell's office had received an official complaint from a solicitor representing the parent of a child attending Saint James's Church, alleging sexual grooming had taken place. Furthermore, the Bishop had also had communication from the 'well-respected Head Teacher of St. Patrick's Roman Catholic High School,' who had expressed concern about the unprecedented personal intervention of Father Morton in a safeguarding issue relating to the same minor. Father Mallon asked Tom whether he had a response to these grave areas of concern.

'Do I need a solicitor?' Tom asked.

'This isn't a formal investigation, yet,' Mallon told him, as ferret-face scribbled away on a note pad.

'Then, I've nothing to say, other than this boy is coming out as gay, and he has the support of his mother, but not the father, who has left the family home and begun a new relationship. The boy and the boy's mother asked me to speak to Headmaster Cooper to prevent any bullying at school. I didn't keep a detailed record of the meeting that I had with Cooper on school premises, but I wish that I had.'

'Why you, Morton?'

'Why not me, Father Mallon?'

'The beautiful teachings of Our Lord, Jesus Christ, are under attack from enemies outside the Church. What a travesty it is that he also has enemies *inside* the Church.'

'I agree,' Tom said. 'The commandment to 'love one another as I have loved you' seems to be being trampled within, and without, the Church. Don't you agree, Father Mallon?'

'Bishop Worrell is going to launch a new safeguarding programme to protect children from homosexual clergy,' Mallon said, leafing through his document folder. 'I thought I'd share it with you first, Thomas. I may call you Thomas, may I? Not Doubting Thomas, of course—he was an invention of John.'

'I'm always partial to a bit of John—some parts more than others. And you can call me whatever you like, Gerry.'

The secretary was fidgeting, looking increasingly uncomfortable.

'The Bishop and I…'

'*His Excellency* the Bishop and I,' Tom corrected.

Mallon stared at him, and Tom stifled the urge to burst out laughing.

'His Excellency the Bishop and I are piloting…'

'Are you a couple now?'

'Father Mallon, I would suggest that you take this seriously. Your future in the Church depends on it.'

'I'm Tom, you're Gerry. How seriously am I expected to take this ridiculous farce? I know what you are going to ask me to do, and I will not be taking any part in it. There is no way that I am going to fill forms in answering questions about my sexual orientation, and neither will I be spending time with a forensic psychologist looking to root out queer priests like this is the Gay Inquisition. All you need to know is that I am currently celibate.'

Mallon banged his fist onto his desk.

'This is about child welfare and ensuring this Diocese does not have any rapist priests bringing our church into disrepute. You will do as you are told, or you will lose your job. Is that clear?'

'This is *not* about rapist priests,' Tom said. 'If it were, I'd be moving heaven and earth to help you. This is an anti-LGBTQ vendetta, with gay priests set up as the fall guys while the real culprits get away scot-free. If we are finished here, I'd ask that your assistant email me a copy of his minutes so I can add my comments.'

'Tell me,' Mallon said, as Tom reached for the door, 'why did you become a priest? I'm intrigued.'

'For the same reason as you, I expect, Father. I wanted to dedicate my life to Christ.'

58.

'What the fuck did you tell Anya that for?' Shaun said, shaking his head.

'Genius, mate,' Michael said, laughing. 'I wish I'd been there.'

'You're not really going to be a priest, are you?' Pete asked.

'I've got two years to pray about it, and then, if I do go to the seminary, that's another five to six years of training and study. Nothing is final for ages yet. I wouldn't be ordained for another seven years, at least.'

'Jesus Christ,' Shaun said. 'Who the fuck would want to be a priest?'

'If nobody did there wouldn't be any.'

'Does that mean no more clubbing, no girls, no e trips n' whizz?' Pete asked.

'A little temptation might make me a better listener in the Confessional.'

'Anything else you want to tell us?' Michael asked.

'No, nothing else,' Tom said, avoiding eye contact with his friend.

'What did your mum say?' Pete asked.

'She's thrilled.'

'I'll bet,' Shaun said, his voice laden with sarcasm.

'Have you seen Ash Burrow?' Pete said. 'It looks like a mansion from a slasher movie. You wouldn't get me staying there… dead before sunrise!'

'Father Worthington showed me around, and I liked the place. Look boys, I could change my mind about this. It's just an option, something that I might do. Something I might not. Chill yer fuckin' boots!'

'What did Shirley say when you told her?' Michael asked.

'She just laughed,' Tom said. 'She said I should train as an exorcist.'

59.

Dear Antony,

Thank you so much for the lovely flowers, which made my day when they arrived, such a lovely surprise. I kept the white roses for the rectory, arranged the lisianthus and bouvardia in vases in the sacristy, and—I hope you don't mind—I put the Calla lilies and eucalyptus on the Lady Altar, which now looks stunning. Everywhere I go in Saint Jimmy's, I am reminded of you!

Pete was very naughty telling you about my recent troubles with the Diocese. There's no need to worry. If the worst happens and they sack me, I think I'd like to be a bus driver so that I can travel the world and see far-away places like Accrington, Burnley, Ormskirk, and Newton le Willows. There will be no stopping me!

Danny, the boy in my parish who came out as gay, is enduring terrible homophobic bullying at Saint Pats, which is shameful. Who would have thought that in this day-and-age, religious freedom of speech could be weaponised to single out and abuse young LGBTQ people? Fortunately, Danny seems to be a tough cookie, and he isn't self-harming or having suicidal thoughts, as far as we know. The father is having none of it and wants his son to have counselling from an evangelical group in Manchester, which sounds suspiciously like conversion therapy to me. I've made my views known to Dan's mother, but it's up to them. I can't really interfere. All I can do is be there for Dan if he needs someone to talk to.

Lent is always a time of reflection and prayer. As Christ spend forty days in the wilderness, fasting and praying, so we, as followers of Christ, try to emulate his example. And, as we approach Good Friday, I'm always reminded of those who have gone before us: your mum and dad, my dad and little brother, our dear friend Shirley, my friend Dan, Pete and Monica's little baby son, Shaun's grandson who died last year. May they all rest in peace.

I hope that the business is still going from strength to strength. I love the online deli, and I placed my first order this morning!

As you know, Antony, I wish you all the happiness in the world from the bottom of my heart. I know snail mail is old-fashioned these days, but there is something special about a hand-written card or letter. I must sound like a bit of an antique.

I miss you so very much, and I promise that I'll come to visit soon. The next few weeks will be busy. This Easter, I'm planning something a little special. I'll tell you more about it, next time, I promise. I think you'll be proud of me. I hope you will. It's all very daunting.

Thank you again for the flowers. They are spectacular, and I was walking on Cloud Nine all week. Even Joan thinks they are beautiful!

All my love,
Tom x

60.

The nightclub was bouncing, lights projecting through the smoke, electronic music pulsed, the bass vibrating through Tom's rib cage. They were deep in Manchester's Northern Quarter, the club's entrance hidden amongst a myriad of ginnels and cobbled streets. Pete was in a booth, snogging a black girl. Michael had reached his drug-fuelled apex, which rendered him incapable of speech and was somewhere in the dancefloor crowd. Friendly Shaun, good vibes ambassador, was talking to a wide-eyed raver in a white T shirt at the bar, the two of them sipping ice cold Buxton Spring from a plastic bottle.

Pete had split up with Monica, temporarily as it later transpired. He had denounced Catholicism, declared himself an atheist, dropped out of Saint Pat's sixth form, and moved to Bussell College instead. Whenever he had the opportunity, Pete would lay into Tom for believing in his 'imaginary best friend in the sky,' reeling out the abuses committed by the Church and the damage religion had inflicted upon the world. Michael kept his head down and said nothing. Shaun shrugged his shoulders and said, though he hadn't believed in God for years, he respected everyone's opinion.

Pete had made new friends at Bussell College, a tall gangly lad with fair hair, called Antony, and a short dark-haired boy, called Gary, who had come with them on the train into Manchester. Antony was a top lad, chatty, funny, and Tom got on with him straight away. Gary, on the other hand, didn't smile and didn't say much.

'Gary's gay,' Antony told Tom, shouting above the noise of the music in the nightclub.

'I'm not,' Tom replied.

Antony said nothing.

That night, the friends crashed over at Antony's house for the first time, sleeping in one of the spare bedrooms or on one of the couches downstairs. Late morning, Antony's mum, made a cooked breakfast for everyone. Antony's mum didn't seem to care about the mayhem caused by six stinking boys with their clothes and shoes littering up her beautiful home. She was cool about everything, even the stench of Pete's cheesy feet, seemingly just happy that her son and his new friends were home and safe.

'Call me Lil,' she instructed the rave-ravaged teenagers.

'The priest thing has made Lisa even more determined,' Michael said, as he chewed his bacon sandwich.'

'What priest thing?' Antony asked.

'Tom's going to be a priest, apparently,' Pete said.

'I'm not even nice to her,' Tom said.

'You're going to be a priest?' Antony asked.

'Yeah.'

'Fucking hell,' Gary said, 'I can't think of anything worse.'

'It's a ruse to get out of dating girls,' Shaun said.

Antony was watching Tom now, appraising him.

'Is that true?' he asked, swigging his coffee.

Tom laughed and ignored the question as he tucked into his eggs and beans.

'All we hear is "Tom said this" and, "Tom said that,"' Michael said. 'It's driving me and Hils crazy.'

'I promise you, I never ever even speak to her,' Tom said.

'Go for it, Tom' Shaun said, 'I moved on long ago.'

'Pass the ketchup, Saint Thomas,' Pete said.

'Fuck off.'

'Yes, Father Morton. No, Father Morton. I will fuck off, Father Morton,' Pete said, chewing his food.

'That's two Our Fathers and one Hail Mary for you, Peter King.'

'Who's going to be a priest?' Lilian Keane asked, entering the kitchen.

'Tom is,' Antony said.

Tom found himself being appraised by eyes the same shape and colour as Antony's.

'That's an interesting career choice, Tom,' she said.

'It is.'

'My dad's a vicar,' Gary said. 'He hates it.'

Tom decided that he didn't like Antony's friend, Gary, very much. Antony on the other hand… well, he was nice.

Really nice.

61.

Danny Arundel was sitting on the sofa watching TV, his arm in a sling, when Tom stopped by.

In the galley kitchen, Danny's mum, Dawn, explained how her son had been deliberately tripped on the main school staircase, had fallen badly, been injured, and then taken to hospital by one of the teachers. 'Prior to this, Danny has been struck in the face, called all kinds of horrible names, and the worst thing is the social media. The parents are even worse, sending me messages defending their vile children, saying Danny is just looking for attention. The school is ticking the boxes, but what is it going to take before they deal with this homophobic behaviour properly? For Dan to die? Even Sophie is getting picked on just because she is Danny's sister.'

'What has Mike said about this?'

'He blames me. He blames you, everybody but himself, or the school.'

'Hello Dan,' Tom said, as he went into the sitting room.

'Hello, Father Thomas.'

'Call me Tom, that's what my friends call me, that and Father Moron.'

Danny laughed, and Tom sat in the armchair opposite him.

'How are you?'

The boy's eyes brimmed with tears.

'You said it would be okay.'

'I did, and, one day, it will be.'

'I don't think God loves me, anymore.'

'Oh, yes she does, Dan. She loves you very much. I would like to ask that you, your mum, your sister all come to church on Easter Sunday. Is that okay?'

Danny nodded.

'Promise?'

'I promise.'

'You might think that no one's got your back on this, but they do. And we need to fight back, whatever the cost. Because that is what the Easter story is all about, facing into power, defeat, then transforming that defeat into a victory that changes the world forever.'

'Make sure that you're in church on Easter Sunday,' Tom told Dawn, as he said goodbye on the doorstep.

'Why?'

'I'm going to pull the pin on a grenade.'

'Bless you, Father. But don't go getting yourself into any trouble. That won't help any of us.'

'As I always say, 'Be there, or don't be there,'' Tom said, smiling, as he unlocked his bike.

'We'll be there. What is your sermon going to be about?'

'Life after death, resurrection, that kind of stuff. It's Ostara's Day, what else would I be preaching about?'

62.

After his A level examinations, Tom found himself a job as an Administration Assistant at Bakerline Trucks in the Direct Sales Department. Direct Sales sold the basic truck chassis—the cab, frame, axles, wheels—to a bodybuilder who put the fire engine, tipper, ambulance body, or crane unit on the chassis and then, sold it as a finished vehicle. As well as the chassis, Tom's department sold spare parts, which were significantly more profitable.

The sales guys—and they were guys, there were no women in the team—were all ex-engineers who had been through the company apprenticeship programme and had never worked anywhere else. They were rough, tough, sexist, homophobic, fierce Northern English bastards, and they made Tom's life hell for three months.

For the first three months he worked there, the question that Tom got asked every Monday morning without fail was, 'Did you get plumbed in at the weekend?'

The expectation was that as a nineteen-year-old, blue-blooded male, Tom should be out shagging every available female in town and then coming into work to regale his married colleagues with all the sticky sordid details.

Tom was a huge disappointment to his manager, Barry, and to his colleagues, Chris and Andy. From asking Tom to go down to engineering and ask for a glass-hammer, to telling him to ring the canteen manager and ask for a chocolate teapot, Tom was mercilessly ridiculed for being an educated space cadet.

To an extent, the Bakerline boys had a point. Tom was the product of a system that had asked him to think in two-and-a-half-thousand-word essays, and he was having to reprogramme his whole processing system, at pace. That said, Tom's treatment bordered on abuse and persecution, and there were some nights that he went home in tears, vowing not to come back the next day.

The breakthrough came when a dead-leg ambulance bodybuilder that Tom had been given to manage (because there was no hope of them ever placing an order) placed an order for five trucks and a shit-tonne of parts to go with the chassis. The trucks were going to Africa as part of an Aid Convoy, and they needed to be bullet proof, which meant more profit.

'How did you do that?' Barry asked, as he stared at a copy of the faxed order with 'For the kind attention of Thomas Morton' written at the top.

'I just answered their questions as best I could and got back to them the same day,' Tom said.

And after that bit of luck, everything changed.

Tom was earning nine grand a year which, even after he'd given his mum bed n' board, was an absolute fortune in terms of disposable income. The priesthood idea soon disappeared into the ether of batshit-crazy ideas that had served their purpose.

Chris later told him that Barry had tipexed out Tom's name at the top of the order before sending it through to the Sales Director, claiming it for himself. Tom told Chris that he didn't give a flying fuck about what Barry had done, all that mattered to him was that the team had won the new business.

He might have won the respect of his colleagues, but the 'Did you get plumbed in at the weekend?' question never stopped.

'You're not queer, are you? One of them shirt-lifters?' soon followed.

Tom tried to explain he was enjoying himself going clubbing with his friends every Friday and Saturday, as well as saving up for his first foreign holiday, but it was to no avail. And that is how he got set up with Tamsin from accounts, five years older, his first girlfriend, and the woman he lost his virginity to aged twenty-years and two-months.

63.

Holy Week, the culmination of the Church year, was the week that saw Tom get suspended from the priesthood pending a formal investigation by the Diocese.

The highlight of Palm Sunday at Saint Benedict's Church was the Passion Story. Emma Morton, Tom's mother, was the narrator and, given that it was a B Cycle year, it was Mark's Gospel that was being used. There was no D Cycle. John's account was never used, despite it being the only first-hand account of the Passion of the Christ in the New Testament. Tom was speaking the words of Jesus, as Father Spence had before him, as countless other priests had before Father Spence. The congregation voiced the crowd, Pontius Pilate, and the disciples.

As he read out English translations of the Greek translations of the Aramaic words that someone remembered Jesus had used, Tom prayed for the souls of Father Spence and Father Worthington and all the gay priests who had devoted themselves to the proclamation of a gospel of forgiveness of sins and to the spiritual welfare of their congregations, despite the personal cost, despite the condemnation they knew they would have faced had they been known for who they really were.

Tom's Palm Sunday sermon was later described by one enraged listener as 'the longest resignation speech they had ever had the misfortune to hear,' and by another perplexed participant as 'gaywashing the gospels.'

'Lazarus coming back from the dead is a story found only in John's Gospel,' Tom said, ignoring the Diocesan instructions on the content for sermons on Palm Sunday. 'This story precedes the triumphant entry into Jerusalem and acts as a reflection of Jesus's own death and resurrection, just a few weeks later.'

The expressionless parishioners sat on pews in familial rows—Tom thought they looked like a human version of Connect 4, a linear insight that filled him with foreboding.

'Lazarus was an unmarried man living with his sisters, and he was dying from a mystery disease,' Tom said, pausing to let the words sink in. 'Jesus, an unmarried man, who lived with his mother, is told, "The man you love is seriously ill." Jesus tells his followers that, "This sickness will not end in death, and God's son will be glorified through it." Jesus hangs around for a few days before setting off, and, when he arrives in Bethany, Lazarus has been in his tomb for four days. Martha, Lazarus's sister, says to Jesus "If you'd been here on time, my brother wouldn't be dead n' buried." Jesus says to her, "I am the resurrection and the life, anyone who believes in me, even though they die, they will still live. And anyone currently alive who believes in me, shall never die." Jesus says that *anyone* who believes in him shall never die... anyone who believes in the logos, in the verb that is full of grace and truth.'

Tom's exegesis had elicited a wave of unease that was rippling through the Saint Benny's congregation. There was coughing, people shifting in their pews, the crossing of legs, the crossing of arms. Tom pressed on, knowing what must be said, what must be done.

'Martha said "Yes, Lord, I believe you are the Messiah, the Son of God who has to come into the world." And then, we are told that Jesus wept. The dam burst, and our saviour breaks down in tears. What does this scene tell us about the nature of God? Perhaps, he was looking ahead to future generations of people who would suffer from terrible diseases and be treated as social outcasts. The heart of our faith *is* the courage to will to love, forgiveness, compassion; not judgement, anger, violence, the will to power.'

Tom looked to his mother to see whether she was hanging her head in shame at his antics. Emma Morton was sitting up straight, listening, watching her son speak in front of his own Sanhedrin.

'Jesus asked for the stone of the tomb to be removed,' Tom said.

Unclipping his microphone and stepping from behind the antique wooden lectern adorned with a carven eagle with its wings outstretched, Tom moved to the bottom of the altar steps so that he was on the same level as the congregation.

'Martha told Our Lord that there would be a smell, the stench of death. And Jesus said, "What did I say to you, Martha? If you believe, you will see the glory of God." Martha wasn't happy about it, but they rolled the stone away. Jesus prayed, "Father, thank you for hearing me. I know you always do. But for the benefit of the people here today, please do this so they may believe that it was you who sent me." Jesus calls out, "Lazarus, come out of the cave." And Lazarus came out.'

The silence in the building was deafening.

'The Secret Gospel of Mark, the unedited version of The Gospel According to Mark, if you will, has further insight into the Lazarus story. What we don't know is how the first-hand account that John had access to links with the Markian version that didn't make it to the final cut. John, the Evangelist, may or may not be the same person as Apostle John—the person many believe was the beloved disciple of John's gospel. He is certainly not the John who wrote the prophetic Book of Revelations. Perhaps, in a time when women were not treated as equals, "John" was a Currer Bell *nom de plume* for one of the female disciples. What is clearly important to our gospel and letter writer is that the homoerotic aspects found in the Secret Gospel of Mark be reflected in their account of the life of Jesus. John develops a "Seven Signs" narrative that demonstrates that Jesus Christ is the child of God. And on Easter Sunday, we celebrate Christ coming out.'

People started leaving, turning their backs on their errant parish priest. Others followed, until only two women remained: Tom's mother, and Joan Bird.

64.

'We've set you up with Taz from Accounts,' Chris and Andy, told Tom.

'What?' Tom asked, nearly choking on his coffee.

'She's a nice girl,' Chris said.

'She's got a boyfriend,' Tom said. 'She was telling me about him. He's a mechanic in Garstang.'

'And?' Andy asked.

'You're taking her out for a pizza,' Chris said.

'I can't drive.'

'You work for a truck company,' Andy said. 'What's wrong with you? I've got my HGV 1 and 2.'

'She can drive,' Chris said. 'Don't worry about it.'

'You can give her the sticky finger,' Andy said.

'What the fuck?' Tom said. 'That's gross. Is Barry in on this?'

'No,' Chris said, 'and don't tell him until after you've been on the date. He'll be sniffing her seat, the deviant bastard.'

'He'll want to know everything,' Andy said. 'All the details.'

'Jesus,' Tom said. 'This is horrific.'

'Chill your boots, big man. Take her out for a meal, shag her, and when it's done, we'll leave you alone,' Chris promised.

Tasmin Jones picked Tom up at his house on a Thursday night. Her car was a wreck, held together by rust and duct tape. Inside, it looked like someone had emptied a dustbin in the foot wells. She drove everywhere at a hundred miles an hour, swinging around corners like she was attempting an Apollo 13 slingshot around the moon. By the time they arrived at the restaurant, Tom was green and trembling.

Taz was a natural extrovert, and she had a conversation with herself, as they ate starters and mains, with Tom nodding his head in the right places so as not to appear rude. He was surprised to find he was enjoying himself.

'I presume those dirty bastards you work with have told you to shag me and report back all the gory details, have they?'

'Err…'

'I'll take that as a yes.'

'I am going to shag you,' Taz said. 'But if you say anything, I'll gouge your eyes out with a teaspoon. Is that fair enough?'

'Err, yeah,' Tom said.

'That Barry needs locking up. I found him sniffing Louisa's seat in Credit Control.'

'I thought that was a joke?'

'No, it's real. He's got a proper seat fetish. Horrible man. He's got a wife and children as well.'

'He stole my export order. Claimed he had sold it.'

'There you go. How old are you?'

'Twenty.'

'How many girlfriends have you had?'

'A few.'

Taz laughed, 'We'll go back to mine, have some drinks, yeah?'

Back at her house, they drank beer and spirits and talked about books and movies. Taz showed him the scars on her belly and then she passed out on the settee. Tom tucked her up with a duvet he found in the bedroom, let himself out the front door, and got a taxi home.

The next day, Tom dodged questions from the Three Dirty Amigos, finding excuses to be away from his desk, divulging nothing for the sake of her honour and his eyesight.

Taz caught up with him by the coffee machine. 'Did we, you know, did we... last night?'

Tom laughed, 'No,' he said, 'we didn't.'

'A real gentleman.'

'Something like that,' Tom said.

Tom went out with Taz again, and, this time, they ended up in bed. Surrounded by Taz's collection of official Winnie the Pooh merchandise, inside pink floral bedding, Tom lost his virginity. Taz couldn't reach orgasm by penetrative sex so Tom had to learn oral sex, but Taz was patient and an excellent teacher.

The romance was a whirlwind. It was all or nothing for Taz. Her previous boyfriend, the mechanic, had been dumped, but his engagement ring still hung on a ring tree that seemed to have a lot of diamond and gold on it.

'How many times have you been engaged,' Tom asked?

'Ten. Do you want to get married?'

'No,' he said. 'I do not.'

Taz came around town with Tom, Shaun, Pete, Monica, Michael, Antony too, drinking with them in their favourite pubs. She was great fun, getting on famously with everyone.

Tom's mum, Emma, however, did not take to Taz, disliking her from the moment they met, asking 'How old did you say you are? Where do you go to church?'

Taz had contracted pelvic inflammatory disease as a teenager, a horrible infection that had left her infertile. She told Tom because she wanted him to know. Then, one night, Taz told Tom about the abortion she had had before getting P.I.D. Tom held her as she wept for the child she would never have and hold.

It was a strange situation for Tom, for a Catholic grounded in the sanctity of human life. As far as he was concerned, in that moment, the sanctity of life applied to the grieving woman in his arms, the victim of cruel fate, of decisions forced by parents, and by boys who didn't wash their dicks properly.

The one thing that really did bother Tom was Tasmin's evangelical leanings. Tom went with her to a happy-clappy church and discovered that she was into the 'hands in the air,' rave Christianity that was the polar-opposite of Tom's experience at Saint Cuthbert's. Taz also seemed to believe that Muslims and Jews were all going to hell, a concept that jarred with Tom's innate universalism and belief in a God who put love at the centre of his corporate policies. Still, the evilgelicals were all smartly dressed, smiley, and they had all been very interested to learn that he was Catholic.

Then, just as things were going well, just as he could look Barry, Chris, and Andy in the face and tell them to mind their own fucking business when they pried into his burgeoning sex life, Tom got hit by a double blow. In fact, 'blow' was the operative word when Tom's subconscious came calling.

He was on top of a barge on the Seine in France for some reason, the sun was shining, and he was having his dick sucked by a... oh my God, that's a man... when Tom awoke to find Taz riding his 3 a.m., hard-on.

'Was that nice?' she asked, as he came.

'Er, yeah,' Tom said, horrified at the trick his brain had played on him.

Then, after six months of physical and emotional intimacy, Taz dumped him. She'd met a butcher called Greg from Stockport, a Led Zep fan with a big cock and enough cash to buy her that elusive eleventh engagement ring.

Tom's mum was pleased that Tasmin was out of the picture. His friends were sympathetic but said it was probably for the best. Chris and Andy found as many reasons as they could to send him to the account's department on errands, laughing as they did so.

The truth was Tom was relieved, relieved it was over, relieved it had happened.

Taz announced to the office that she was getting married, that she and her new fiancé had set a date for next summer, which seemed like an awful hurry to Tom, but what the hell did he know? Things settled down. They were polite to each other in the lift and in the canteen. An equilibrium was reached. Then, she handed in her notice and moved to a new job in Didsbury.

Tom thought that was the last he'd see of Tasmin Jones. Which was a shame because she had been an important part of his life, and he did love her, just not like that.

65.

'Let the words of my mouth and the meditations of our hearts be acceptable in your sight, O Lord, our strength and our redeemer. Amen.'

'As you probably know,' Tom said, addressing the congregation at St. James', 'there is a special place in my heart for John's Gospel. John presents Jesus as co-existent with God, as the bread of life, the source of love that belongs *inside* of us, transforming us, the actuality that becomes our actuality, working through us, changing everything around us.

'Today is Maunday Thursday, or Mandate Thursday as it should be known, not because we are going on a date with a man, which is a pity, but because in John's Gospel we hear Jesus giving us a new commandment—that we should love one another as he loves us. Jesus knows he is going to get arrested because of his teachings, because of the trashing of the temple, because he raised Lazarus from the grave. This mandate is the essence of who he is, everything he has taught. God loves each one of us regardless of our race, gender, or sexual orientation. God sent his only child into the world because of this love, and, therefore, we should love each other. But do we really love each other that way?

'Jesus washing the feet of the disciples is another event recorded in John and nowhere else, and it is a story in line with John's existential philosophy, some might say his individualistic outlook on faith. Christ is turning the master-servant relationship upside down, reminding us that we are here to serve others. By putting others at the centre of our lives, we actualise ourselves.

'There are seven 'I am' statements used by Jesus in John's gospel: I am the bread of life; the Good Shepherd; the Resurrection and the Life; the true vine; the light of the world; the gate; the way, the truth, the life. All seven reveal Jesus as the source of eternal life. An eternal life that is ours *if* we want it. The trinity of Father, Son, and Holy Ghost is 'be, being, and becoming.' Change is at the heart of this equation, so please, everyone, harden not your spiritual arteries.

'To love each other as Jesus loves us is an incredible message, a real challenge that we lose sight of as we get wrapped up in the things that divide us rather than the things that unite us. Some may call us liberal Christians for emphasising a God of Love over a God of

Judgement. Some may call us vile heretics for daring to love instead of striving to condemn.

'As we meet this night in a building built by the Jesuit order, it is perhaps worth asking whether John the Evangelist was the philosophical founder of the Society of Jesus. I don't know about you, but I'll take my chances following those who follow Jesus and not the buffoons writing offensive articles in vitriolic rags like *This Partisan Church*.

'The grace of the Lord Jesus Christ and the love of God and the fellowship of the Holy Spirit be with you all... Apparently, the English word "goodbye" is a contraction of 'God be with ye.' So, goodbye, everyone.'

Tom was shaking hands on the church steps, wishing people goodnight, when the couple he had spotted in the back of the church approached him.

'Hello, Tom,'

'Hello, Tasmin. Hello, Greg,' Tom said. 'It's good to see you both. I'm really pleased you made it.'

'Thank you for inviting us,' Taz said, 'I couldn't believe it was you when I saw you in the hospital.'

'Omnipresence,' Tom said, 'that's the secret. How is the chemo, Greg?'

'Gruelling.'

'You're both in my prayers. If there are any jobs that need...'

'We're fine,' Taz said, 'thank you. That was quite a sermon. We don't get many like that at the Community Church. How do you get away with saying stuff like that?'

'Stuff like what?'

'Like the man date mandate.'

'You know us indulgence-selling Papists,' Tom said, 'we like what we say, and we say what we like.'

He could see that Taz was unconvinced by his fake bravado.

'I know what I'm doing,' he said, 'promise.'

'Look after yourself, Father Thomas,' Greg said, offering his hand, 'and thank you.'

Taz kissed his cheek.

'Take care of you,' she whispered.

66.

The film nights at Antony's house were always special: two VHS rentals: one decent, one trashy, plenty of tinnies, carefully constructed joints, lots of snacks. Tangy Toms was a particular favourite when it came to managing the midnight munchies. Then, the five friends would head for bed in the early hours, sleeping wherever there was space to crash out.

Tom shared Antony's bed some nights, and, as much as he was tempted to reach out, he managed to restrain himself. Afterall, he was not gay, and neither was Antony as far as he knew.

After breaking up with Taz, Tom had had an ill-advised fling with Lisa, Michael's girlfriend, Hil's best-friend. One minute, they were chatting in a club, Tom off his face on acid, the next minute, they were snogging. Tom had been woken up by his mobile phone ringing. As consciousness crept up on him, Tom realised that he was in bed in a strange house with a naked Lisa. He woke her up, telling her he had to go. She put her arms around him, kissed him, telling him, 'Don't come inside me. I'm not on the pill.'

Tom swore to himself that he was never going to sleep with Lisa, again. Two weeks later, he was in town, pissed out of his head. Lisa was there, and one thing led to another. There was an anxious wait for Lisa's period which, when it finally came, was Tom's cue to dump her. He knew it was a bastard's trick, hated himself for becoming everything he had seen and despised in other men. He also knew the pair of them had no future, that it was kinder to be cruel. But when he saw her again, he chickened out.

Antony didn't seem to have a love life. Tom could just about acknowledge his physical, sexual, and romantic attraction to Antony, but the all-encompassing "G" word? Definitely not. The implications were life-shattering. Masturbation became Tom's strategy for managing his burgeoning same-sex attraction.

Tom met curly-haired Roberta from Bristol in a nightclub in Deansgate. Roberta was doing a psychology degree at the University of Manchester and living in Halls of Residence, near Hulme. Like Taz, she was a ball of energy and life, brash, smart, sexually confident. Roberta became the third, and last, woman with whom Tom would have sex. Within a week, she had kicked him into touch, telling him she had met someone else. Then began a cycle of getting back with her, splitting up, and doing it all over again.

It was an addictive misery. Tom didn't know whether he was straight, bisexual, gay, or just totally fucked-up. Every day, he woke up with the resolution to change his life, only to crash back down into confusion and self-loathing. What he did know was that God had made him. What he did know was that he was falling in love with Antony.

Then Taz, newly married, came back into Tom's life.

67.

The fourteen black paintings hung on the red brick walls of St. Benedict's Church, seven each side, icons illuminated by electric chandeliers that hung from the pine clad ceiling. Fourteen Stations of the Cross, landmarks for pilgrims travelling the Via Dolorosa: condemnation, three falls, four meetings, stripped, nailed, dies, taken down, buried. Jesus who was murdered by the authorities, Jesus who stood up to the will to power, Jesus who gave his life for others, depicted on his path of torture and sorrow, ancient Jerusalem represented in modern Lancashire.

No Greater Love, Tom reminded himself, as his mum, Joan Bird, and the handful of people who had braved Good Friday hailstones and torrential rain, circumnavigated the church building praying, listening to readings, following the way of suffering.

What is truth? an exasperated and incredulous Pilate had demanded.

The truth, Tom thought, *is the joy that fired up the Big Bang, the joy that does not discriminate between gay and straight, trans and cisgender, the light that shines in the darkness and the darkness cannot understand it.*

'Ecce Homo,' the Roman Governor told the crowd. 'Here is the man.'

Did Christ set himself up, did he commit suicide by attacking organised religion?

The answer is yes, Tom decided. *One man against the establishment doesn't stand a chance. A Ford Capri can't take out a truck. A man who drives himself and his two children into the path of oncoming traffic is unwell, mentally unstable... Fuck, not now, not here.*

Tom could feel the tears falling as he led prayers at Station Nine.

'Are you okay?' his mother mouthed, touching her son's arm.

68.

Father Dean made him a cup of tea in the kitchen of St. Cuthbert's.

'It's coming up to two years of discernment, Tom,' Father Dean said. 'You need to make a decision on whether you want to continue with formation, whether you've decided to work towards becoming a priest, or not.'

'Yeah, I know,' Tom said.

'You stink of booze, and it looks like you have vomit on your shoes. Is everything okay?'

'Yeah, I'm fine.'

'How has the past two years deepened your faith?'

'Err... I've been experiencing life.'

'I can see that. What skills do you think you will bring to the priesthood?

'I don't know.'

'Have you thought about what subject you would like to study for your degree: theology, philosophy, social sciences?

'Do I need to do a degree? That sounds really boring.'

'These are the questions the Vocations Director will ask you. He will make a recommendation, and then, it is up to Bishop Nigel to make a final decision. Based on what I can see right now, you've got about as much chance of getting into the seminary as I have becoming the next England Football manager.'

'I spoke to Miss Worthington.'

'When?'

'I rang to speak to Father Worthington, and he is sick. Miss Worthington says he is dying.'

'Everyone is doing everything they can to make him comfortable.'

'You know that it is AIDS, Father, and that Father Spence died from it too?'

'Do you really want to be a priest, Tom? Do you really want to leave your job, your friends, your social life to devote yourself to God and to the service of your community?'

'Dean, I'm confused, really confused, about whether I'm attracted to girls, or boys, or both. It's driving me crazy. I don't know who I am, what I am. Thinking about the priesthood is the least of my worries. I just need to make it through to tomorrow.'

'Tom, if the Catholic Church got rid of all its gay priests, we'd have to switch the lights off and lock the doors of three quarters of the churches across the world. What matters is whether you love God and whether you are prepared to dedicate your life to him. Sexual orientation is precious, but it comes a distant second to the love of Christ.'

'I'm not gay,' Tom said.

'I am,' Father Dean said.

'What?'

'I'm gay.'

'Yeah, well, that ain't much of a surprise.'

'And why is that?'

'You're so...'

'What?'

'Gay.'

'The seminary isn't a prison. You can leave at any time if you find that it is not working for you.'

'Does anyone know?'

'You do.'

'That's not what I asked.'

'I'm discreet. We all are. But, when I meet a Catholic priest, I automatically assume he is gay, unless I learn otherwise.'

'Jesus.'

'Please stop taking the name of the Lord in vain, Tom, it's rather offensive.'

'I'm sorry.'

'Once you are in seminary, you'll be given a Spiritual Director, someone who can help and advise you.'

'Can't I just speak to you?'

'Of course, you can. Your sexuality isn't the issue here, neither is the colour of your skin, or the colour of your hair. What is important is whether you want to live for yourself, or whether you want to live for God.'

'I'm not perfect, not like you, Father.'

'Believe me, Tom, I'm far from perfect.'

69.

'The happiest day of my life was…'

'The day that I was born,' Tom said, smiling at his mother.

The Herb Garden was an old pub made to look like a taverna. The Mediterranean style plants were made of plastic. The floor tiles were cracked. The EDM music was loud, and the passage to the unisex toilet with no cubicle door was to the side of their table. That said, the restaurant was only a short walk from his mum's house, the service was usually good, and the 'Three Courses for £12' lunchtime menu was great value for money.

'How's the calamari?' Tom asked.

'Lovely, how's yours?'

'Lovely,' Tom said, ladling his spoon through the remnants of his extremely salty tomato and basil soup. 'I've got Benny's at eight, then I'm doing Jimmy's at ten-thirty.'

'I'm coming to both.'

'Are you?' Tom asked. 'It sounds like your parish priest has given you some extra penance.'

After they had finished their starters, the waitress collected the plates and bowl and asked if they wanted any more drinks. Tom asked for some table water.

'I'm not going to change it into wine,' he joked, as the waitress stared at his dog collar.

'You shouldn't say things like that,' Emma said.

'If we can't laugh at life's ups and downs, what can we do?' Tom asked.

'I'm worried about you.'

'There's no need.'

The carafe of water arrived first then, ten minutes later, dinner plates were set in front of them. Tom waited until his mum had started her seafood risotto, then he cut into a vegetable lasagne that looked like it had been welded to the brown bowl.

'I love you, Mum,' he said, 'and I'd never do anything to deliberately hurt you. You know that don't you?'

'I know,' she said.

'Good.'

'I know.'

'You know what?'

'I know that you are gay.'

Tom stopped eating and gazed at his mother, unable to speak or move. He looked around the busy restaurant, but no one was paying them any attention.

'What?'

'You're still my son, and I love you.'

'What about gay people being vile creatures, living abhorrent lifestyles, homosexuality as a cancer in the bowels of the church, the pink homolobby in the Vatican... all that stuff I've had to listen to over the years, Mum?'

'I don't agree with anyone choosing a homosexual lifestyle, but you're my son.'

'I didn't choose to be gay, Mum. No one does.'

'As I said, you're my son, and I love you with all my heart.'

Stevie Wonder's *Happy Birthday* burst through the speakers at top volume, and an ice cream sundae with a sparkler set alight was carried through from the kitchens to a table of fifteen ladies sitting in front of the window overlooking the main road. Tom and the other diners joined in singing Happy Birthday to the birthday girl.

'You don't know how many times I wanted to tell you,' Tom said.

'What are you planning, Tom? I can always tell.'

Seventy-two years old, and she's still razor sharp, he thought.

'There is a boy, an altar server at Saint James' called Daniel, who is twelve going on thirteen years old. He came out as gay a few months ago and is having an awful time being bullied,' Tom said. 'He's being bullied to his face, *and* he's being bullied online.'

'Maybe he should have said nothing.'

'He's a brave lad, braver than me.'

'What are you going to do, Tom?'

'I'm going to out myself tomorrow, during the sermon.'

'On Easter Sunday? That is unforgivable, Thomas.' Emma Morton said, horrified.

Tom thought about what he was going to say next. Was a Mediterranean themed restaurant run by two Lithuanians the right place to tell his mother about the disease he had contracted? Would it be easier to tell her at home... or would he chicken out, again, and leave his mother to hear his bombshell announcement during the sermon like everyone else?

'Mum,' Tom said, 'there is something else you should know. I am HIV positive, and I have been for nearly twenty years. I take medication. The virus levels in my blood are so low that they are almost undetectable. As far as anyone in the medical profession knows, this will not affect my health or my lifespan.'

Emma reached for his hand.

'What happens if you stop taking these drugs?'

'You already knew, didn't you?' Tom asked, 'Joan found the tablets, I take it?'

'What happens if you stop taking the drugs?'

'Then, I will die, like Father Spence, like Father Worthington.'

'Did they ever…'

'Absolutely not. Don't even ask that. They were, they are, two of the greatest men that I've ever known. You know that.'

'It is Satan's lavender mafia at work, corrupting good men and turning them queer.'

'There is no lavender mafia, only scared men, isolated women, human beings terrified of being found out and kicked out of the job they love.'

Tom dragged his chair over to his mother and hugged her. They cried in each other's arms.

'I hope the other guests don't think it's the food,' Tom said, and Emma laughed.

'I still don't approve,' Emma said, wiping her eyes with a handkerchief, 'God made man and woman to be together.'

'She made me,' Tom said. 'I was beautifully woven inside your womb. Some people are gay, some are straight.'

'This boy, Daniel, he won't want you to destroy everything that you have worked so hard to achieve. What good is getting yourself sacked?'

'I can't teach the things that the Bishop wants me to teach. It is a distortion of the truth. Standing up, speaking out, is a matter of principle to me.'

'And you think Easter Sunday mass is the right time and place to make such a personal statement? It smacks of arrogance, of grandstanding, instead of humility before the miracle of the resurrection.'

'I'm coming out of the tomb with Jesus to a new life.'

'I was so proud on the day that you were ordained,' Emma sighed.

'Be proud of me, now, Mother. Because I need you more than ever.'

70.

The Kiss by The Cure was reverberating through the walls as Tom fell out of The Basin, promising himself that he would never ever, fucking ever, return. The music was still top drawer, but the place was full of kids these days, and the watered-down beer was an insult to anyone with a modicum of taste. Michael and Shaun were refusing to run the gauntlet of psychopathic bouncers and idiots out on the lash looking for a fight. They now steered clear of the town centre, preferring the nightclubs of Manchester and Liverpool instead. So, it was just Tom, Pete, and Antony out in Bussell that Wednesday night.

Pete and Antony were across the dual-carriageway, sitting on the low wall by the burger van, tucking into greasy quarter-pounders with chips. Tom bought himself a cheeseburger and stood beside them.

'Antony's got something to tell you,' Pete said.

'Oh yeah?' Tom said, his mouth half full.

'I'm gay,' Antony said.

'Yeah?' Tom said, taking another bite.

Antony shook his head, laughed.

'What?' Tom asked.

'He's just told you something really important, and you just carried on eating your burger, you fuckin' twat.' Pete said.

Tom put his polystyrene tray on the pavement, lit a cigarette, and shrugged.

'Have you rung for the taxi?'

'Yeah,' Pete said, 'Templar Cabs.'

The taxis in other local towns were usually Asian, but not in Bussell, not in the early '90s. Templar Cabs with their flag of Saint George livery—a knight with a sword and shield emblazoned with a red cross—were a hundred percent white drivers. The opening line as customers crowded into the seats was always the same.

'Had a good night, lads? Where we off?'

Bussell, as a working-class, ex-mill and pit town, always elected a Labour Party Member of Parliament, and was a solid red wall, socialist seat. Independent thinking? Absolutely. Insular focus? Oh yes. The inherent contradiction was that had anyone pointed out the racism inherent in the town's number one taxi firm, it would have been met with puzzled looks and a 'I don't think so, love,' shrug of the shoulders.

The same inherent contradiction would lead the town to vote overwhelmingly to leave the European Union in 2016, despite three decades of Brussels inward investment in Bussell.

The three young men, children of that same northern town, bundled themselves into the white Templar Cab, answered the 'had a good night, lads, where 'we off?' question, and were then whisked through deserted streets towards Antony's house.

Tom sat in the front passenger seat, spouting drunken nonsense to the driver. Pete and Antony were in the back, stony-faced, saying nowt. Tom paid the fare, tipping the driver two quid for being a good lad and listening to his drivel.

Antony opened the front door of his house, staggered inside, and announced that he was going straight to bed.

As they waited for the kettle to boil, Pete accused Tom of being a callous wanker, an accusation that was unfair and uncalled for, in Tom's opinion.

Tom told Pete to fuck off, then wandered off to bed.

Tom saw that the door of Antony's bedroom was open. Antony was curled up in bed, unconscious. Swaying, Tom lit a match and threw it at Antony's sleeping form. The burning match smouldered and flicked into flame against the bedding. Tom reached over, picked up the match and blew it out. There was a charred hole in the blue duvet.

I am a twat, Tom thought, *I could have burned Antony alive in his bed.*

Nursing his own myriad inherent contradictions, Tom collapsed onto the lumpy mattress in the spare room.

71.

The Church of Saint James was full to bursting, filled with families, the old and the young. Dressed in white robes, Father Thomas celebrated mass with his parishioners, recounting the story of the resurrection, reading from the Gospel according to Saint John.

'In his writings, John presents Jesus as the source of life and love,' Tom said, as he began the sermon that would change his life and the life of Saint James' church, forever. 'Jesus is the bread of life, the resurrection and the life, the Good Shepherd who lays his life down for his flock. It is Mary Magdalene who takes centre stage as the key witness to Jesus's death and resurrection, for it was Mary who found that the stone had been rolled away from the entrance to the tomb. She meets a man who she thinks is the gardener and asks him if he has taken the body away. "Mary," Jesus says. She recognises him and gasps, "Teacher?!" Jesus then says something interesting. "Don't cling to me," he says, "for I haven't yet ascended to the Father. Go and find my brothers and tell them, 'I am ascending to my Father and your Father, to my God and your God.'"

'Many of you here today will have had brushes with death,' Tom said, 'either your own experience or because someone you loved has passed away. I speak of an event from my own life with trepidation because my mother is here today, and this affects her deeply through the loss of a husband and a child. My father was a troubled man. My recollections of the event as a young boy are hazy, and I am never sure how much of what I remember is real or a dream. The facts are that my dad put me and my brother in the back of his car and drove in front of a truck with the intent to kill us all. Somehow, despite the severity of the impact and the car ending up on its roof, I escaped with minor bruises while my dad and little brother... my brother, Colin... were killed. In my memory of the event, I walked down an empty road with a girl holding my hand, and she was my friend. I knew that instinctively.

'Somehow, I was alive, back from the dead. I've always felt that I was meant to do something with my life, something for my God and your God. Pope Benedict used these words, "a bearer of something another has committed to my charge." My life has had many twists and turns, many ups and downs, just like everyone else's has, but deep in the centre of me is a conviction that Jesus is the logos, and that, by his death and resurrection, we are set free from the bondage of sin. Nothing else matters—the brand of Christianity we buy into, or, indeed, whether a person is a card-carrying Christian or not. Because the verb is at the heart of all. We cannot escape the fundamental equation that existence is built upon. "No one comes to the Father except through me," Jesus said, and he was right. If you want to call yourself good, *be* good, *become* goodness... die a little every day to be reborn of grace.

'I wanted to share another story, a story about a friend of mine who came out as gay some thirty years ago. I ignored what he was saying to me because I was scared, because I knew that I was gay too. I was scared for many years. When I finally accepted who I was, I kept it hidden from everyone—my mum, my friends, from all of you. By not telling the truth, I was living a lie. I am not prepared to lie any longer because I cannot accept that the Jesus, who died for me, would condemn me, and others like me, as being inherently disordered and sinful, just because we are born homosexual instead of heterosexual.

'I have also been living with HIV for the best part of two decades. I am alive thanks to the miracle of science and medicine. I have no idea what will happen to me now that I have made this known to you all, but it is important to me that other LGBT Catholics realise that they are not alone, that God loves them too.

'On this Easter Day, we celebrate the Good Shepherd who lives, dies, and lives again for their flock, this timeless love that is at the heart of all creation, and is the source of all goodness. I know they are my friend. I know this instinctively. Amen.'

The clapping started slowly, and then it built until the congregation of Saint James were on their feet, demonstrating their support for their tearful and humbled parish priest.

Over the days that followed, the Diocesan authorities took counsel together about how they might deal with the outbreak of neo-liberalism in Bussell, that god-awful, industrial town in the south of the county. They moved swiftly to limit the spread of the contagion, suspending Father Morton, and closing the Jesuit-infected Church of Saint James, announcing that all services would be held at Saint Benedict's until further notice.

However, what Bishop Derek Worrell had not counted on was the inherent contradiction of a town ambivalent about faith but extremely protective of those it regarded as its own.

It was game on.

72.

The morning after the night before was a mixture of euphoria, fear, and revelation for Tom. He woke with Antony cuddled into his chest with the realisation he had had sex with a man, a man with whom he knew he was in love. The connection with another man was real, more real than anything he had ever experienced in his life before. He was alive and ecstatically happy for the first time. Antony's mum made breakfast for the five lads: one of her own, four who were now semi-permanent weekend residents. No one said much as they ate, and the other three made their excuses and hit the road in Shaun's car, thanking Lillian Keane, once again, for her hospitality.

Tom and Antony showered together, had sex together, and before Tom left to catch the bus home, the two young lovers kissed goodbye in the doorway.

As Tom walked from the bus stop up the street to his house, he was stunned to see Tasmin's car parked outside. Taz was having a cup of tea with his mum in the front room, which was even weirder.

'I'll leave you to it,' Emma Morton said, as she disappeared upstairs.

'Do I get a kiss?' Taz asked.

'Yeah, of course,' Tom said, mindful of where his mouth had been earlier that morning.

'I thought I'd drop in.'

'Great. How is being married treating you?'

'Good thanks. How are things at work?'

'Yeah, okay. Everyone misses you. How's Greg?'

'He's great.'

'He's still got a really big dick, then?'

'Tom! Size isn't everything, you know. There's a girl with red hair at your front door.'

'Jesus,' Tom said. 'It's Lisa.'

'Is she your girlfriend?'

Tom heard his mother's steps coming down the stairs, and the front door opened. Seconds later, the door from the hall opened, and Lisa came into the front room.

'Oh,' she said, seeing Tom and Taz sitting in the front room together.

'I was just leaving. I'm Taz, by the way. See you again soon, Tom.'

'See you.'

'That was awkward,' Lisa said, as Tasmin's ancient car roared away down the avenue.

'I haven't seen her for a year,' Tom said. 'I had no idea she was here 'til I got home. How are you?'

'Do you want to come out with me? I thought we could go out for a meal in Preston.'

The phone rang in the dining room. Tom knew his mum had an extension up in the bedroom, so he ignored it. Then, he heard the thump-thump of his mum coming down the stairs.

'Tom,' his mum said, opening the door, 'it's Antony on the phone.'

'Tell him I'll call him back,' Tom said to his mum, then, 'I'd like that, Lise, I can't do next weekend, but maybe the weekend after, is that okay for you?' he asked.

'You're definitely not back with her?'

'I'm definitely not back with her,' Tom said. 'Fuck knows why she showed up today.'

After Lisa had gone, Tom rang Michael and arranged to meet him at the Lychgate, a pub strategically positioned halfway between their homes, no more than a fifteen-minute walk.

The phone rang again, and Tom picked up.

'Hi Tom,' Roberta said. 'How are you?'

'Hi Bobbi,' Tom said. 'Long time no see.'

'Do you want to come over tonight, stay over?'

'It'll be later, about ten-thirtyish. That work for you?'

Tom had his second shower of the day and got himself ready for the pub.

'She said she had some wedding pictures to show me,' Emma Morton said, as he came downstairs.

'Who did?'

'Tasmin. That's why I let her in.'

'Beware of Greeks bearing gifts, Mother,' Tom said.

'Antony called again.'

'I'm off out. I'll call him later.'

Michael was sitting at the bar in the Lychgate. There was a pint of bitter waiting for him as Tom came through the door.

'How are you doing?' Michael asked.

'Fair to shit,' Tom said. 'You?'

'Just want to make sure you're okay.'

'Mike, that's Shirley in the corner. I'm going to go over and say hello. I haven't seen her in ages.'

'She's with her fella, Tom, and he's a notorious meathead professional footballer. I'm sure she'll come over and say hello once she's clocked us.'

'Nah, fuck it. I've known her for years.'

Tom took his drink and pulled up a chair at Shirley's table.

'How are you, Shirley?' he asked, 'I haven't seen you in yonks.'

Shirley was rigid as she introduced Tom to her boyfriend, Gareth.

'Hello, mate,' Tom said, shaking Gareth's hand. 'Me and Shirl go back years.'

'Do yer?' muscular, tattooed Gareth said.

The conversation stalled. Gareth was staring at Shirley.

'Me and Gareth were just having a private conversation,' she said. 'It's lovely to see you and all, but do you mind?'

'Err, no,' Tom said. 'Of course not. Good to see you, Shirley. It's been too long. I miss you. Good to meet you, Gareth. You've got the best girl in Lancashire there.'

Tom noticed the blue vein on Big G's temple looking like it was about to burst and go supernova.

'That was fucking weird,' Tom said, as he sat back at the bar, next to Michael. 'What a bitch. It was like she couldn't wait to get rid of me, like I was a piece of shit or something.'

'Maybe, you got it wrong,' Michael said. 'Anyway, on to more important matters. It's your round, Morton.'

Tom ordered more drinks, paying with the shrapnel in his pockets– fifty pence pieces and old coppers.

'Have you robbed a charity box?' Michael asked.

'Piss off.'

'What time did you get back from Antony's?'

'One-ish.'

'He's a top guy.'

'Yeah, I guess so.'

Tom walked home after sinking seven pints in the Lychgate with Michael, arriving back at his mums' around 10 p.m.

'How is Michael?' his mum asked, as Tom took his shoes off at the back door.

'Good.'

'Does that poor use of the English language indicate that he is well, or that he is a good person?'

'He's well, Mum.'

'Antony rang again.'

'Did he?'

'And a girl called Roberta. I told her you were at the pub.'

'Mum,' Tom slurred, 'I'm going to use the phone upstairs, is that okay?'

'Of course, but don't be on too long.'

Tom dialled the number for Saint Cuthbert's. A tired sounding Dean Wesham answered the phone after half a dozen rings.

'Dean, it's me, Tom, I've made my decision.'

'Are you drunk, Tom?'

Tom wiped the tears from his eyes. 'I want to be a priest. I've had enough.'

'Tom, you don't become a priest to escape from life, you become a priest to join with life.'

'Either they let me in, or I'll become a Buddhist monk, or a fucking Satanist, or something.'

'It's not up to me. It's a decision for the Vocations Director and the Bishop…'

'But they'll listen to you, right?'

'They will.'

'Then, get them to let me in,' Tom cried, in floods of tears. 'Let me in for Christ's sake. I can't go on like this much longer.'

Part Three

Teardrop

73

The redundant Bussell International Swimming Pool building had been provided free-of-charge by the town council while the ex-Saint James' congregation found a more permanent building in which to worship. The pool had been drained years before, and the building stood empty while the machinations of local government moved towards a decision on what to do with their white elephant edifice.

Tom preached down at the deep end, beneath the decommissioned diving boards: stage one, stage two, and the dizzy heights of stage three. His congregation sat on metal deck chairs, sloping up towards the shallow end.

'Paul Tillich escaped the Nazis and fled to America,' he told his renegade congregation of Catholic dissenters, his voice booming inside the cavernous 1960s concrete building. 'In his writings, Tillich describes God as 'being-itself' rather than 'a being.' God is not top dog in a list of archangels, angels, and deities. God is not a petty Monad, a cosmic tyrant who delights in torturing the disobedient for eternity. God *is* the God who appears when the God of earthly religion disappears in the anxiety of doubt. God is beyond Jean-Paul Satre's existence versus essence debate. God is not the content. God is the Platform itself.'

The locked-out flock, the parishioners pushed-out of their church *by* the Church, listened to their priest, watching from inside their goldfish bowl as the townsfolk hurried past the huge glass windows or stopped for a moment to peer at the strange goings on inside the abandoned Bussell Baths.

'Martin Heidegger joined the Nazi Party,' Tom said, 'even though they laughed at his ideas. Heidegger used the term "Dasein," which roughly translates as "being-there," or "being-in-the-world." Karl Barth refused to sign an oath of loyalty to Hitler and was forced to leave Germany. Barth wrote that grace is at the heart of the Christian message. Grace is light. Grace is change. Grace is the dynamic. Being-itself, Being-there, Being-born, these are our ontological trinity, our three stages. Or to put it another way: being, be, becoming. Biology is sandwiched between being and non-being, just as Freud's concept of the ego is sandwiched between the super-ego and the id. Biology is sandwiched between the will to love and the will to power.'

The sun shone through blue glass, warming the air inside the building. Cars sped around the one-way system, the noise reverberating through the cordoned-off seating area with its defunct vending machines. Tom could see the broken white tiles beneath the chairs of his parishioners: families, the elderly, all those who had followed him after the closure of Saint James, all those who had refused to worship at Saint Benedict's. Blue lines ran like veins from one end of the swimming pool floor to the other, connecting their hearts to his.

'William Blake wrote in his epic poem *Jerusalem* that "negations are not contraries, contraries co-exist." Emanuel Swedenborg wrote of correspondences, that love comes into being when it is of service to others. Quantum Mechanics teaches us about entanglements and challenges, our binary assumption that information is either a zero or a one. We know it can be both. Nature is gloriously non-binary, which suggest that God, being-itself, is both our Father and our Mother.'

Tom's worry had been that his tribe would perish in the wilderness once they had made their escape from Pharoah Worrell's grasp. But the exodus, and the publicity that followed, had swelled their numbers. Now that the die had been cast, Tom was determined to agitate for a new Vatican Council, for the Catholic Church to reposition itself from being an organisation that stands *between* the individual and their God, mediating on their behalf, to one that stands *with* the individual, supporting, coaching, and encouraging. That idea had seemingly struck a chord with many who had left the Church disillusioned with rampant misogyny and homophobia.

A plastic decorator's table was being used as a makeshift altar.

Tom took bread, broke it, blessed it, saying, 'God our parent, source of all being, you are holy indeed, and all creation rightly gives you praise. All life, all holiness comes from you through your being-in-the-world, Jesus Christ, our Lord, by the working of the holy becoming. From age to age, you gather a people to yourself, so that, from east to west, a perfect offering may be made to the glory of your name. And so, we bring you these gifts. We ask you to make them holy by the power of your Spirit, that they may become the body and blood of your child, our Lord Jesus Christ, at whose command we celebrate this...'

The first shot shattered the window to Tom's right, showering him and the altar with fragments of safety glass. The second shot blew out a huge pane halfway down the building, scattering shards over panicking people. There were screams from inside the building, cries from the road outside, followed by the wail of police cars from Bussell station, which was situated directly opposite the swimming baths on the other side of the dual carriageway.

Tom would later learn that the shooter had waited patiently by his vehicle to be arrested, that he was a carrot farmer from Burscough, a church-attending Catholic who had blown the windows out of the temporary church to make a point about the 'discipleship of Satan that had taken root in Lancashire.'

74.

'Call for you, Mary,' Paddy Mulhern shouted, banging the door with his fist.

Tom put his pen down, pressed pause on the Lisa Stansfield CD, and made sure he locked his room in the Chadwick Wing of Ash Burrow Catholic Seminary on the way out, just in case one of the other fuckwits he lived with trashed it or threw his clothes out of the window.

'Who the fuck is Mary?' Pete asked, as Tom picked up the phone attached to the wall in the communal stairway.

'That's Paddy's idea of a joke,' Tom said.

'Is that idiot really going to be a priest?'

'That's the idea.'

'Jesus.'

'What do you want, Pete? I've got an essay deadline,' Tom said, conscious that the other nine rooms on his corridor could all be listening to his conversation.

'Sorry for bothering you,' Pete said, and Tom heard the anger creeping into his voice. 'What are you writing about?'

'Was Socrates a historical figure or did Plato invent him?'

'Like Jesus and Saint Paul?'

'Fuck off, Pete. That's totally different.'

'I was ringing to tell you, that me and Monica are engaged.'

It was the news that Tom had been dreading. It was selfish, it was immature, but it was another strand of a previous life that was rearranging itself behind him, closing the door on any possible return to carefree teenage hedonism with his friends.

'Congratulations, mate,' Tom said, after a moment's pause, 'I'm really pleased for you.'

'We are getting married, next year, August 11th at Saint James' in town. You know it?'

'I've been past it, never been in. You're getting married in a Catholic Church, Pete?'

'I'm doing it for the outlaws. They're paying, and they want the whole God-shebang. The stag will be in Barcelona, next June. Michael and Shaun are coming.'

'How are they?'

'Shaun's got that job in Bedford, and he starts in a few weeks. So, he'll be the second one to fly the coop.'

'Who was first?'

'You were, Tom. You fucked-off and left us,' Pete said, the aggression returning to his voice. 'Michael is finishing his fine art foundation course, then he's off to London if he can find somewhere to live.'

'And Antony?'

'None of us have seen Antony for a while. I sent him a text message, and he said that he'll be coming to the stag and the wedding.'

'You've got a mobile phone, have you?'

'A Nokia 101, top of the range, and I've got a cigarette lighter charger for the car, too. The only problem is my phone will only hold thirty contacts in the memory, which is a right-royal pain in the arse.'

'I'm still in there?' Tom asked.

'You're one of my thirty,' Pete said. 'So, how about Barcelona?'

'I'll do my best,' Tom said, knowing full well that he wouldn't be able to go.

'Good man. See you, Mary.'

'Fuck off, Pete.'

75.

Tom could see a brown paper file with a photograph of his ordination stapled to the front and the reference code 400-157i written in black pen beneath his name. Father Mallon sat on the opposite side of the mahogany table, a framed portrait of John Paul II hanging on the striped wallpapered wall behind his head. The file lay unopened in front of the Bishop's hatchet man.

'Resign, Morton, that is the only option you have,' Father Mallon said, his arms beneath the table.

'I'd say you're in a bit of a pickle,' Tom said. 'Suspending me and closing Saint James might look bad in an employment tribunal, and goodness knows what other negative public relations coverage you may get as a result.'

'Are you threatening the Church?'

'You have deprived me of my mobile phone, you have checked me for recording devices, you have not allowed me to bring a colleague into these proceedings. I'd say you are indulging in paranoia and ignoring legal, ethical employment practices, Father.'

'Resign, and all this unpleasantness will end. If you do resign by the end of this meeting, we will protect your pension for the years that you were employed by the Church. We will also pay you three month's salary in lieu of notice, as well as providing you with a satisfactory reference for a job stacking tins of paint in your local home and garden centre.'

'And if I don't take you up on this most gracious and generous offer? Are you going to get another farmer to shoot out some glass?'

'There is a young man who has been through a terrible ordeal, a brave soul ready to make a formal complaint to the authorities, an abuse survivor ready to share his story about the homosexual priest who stole his innocence.'

'You wouldn't dare,' Tom growled. 'I'd appeal directly to the Pope if I had to.'

'We have witnesses, and just think of the hurt and humiliation for your poor mother. As for Bergoglio, that Marxist, Freemason, friend of homoheretics, is Catholic in name only. We pray that God will see fit to end this Jesuit Pope's calamitous reign and guide the hearts and minds of pious cardinals to elect a man who will cleanse the Universal Church of the disease that besets it.'

'I seem to recollect that you yourself were once fond of a sauna with a seminarian, Father Mallon.'

Mallon struggled to control himself, biting back his anger.

'I am an ex-gay. Our Father in heaven did not make me gay. God did not love me when I sinned. I hated myself for it. The reason I fell into sin was because of men like you, Thomas Morton. The reason for my wrong choices, choices that caused me nothing but pain, was because of the homosexual culture infesting our seminaries, an infection that needs cleansing immediately.'

'And self-hate focuses your hatred of others.'

'I have taken the liberty of drafting out your resignation letter, all you have to do is sign it.'

'And the poor child you have persuaded to commit perjury? Surely that sin will rot away what little is left of your foul heart, viper.'

'Oh no. This isn't a child. This is a man, and the accusations against you are of a historical nature, over many decades. Why would you inflict that on yourself and the other queers we have yet to root out? Go quietly, Morton,' Father Mallon said, as he opened the file on the table and started leafing through the papers. 'For the sake of you and your friends, Fathers Mulhern, Denton, Doherty and the rest.'

'Don't forget Bishop Derek,' Tom said, 'or Priscilla as he was known, back in the day. I think you can stick that letter up yer arse, Gerry, don't you? Let me tell you what *I* want. I want my church back— immediately. In return, I will retire, but at a point no earlier than two years from today's date. I want my pension in full. *And* I want John Cooper removed as Head Teacher at Saint Pats.'

Mallon studied the man in front of him.

'You wouldn't have the balls to accuse the Bishop,' he said.

'I'm from Bussell, me,' Tom said. 'So, fuckin' try me.'

76.

Tom, Paddy Mulhern, Alastair Denton, and Steve Carlyle were in Paul Doherty's room, taking turns on Paul's bong. Alastair was sitting on Paul's bed, giggling to himself. Steve had gone quiet and was quashed into the orange beanbag next to the sink. Paul was sitting on the cream rug, smiling as the smoke escaped his nostrils. Paddy was on Paul's desk, legs apart, his shirt unbuttoned.

'Jezebel's feeling horny,' Tom said. 'Watch out, boys.'

Paddy grinned. 'Fuck you, Mary Morton,' he said.

'I've got the munchies,' Tom said, standing and opening the door of bedroom five.

'Shut the *bloody* door,' he heard Alastair shout as he stumbled into the corridor.

Tom had lost his ankles, which was a perplexing conundrum. His legs were there down to his shins, but his feet had become disconnected. Outside Paul's room, swaying from side to side, Tom contemplated the alarmed fire door, portal to another world, escape route back to a previous existence.

Walking like a marionette past the ten bedrooms—five black doors either side of the purple carpeted divide—Tom saw the door to bedroom eight was wide open, which meant Derek, the cunt, was either taking a shit or in the kitchen.

'Cilla!' Tom said, as he staggered into the communal kitchen, and found Derek eating a plate of spaghetti.

Derek Worrell stared at him with abject contempt, then carried on with his pasta drenched in tomato sauce.

'Cilla,' Tom said, 'I've run out of milk for my Corn Flakes, can I borrow some of yours?'

'Be my guest,' Derek said, 'Mine's the semi skimmed on the fourth shelf.'

'Cilla,' Tom said, knowing full well that Derek had directed him to Fraser in room nine's supply, 'I've run out of Corn Flakes, can I borrow some of yours?'

Before Derek could respond to Tom's plea for nutrition, Paddy and Paul fell through the kitchen door and collapsed onto the tiled floor.

'Hello, Cilla,' Paddy squealed, as he dissolved into laughter. 'Don't be mad at us.'

'One day, when I'm Pope,' Derek said, 'I'll send all of youse to the most inhospitable part of the planet, somewhere uncomfortable where there are plenty of horrible diseases and people who'd delight in peeling the skin from your bones. If I thought anyone in this hideous Gomorrah that they call a priest training college would listen, I'd report you all. But they are as bad as you are. filthy perverts, fucking each other like dogs in the street. Douglas and Eden, Spiritual Directors? Don't make me laugh.'

Derek pointed his fork at his fellow seminarians.

'Enjoy it while you can, boys. Judgment comes.'

Paddy looked at Tom. Tom looked at Paul.

'He certainly does,' Paul said, and the three burst out laughing as Derek threw down his fork and strode from the room.

Tom lifted open the window and sat on the sill, swaying.

'You do know we're on the first-floor?' Paddy asked.

'He fell out of that window holding a pint of Guinness the other night,' Paul said.

'Did you spill it?' Paddy asked.

'Of course, I fucking spilt it,' Tom said, 'Jesus, what kind of question is that?'

Tom had spotted the remains of Derek's pasta, and hunger overcame reason and self-respect as he sat down at the table.

'No, don't,' Paul gasped.

'Too late,' Paddy said, as he watched Tom shovel the remains of the Spaghetti Bolognese into his mouth. 'That's *so* gross!'

Paul had his arm around Paddy's shoulder and the two men kissed.

'Get a room,' Tom said. 'I'm trying to eat.'

'You know the rules, Mary,' Paddy said. 'Lock your door if you're busy or too tired. An open door means an open heart.'

'Unless that's room four, eight, or ten,' Tom said, 'in which case an open door might mean a week in intensive care for any unwise intruder.'

'Miriam and Martha are just playing hard to get,' Paddy said, 'and as for Cilla, I think there's more to Godgirl than meets the eye.'

'What about room six?' Paul asked. 'You didn't mention your room?'

'If one of you slips into my bed,' Tom said, 'I'll fucking...'

'You'll fucking what?' Paddy asked.

'Scream blue murder. My rectum is my own, thank you very much.'

'I told you,' Paul said to Paddy.

'Told him what?' Tom asked.

'Ruthie says you've got a preference,' Paddy said. 'Don't you?'

Paul smiled as he put his head on Paddy's shoulder.

'Ruth says *everyone* has a preference,' Tom said. 'The other night, he was telling me that George Michael is gay. That guy has shagged more women than I've had hot dinners! My preference is going to bed on my own. We have three hours of Epicureanism tomorrow morning, then three hours of Anselm of Canterbury. And before you ask, my door will be locked with the key firmly in the door.'

'You can put your key in my lock, anytime,' Paul said, as Tom staggered from the kitchen.

Tom fell onto his bed. Looking up, he noticed the door was ajar and his keys and wallet were on the desk.

He waited, breathing into his pillow, lying on top of the duvet.

Steve Carlyle, Tom's next-door neighbour in room seven, dressed in a t-shirt and boxer shorts, came in and closed the door softly behind him.

'Hi Sarah,' Tom said.

'Don't call me that. I'm gay because I am sexually, romantically, emotionally attracted to men, not because I want to be a woman.'

'Sorry.'

'Do you want a cuddle, Tom?' Steve asked, kneeling beside him, stroking his hair, kissing his lips.

'Yes,' Tom said, reaching out, kissing Steve on the mouth, 'I do. Lock that door, take those pants off, get yourself into my bed.'

77.

Fathers Morton and Mulhern sat together on the lichen-stained, wooden bench outside the building that had once been the Catholic Church of Saint James. The ground floor windows of the church, the rectory, and the sacristy had been fitted with grey metal covers with the name of a security company and a phone number stencil-painted in black lettering. The church doors had a padlocked, metal chain threaded through the handles. The building was dead-eyed, lifeless, with a 'For Sale—Former Church' sign planted in the dried-up flower bed.

'I cannot bear to see deconsecrated churches,' Tom said, 'and this church was my church, full of life, full of love, full of grace. Shutting us down is an act of vengeance.'

'It took him thirty years, but he finally got you back for finishing off his pasta,' Paddy said.

'Hello, Father, see you Sunday at the Ritzy,' a woman holding a child by their hand said, as she hurried past the two priests.

'See you Sunday,' Tom said, smiling and waving.

'I watched *Predator* and *The Untouchables* in that cinema,' Paddy remarked, 'I can't believe it is still standing.'

'It's due for demolition,' Tom said, 'but with the swimming baths now permanently closed thanks to our zealot farmer, we haven't got many options, unless we move outside of the town centre, which I don't want to do.'

'Your congregation has been remarkably loyal. I'm not sure my flock would walk over hot coals for me. They really love you, Tom.'

'It isn't about me, Paddy. It's about Jesus.'

'Of course, it is. I apologise. It's *always* about Him.'

'What do you think my church will look like once they've converted it into flats, or a gym, or a shoe warehouse?' Tom asked, ignoring the sarcasm.

'Don't torture yourself, Father. Move on.'

The sound of joyful children running and jumping in the playground of the nearby primary school mingled with the noise of cars and buses making their way down Greengate towards the ring road. People were coming in and out of the glass reception area in the brutalist Bussell Council building. The electric door of the Dental Practice swished open as an elderly man, supported by a woman, walked towards a parked car on Stonebridge Terrace.

'Will anyone mourn when the church has gone?' Tom asked. 'Will anyone mourn when we're gone, when the Catholic Church cleanses the last gay man and woman from its employee database?'

'They think we are a gay cabal,' Paddy said. 'We are a grey cabal of survivors, doing our best in difficult circumstances, scattered, afraid, never able to fully be ourselves, giving our lives for God, for Jesus, for our fellow human beings.'

'If I don't resign, they have a witness who will testify that I abused them.'

'And did you do anything... inappropriate?'

'I can't believe you asked that, Paddy,' Tom said, bitterly.

'I'm sorry! I just know they'll get us, one by one.'

'You need to warn the others: Alastair, Sam, Fraser, Paul.'

'What if we stand together?' Paddy asked.

'Father Mulhern, you will be risking your livelihood, your parish, your comfy armchair by the fire in that nice priest's retirement home in Southport. *I* made the decision to out myself. I'm not expecting the gay Avengers to assemble.'

'We need Father Flynn to box Bishop Worrell's ears,' Paddy said, 'like the time fuck-features called Tarry an IRA sympathiser.'

'God, Tarry Flynn was fit!' Tom said. 'That Cork accent, those tight jeans, that arse, I used to daydream about what was inside his pants during Holy Mass.'

'We all did,' Paddy said. 'But, alas, Tarry's bride was the Church of Rome.'

'He must have had the patience of a saint living next to Paul all those years.'

'I never once saw Tarry drink or smoke or heard him swear.'

'That punch on Derek's jaw was a wonder, knocked him backwards off his chair,' Tom said, laughing. 'You know who I heard from the other week?'

'Who?' Paddy said.

'Steve Carlyle.'

'Is he still working in television?'

'He and his husband run a digital media company in Manchester.'

'He was never cut out for the priesthood… too assertive, as Father Douglas would say.'

'I liked Steve,' Tom said.

'I know you did,' Paddy chuckled. 'How is living at home with your mother?'

Tom shook his head. 'Awful. I try to get out as much as I can. It's like I'm five years old again.'

'I keep thinking about poor Marcus, fit as a fiddle, dead at forty-two from a heart attack.'

'Him and Tarry were great friends, going backpacking together in the Lake District.'

'Walking holidays in Austria?' Paddy asked, smiling.

'No, never like that,' Tom said. 'They were the only two straight seminarians in Ash Burrow.'

'Rooms four and ten, Father Morton. We all tried to get in there, but alas, 'twas to no avail.'

78.

Tom and Steve were in bed, the gentle breeze lifting the bottom of the yellow and orange curtains, then letting them fall back onto the sill.

Tom was on the outside of the single bed. On the shelf above the desk were his precious books, and the thought came to him that he was turning into a book hoarder, just like his mother.

Steve lay between him and the painted brick wall, his fingers running up the small of Tom's back, from his buttocks up to his shoulder blades, and it felt divine.

'Who's the man with the lantern?' Steve asked.

'You mean the print on the wall? It is Los, from Blake's *Jerusalem.*'

'I hate that song, all that bullshit nationalistic jingoism at the *Last Night of the Proms* and rugby matches.'

'The verses for the hymn *Jerusalem* are taken from another poem Blake wrote called *Milton.* You should definitely read *Jerusalem, the Emanation of the Giant Albion,*' Tom said. 'Everyone is reading Blake wrong in my less than humble opinion. Jerusalem is the female spirit of creativity. Emanation is about identity. Albion is England, of course. *Jerusalem* is a non-binary anthem, and you should be delighted that the establishment are belting it out at the top of their voices completely oblivious to Blake's queer intentions.'

'I think you're reading too much into it,' Steve said.

Tom turned around and reached for Steve's cock, giving it a little squeeze, feeling it go hard in his hands.

'The spirit of Jesus is continual forgiveness of sin,' Tom said.

'And are we sinners?' Steve asked.

'I am perhaps the most sinful of men, 'Tom said, playing with Steve's nipples with his tongue. 'I do not pretend to holiness, yet I pretend to love, to see, to converse with daily, as man with man, and the more to have an interest in the Friend of Sinners.'

'As man with man?'

'As man with man,' Tom said, as he disappeared beneath the covers.

79.

'Hi,' Tom said. 'Sorry to bother you, have any of you seen Rosie lately? She's usually around the railway station, but nobody there has seen her for the last few days.'

The three homeless people sat together outside the coffee shop on Market Street, eating hot food provided by the owner. The two men shook their heads, looking at Tom with suspicion.

'If you see her, ask her to get in touch with Father Morton,' he said.

The woman in the sleeping bag shouted, 'Hey you,' as Tom turned to leave. 'Try the infirmary. She was taken by an ambulance. I saw them.'

'Thank you,' Tom said.

'And who did you say that you are? the hospital administrator asked, when Tom managed to get through by phone.

'I'm Father Morton of Saint James' Church, Greengate. Rosie is a friend of mine.'

'The queer priest whose church has been shut down?'

'Yeah, that's me.'

'I read about you on the Bussell News app.'

'Can you tell me how is Rosie? Can I visit her?'

'I'm afraid that Rosemary Brennan died two days ago. She was in intensive care with tuberculosis.'

'Rosie died... from TB?' Tom said astounded. 'That's a nineteenth century disease.'

'Homeless people are particularly susceptible to respiratory diseases like TB, pneumonia, and influenza. Smoking tobacco doesn't help, and smoking drugs has a catastrophic impact on the lungs. You are not family, so I cannot share any more details over the phone. We have a Hospital Trust data protection policy to which we need to adhere.'

'I understand,' Tom said, 'and I appreciate you helping. What will be done with her body if no one comes to claim it?'

'If there is no next of kin, then teaching hospitals can use the body for research, or we can use the body for transplants. In this case, given the cause of death, we will most likely move the body for cremation as soon as we can.'

'There is no next of kin. What if I were to pay the funeral costs and have her buried?'

'You will have to make a formal application, Father Morton.'

80.

'Bless me Father for I have sinned. It is one week since my last confession,' Tom said, as he knelt on the *prie-dieu.*

'Go on,' said the voice of Father Douglas from behind the screen.

'Father, my sins are... I... err...'

'Go on.'

'I got angry at one of my fellow seminarians.'

'Is there anything else?'

'I... well'

'Go on.'

'I have... feelings... for one of my friends.'

'What kind of feelings?'

'I have... romantic feelings.'

'Is this friend a boy that you know?'

'Yes, Father.'

'Thomas, it is known.'

'I'm sorry, I don't understand.'

'It is known.'

'What is?'

'True faith is the realisation that we are loved despite being unlovable. The Church needs priests who are broken, in pain, tortured by their love of God and the urges of biology. If we were not so, how could we relate to the rest of the world?'

'Fuck you, and fuck the damn Church,' Thomas spat.

'One day, you will be a fine priest.'

'How?' Tom cried. 'This is torture!'

'Did you leave someone behind?' the voice of the confessional box asked.

'I fell in love, panicked, ran out on him, and came here to hide. I haven't spoken to him since.'

'Time is a great healer.'

'I don't think this will ever heal,' Tom said. 'I'm not sure I want it to.'

'In time, you will move on,' the unseen Father Douglas said. 'Friendships with other priests are not uncommon, only take care not to be seen as a couple. Be discreet. One day, we hope the wider Church will be more tolerant in these matters.'

'Why should a priest not marry? Where does it say in the Bible that a man can't love another man, that a woman can't love another woman?'

'Do you like life here at Ash Burrow?'

'I love it here.'

'It feels like home?'

'It feels more like home than home.'

'I'm glad to hear it.'

'What about you, Father? How do you manage the conflict of love of God and the urges of biology?'

'I subordinate my ego to the greater good of the Church. I have a job to do, a vocation to teach and to train. While you are with us, Thomas, we will educate your mind and prepare you to be the best priest that you can possibly be. All of us are here to serve, just as Christ taught us.'

'But I want to sleep with men, Father. How can God still love me?'

'We are all pragmatists here at Ash Burrow, Tom. And I have a suspicion that God is too.'

81.

'It is unfortunate,' Tom told the ex-Saint James congregation the following Sunday, 'that we followers of Christ have to endure being targeted by toxic Christians, such as those protesting outside here this morning. I am sorry that you were verbally abused and heckled on your way in. I am grateful that you have supported me. I am grateful that you have supported each other.'

The crumbling Ritzy cinema was illuminated by strip lighting, the old projection room was boarded up, and the ripped seats still had numbers printed on metal tags screwed into the top of the faded upholstery.

'I remember when Screen One at the Ritzy was the main event,' Tom said, 'the blockbuster billing. It is sad to see this once proud building in such a perilous, dilapidated state. And it is sad to see our Church in such a perilous, dilapidated state. Like Francis of Assisi before us, our job is to rebuild San Damiano, to rebuild the church here in Bussell.

'The Blockbuster billing this morning is the story of Christ and the "Woman caught in Adultery," another narrative found only in John. Jesus is shown as the friend of sinners, saying, "Where are those who accused you? I don't condemn you either. Now go and live a life of love. Love as meaning, love as change, love as actuality, together these are the holy trinity." As the Letter of St James tells us, "Faith without good works is dead."'

'A friend of mine called Rosie died this week. She was a homeless woman, and she contracted TB, here in our town, which is staggering in this day and age. I am delighted to announce the formation of a new social enterprise, a new community interest company to be led in faith and hope by a board of directors made up of people in this room. I would ask that each of you think about whether you would like to be part of this. It will require you to give of your most precious resource, time. We will be getting out into the local community, not to throw the words of Jesus at people, but to *do* the things he commanded us to do—to love the Lord, our God, and to love our neighbour as ourselves, to love people like Rosie Brennan.

'Our aim will be to reduce inequalities across this town, to help the vulnerable, the marginalised, the lonely, those with the deepest social issues. We will work in partnership with Bussell Council, with other providers, other faith groups to care for refugees, asylum seekers, the homeless, sex workers, people with mental health issues, those struggling with substance abuse. We will operate with compassion and resilience, and we will be diverse and open to all. We will be Catholic activists in the true sense of the word—universal—but we will not preach, we respect both belief and non-belief.

'Love is not an abstract noun. Love is a verb. It is the person in front of us. Rosie Brennan helped me when she had every reason to hate me. Her brother, Daniel, my friend, committed suicide when we were teenagers, and I should have been there to help him. My faith has been dead and buried for many years, but now, now, it is alive. Let us pray, using the words our saviour gave us. Our Father, which art in heaven…'

82.

'I am sorry,' Steve said, as he stood inside the doorway of Tom's bedroom. 'I didn't mean for you to find out like that.'

'No. It's okay,' Tom said, sitting at his desk, scribbling furiously. 'I hope you and Sam are happy together.'

'It was just sex, Tom. For fuck's sake, and we used protection. It wasn't like being with you. I've got something else to tell you as well—I'm leaving.'

'What?' Tom said, putting down his pen.

'I've had enough. I can't be myself here. I'll miss you like hell, but I can't carry on cooped up inside this concentration camp.'

'Don't go, please.'

'You like it here for some reason, Tom. But I don't.'

The tears came, and they wouldn't stop. Steve put his arms around Tom, kissing him and holding him as he sobbed.

Tom was taking a shit in trap one when he heard the door open.

'Anyone in?' Alastair shouted.

Tom kept quiet.

'Come on.'

The shower started, and soon Tom was wishing he had said something as the noise of urgent lovemaking rang throughout the toilet and shower block. The question now was whether to keep quiet or to go for the flush and reveal his presence. Tom wiped his arse, flushed the toilet, washed his hands, and said, 'Carry on, lads, don't let me stop you,' to a startled Alastair and Fraser as they poked their heads through the shower curtain.

Inside the kitchen, Tarry was eating breakfast with Marcus.

'Morning, Thomas,' Tarry said.

'Morning, Tom,' Marcus added.

Tom was always bowled over by how beautiful a man Tarry was, and he was always bowled over by how nice a man Marcus was.

'Can I join you?' Tom asked.

'Of course,' Tarry said.

'Pull up a chair,' Marcus said.

Tom made himself a coffee and some toast and joined the two friends.

'How are things with you and our friend in room three?' Marcus asked. 'Frosty,' Tom said, speaking with his mouth full of toast and butter.

'Poor Sam,' Tarry said.

'He fuckin' deserves to be frozen out,' Tom said. 'He's a bitch.'

'Forgiveness is divine,' Tarry said, smiling.

The room went quiet as Derek strode through the door and started unlocking the padlock on his food cupboard.

'How are you, Derek?' Tarry asked.

'I'm good, thank you, Tarry,' Derek said, breezily. 'The door to the toilets is locked again, and I've had to piss in my sink for the third time this week. I take it there are two of our esteemed brethren committing the sin of sodomy in there. I see Princess Thomasina can be eliminated from our enquiries, that leaves just five faerie-folk suspects now that Sparkly Steve has fled the rath.'

'You're a cunt,' Tom said.

'At least I know what one is,' Derek said.

Tom flew at Derek, knocking the can of baked beans out of his hands and sending him sprawling across the lino-tiled floor. It took Tarry and Marcus to drag him away.

'Oh, by the way,' Derek said, standing up, dusting off his clothes, 'I took a message for you, Thomasina. Somebody called Peter rang this morning. He said to tell you that your friend Shirley is dead.'

83.

Twenty-eight years after her funeral, the memorial for Shirley Benton was unveiled in the walled rose garden, Bussell Park. The memorial was a cone-shaped cairn made from local stone, set at the centre of a circular flower bed divided into four quadrants. In each quadrant, roses of differing pink hues swept around the monument dedicated to a woman, to all women, murdered by men.

The memorial unveiling day was to be the celebration of a life. With Shirley's mum and sister, their extended family, friends, well-wishers, Tom read out the prayers and dedication, and then Bussell's Mayor pulled back the covers over the cairn to tumultuous applause.

Standing with Michael, Shaun, Pete, and Antony, Tom grimaced at the injustice that Gareth Hughes, the jealous former boyfriend, who had murdered Shirley, had been released from prison after eighteen years and was now enjoying his freedom while Shirley was six feet under. Children played, a string quartet were playing renditions of rock n' roll classics, and the wind rustled through the leaves and branches around the beautiful park that had been a spoil heap at the side of the west-coast mainline until the early 1900s.

'Lisa is here, Tom,' Antony said. 'I haven't seen her for years.'

'Her husband expelled Daniel Arundel from school two weeks ago,' Tom said. 'Apparently, Dan was being disruptive and in conflict with the school's mission and values.'

'Acting too gay?'

'Something like that.'

'I warned Headmaster Cooper what I'd do.'

'Which is?'

'Lisa and John are getting divorced. I'm ninety-five percent certain that he's boffing his secretary. Lisa deserves to know.'

'What evidence have you got?'

'None. But the nose knows. I can sniff out sin.'

'Spoken like a true priest.'

'What are you two plotting?' Michael asked, as he, Pete, and Shaun gathered round.

'Tom reckons John Cooper is having it away with his PA,' Antony said, 'and we are not sure if Lisa knows or not.'

'In these circumstances, I think it only right to ask, "What would Shirley do?"' Pete said, a wry smile on his face.

'In that case, nail the bastard!' Shaun said.

'Be as wise as a serpent,' Michael said, 'fuck the doves.'

'Yeah, Tom said. 'Time to pull the pin. Antony, you can come with me. You're always very diplomatic, not like these three muppets.'

84.

The deposit for the flights to Spain and the hotel had been due at the end of November, and Tom had had to ring Pete and tell him that he wasn't able to go, that he would miss the stag-do in June.

The clock ticked inexorably towards midnight and the start of another year. Alone in his room at Ash Burrow, Tom flicked through the numbers on his mobile phone, the birthday present to himself: his mum, his friends, the doctor's surgery, the dentist, the bank… and still he had room left on his contacts list, more space for the acquaintances he didn't have.

The digital reader clicked 00.00 01/01, and Tom began sending out text messages, wishing everybody peace and joy, and a happy new year.

Shaun responded first, 'Happy New Year, Friend,' the text message said, and the realisation crept in that Shaun didn't know who had sent it. Tom's number was unrecognised. He was an unknown caller, not present in Shaun's prioritised address list.

It was an earthquake moment. He was out, separate from the friends that he loved. Pete's stag-do would be a shared experience from which Tom would be forever excluded, and, over time, more events would follow until he was no more than a memory… Do you remember Tom? That lad that became a priest? Yeah. Whatever happened to him?

Would it be better to never speak to them, again, he wondered, to spare himself the pain of being the shadow of someone they used to know?

Tom decided that he would stay away from Pete and Monica's wedding, stay away from Bussell, stay away from men, that it was time to devote himself to God and to God alone. This was his promise, his solemn vow, a sacred resolution before the throne of the Almighty.

And he wasn't going to change his mind.

85.

Tom and Antony were in Tom's mum's house in the dining room, surrounded by the volumes and tomes collected over the course of a lifetime, paperbacks and hardbacks stacked two-deep on bookcases and shelves.

'I think your antics with Lisa Cooper may have backfired, Father Morton,' Antony said, as Tom read out the details of the solicitor's letter sent on behalf of the Catholic Diocese of Preston. 'Our Headmaster seems to be rather miffed at your intervention in his complex love life, and has no doubt picked up the phone to the Bishop's office to expedite your departure, *post haste!*'

'Thank God my mother is out for the day on a coach-trip with the Catholic Grannies,' Tom said, shaking. 'She'd have a fit if she knew that I'd been charged with Gross Misconduct by the Church. I get nothing. They are going to return my pension to me, minus income tax. Is that even legal?'

'You need a solicitor, Tom. If the Alt-Christians in the Bishop's office start to play dirty, you need to play dirty too. Screw turning the other cheek.'

'I just can't believe it… instant dismissal.'

'What did you think was going to happen after you led a revolt and started a breakaway church right under their noses?'

'They started it.'

'You called out the faith fascists, and they were always, *always,* going to get you back,' Antony said.

'I think it is important that we understand the attractions of fascism and the root Latin word *fasces* that signifies a bundle of sticks—sticks that, on their own, could be broken, but together are strong,' Tom said.

'Jesus, Tom. This is not a theology dissertation. They are chucking you out, defrocking you, leaving you unemployed and penniless.'

'We all, in some way, long to belong. We all need to think about what it is in our own Church organisation that we want to be part of. Are we looking for certainty, for collective strength, for freedom from freedom, or are we prepared to trust in a reasoned uncertainty? Do we walk with Christ on the waters of doubt, or do we stay huddled together inside the boat of organised religion?'

'Writing a thesis on Kierkegaard and the role of the individual versus the role of the Church is *not* going to help you to get your job back.'

'Kierkegaard was gay,' Tom said.

'Are you sure?' Antony asked.

'Why do you think he ended his relationship with Regine Olsen?'

'You think everyone is queer: Blake, Swedenborg, Kierkegaard, the list goes on.'

'We are one in five,' Tom said, 'not one in fifty.'

'We?

'Yes, we.'

'I am proud of you, for what you've done, for the risk you've taken. You didn't have to.'

'I had to. We both know that. And if I hadn't? Well, that doesn't bear thinking about. As for these snakes, their venom just makes me even more determined to step on their tails.'

'I love you,' Antony said.

'I love you too,' Tom said, 'so very much. I always have, I always will.'

'I've got to leave soon. You know that, don't you? I have a business to run in the South West.'

'I know. But my heart goes with you.'

'Blrrrgh…' Antony said, laughing, 'where did you read that slushy line.'

'I mean it,' Tom said, 'every word.'

86.

Tom sat at the back of Saint James' Church, mesmerised by the beauty, the mathematical precision of the building. He had walked past the entrance, sober and drunk, a thousand times. But, until this day, he had never taken the time or the trouble to venture inside the house that the Jesuits built.

Around him the theatre of marriage was taking place. Tom could see Pete and his brothers, all dressed in wedding suits, at the front of the church. He recognised the faces of Pete and Monica's friends, family, and neighbours. Michael and Ruby waved at him from their seat three rows ahead. He could see the back of Shaun's head and wondered if the girl sitting next to him was his new girlfriend, Isla. He saw Steve Fairfield and Will Scholes, lads from primary and secondary school that he hadn't seen for ten years. As the ceremony began, and, as Joe Gallagher led his beautiful daughter down the aisle, the enormity of how different his life was compared to his childhood friends hit Tom.

The marriage ceremony was perfect in every way, every detail in the dresses, the flowers, the readings, the exchange of rings, the photographs—everything was exquisite, which made Tom wistful for the experience of marrying his beloved in a building as wonderful as St. James' Church.

As the bride and groom made their way outside for the obligatory post-service photographs, Tom heard Antony's voice.

'Hello Tom. How are you.'

'I'm good,' Tom said, turning around, reaching out to shake Antony's hand, faking the smile as he was introduced to Antony's plus-one, Nick, a spikey-haired brand manager at a detergent company.

'Tom's training to be a priest,' Antony explained.

'Really?' Nick said. 'That must be… interesting.'

Tom nodded, 'Yeah. It's… interesting. How are things in toilet cleaners?'

'How's your mum?' Antony asked.

'She's fine. How's yours?'

'Are you coming to the reception at Bradshaw Hall?'

'I am, yes,' Tom said.

'We'll see you there,' Antony said. 'Do you need a lift?'

'No, I'm fine. I'm treating myself. I've got a taxi booked. Thank you.'

'Crusader Cabs?'

'That's the one.'

'You still don't drive?'

'Nah, not interested. If God had wanted us to drive, he'd have given us wheels instead of legs.'

'Jesus,' Nick said, 'did you just really say that? What about evol…'

'He's joking,' Antony cut in. 'We'll see you later, Tom.'

'Yeah, see you, guys,' Tom said.

As he watched Antony and Nick, the Prick, leave the church, Tom thought seriously about throwing a sicky and going home.

'You made it,' Joe Gallagher said.

'Hi Joe,' Tom said. 'Good to see you. Monica looks amazing. You must be really proud.'

'How is the priest training going?'

'I'm happy at Ash Burrow.'

'How so?'

'The first thing they said to me was, "Just be yourself."'

'We'll talk later, you and I. We'll have a drink.'

'That would be great, Joe. I'll look forward to it.'

Like a hole in the head, Tom thought, as he watched Joe make his way towards the sacristy.

'Hey, Tom!' Michael shouted from the church entrance. 'You're needed outside. Pete wants a picture with the boys.'

'Yeah, I'm coming.'

Tom took at a last look around, soaking in the ambiance of the square stone church that rose to a pinnacle pointing towards the sky, letting himself be absorbed by the almost Egyptian feel of Saint James', imagining himself as a priest in a church that held such a visceral connection between the earth and the divine.

Tom was out of drinking practice, and he felt tipsy after one glass of wine. The table plan displayed on an easel in the hallway of Bradshaw Hall informed him he was going to be sitting with Shaun and Isla, Michael and Ruby, Antony and Nick, and a friend of Monica's called Zia, who he hadn't met before.

At the bar, Tom said a guarded hello to Shaun, introduced himself to Isla, caught up with Michael and Ruby, all the while making sure he kept his distance from Antony and Bobby Bleach. As the conversation turned to stories from Barcelona, he made his escape.

The guests were called in for dinner, and Tom found out that he was seated between Michael and Zia on a circular table directly in front of the bride and groom's top table. Zia, a tattooed, pink haired, guitarist turned out to be a hoot, and, over three courses, the speeches, the endless toasts, Tom was grateful for her company. He drank considerably more than he was planning to, all the while keeping an eye on Antony, watching as he interacted with the others around the table.

The meal ended and the music began in another room. The other three couples drifted away—to the bar, to the bedroom to freshen up, to the outside seating area for a cigarette break, and to check the football scores.

'So then,' Zia said, sipping a double vodka and lemonade, 'what's with you giving Nick the daggers? Don't you like him?'

'I wasn't, was I?'

Zia raised her eyebrows.

'He cleans toilets—that's nasty.'

Zia laughed.

'And he uses too much hair gel—never a good sign.'

'Do you disapprove of him because he is gay?' Zia asked.

'Christ no! It's nothing like that,' Tom said.

'Really?'

'Really.'

'Do you dislike him because you're jealous?'

'Of course not.'

'Come on Mister Priest, confess!'

'Maybe just a little.'

'I knew it,' Zia said. 'How long have you lusted after Antony?'

'Oh, my God, forever,' Tom said, as he reached across to another table and stole their red wine. 'Always and always.'

'Does he know?'

'We slept together once, a long time ago. Since then, we haven't really seen each other.'

'I didn't know there were gay Catholic priests.'

'I'm not a priest yet, but there are *loads* of gay ones, believe me. Great men doing God's work. We try to be discreet.'

'Have you ever slept with a girl?'

'Yes,' Tom said, 'three—not at the same time! I have a preference, and it took me a while to work that out. Anyway, answer your own question, Zia, have you ever slept with a girl?'

'Lots. Men too.'

'And do you have a preference?'

'I prefer the ones who have a shower each morning.'

Tom laughed. 'That rules me out.'

'It looks like your ex and Mister Harpic are falling out... Have a look outside at the car-park.'

Tom turned around for a good nosey. He could see the facial expressions and the body language, whatever was being said, it wasn't going well for Antony and Nick.

'Weddings,' Zia said, 'they bring out the best and the worst in people.'

'You've been practicing,' Antony said.

'Fuck, I've missed you,' Tom said.

'You broke my heart.'

'I broke my own heart in the process.'

'What a mess.'

'I'm sorry that you and Nick fell out... Actually, I'm not sorry at all.'

'What are we going to do?'

'Probably, going back downstairs and rejoining the wedding would be a good place to start.'

'Or maybe, we could just stay here.'

'Nick paid for the room, did he?

'He did.'

'Let's stay here, then, dirty those sheets for a second time.'

87.

'I see your church has been sold,' Joe Gallagher said, as he painted the exterior of Monica and Pete's bay window with white undercoat.

'Who says?' Tom said, leaning against the front wall.

'It was in last night's paper, and, this morning, I went past, and it had a sold sign on it.'

The grief was like a dagger through Tom's heart—some arsehole developer was going to buy Bussell's monument to God, cut it into little one-bed apartment pieces, put in plastic windows, laminated floors, open-plan kitchens.

'Thanks for telling me, Joe.'

'It seems like yesterday, Monica and Peter were getting married in there.'

'It seems like yesterday that I arrived as parish priest.'

'Your man, Bishop Worrell, was on the TV and in the newspapers damning gay priests to hell, saying that homosexual clergy are child-abusers, that he is going to do a root and branch review, and fire the filth.'

The anger began rising inside Tom.

'I saw him too, Joe. There are two types of Christians: those who believe the debt of sin should be punished, and those who believe it should be forgiven.'

'How are you surviving, lad?'

'Day to day, Joe. But I celebrate the small wins. I had a letter from one of the St. James' dads who was trying to get his gay son into an evangelical conversion therapy programme, saying that he now accepts and loves his son as he is.'

'That's a result. Your friend was buried, I hear, the homeless lady.'

'Paddy Mulhern led the service, at Saint Cuthbert's. We failed Rosie in life, but we did her proud in death.'

'What about the big wins?' Joe asked, putting his brush down and facing Tom.

'What do you mean?' Tom replied.

'Why did you come and see me?'

'I was just passing by… Okay, I wanted to chat with you.'

'You already know what you need to do, don't you? It's time the world heard the truth about Bishop Derek Worrell.'

88.

Tom was in the kitchen, sitting on an orange plastic chair texting Antony, planning their next date. Tarry Flynn was frying eggs and Alastair Denton was guzzling chilli and rice. Tarry's CD player was on the windowsill playing Stereophonics.

'Messaging your boyfriend, Moron?' Derek Worrell said, as he burst through the door.

'The last time someone called me that name, I was about ten,' Tom said. 'Fuck off, Derek.'

Worrell's face turned crimson.

'I'm going for a shower,' Tom said. 'I'm not staying in the same room as this arsehole.'

Tom got undressed in his bedroom, wrapped a towel around his waist, took his shampoo and shower gel, locked his bedroom, and padded across the carpet to the showers and toilets. He chose the shower next to the door, the one furthest away from the two toilet cubicles, turned on the tap, drew the curtain around him, and absorbed the delicious heat as the warm water cascaded down his body.

He heard the door open, heard the lock snap into place, and then there was an explosion of pain in his head, and he was in the shower tray being kicked and punched. He lost consciousness, and, when he awoke, there was blood everywhere and he was being anally raped.

'Stop,' Tom whispered.

'Fucking queer bastard,' his attacker said. It was Derek Worrell's voice.

When the assault finally ended, Tom was left in a heap, the water still running.

It was Paul Doherty who found Tom and raised the alarm. The others: Paddy, Sam, Alastair, Tarry, Marcus, and Fraser did what they could to help.

Tom was taken by ambulance to Saint Helen's General Hospital. For a reason that he could not explain afterwards, Tom covered for Worrell, telling the disbelieving doctors and nurses that he had slipped in the shower. He told Fathers Eden and Douglas the same story.

The other seven seminarians were under no doubt as to what had happened and by whom. Despite their best efforts, Tom would not change his story.

Tom cancelled his date with Antony, deleted his contact details from his phone, and descended into the bleakness of a lingering depression that lasted, if Tom was honest, for years, even decades. What Derek Worrell did that day changed the course of a life, destroyed a man's sense of self-worth, killed his hope, diminishing his capacity to love and be loved. Tom was left with a fear of enclosed and confined spaces: changing rooms, lifts, cupboards, cars, even confessionals. Tom was left with a fear of people coming up from behind him.

Tom was left with fear.

Fate provided another ironic twist when Derek Worrell transferred himself to another seminary, this one called Saint Antony's, near Birmingham.

89.

Police Constables Russell and Arkuss took Tom's statement.

'You realise that allegations of historical sexual assaults going back twenty-five years are notoriously difficult to prove and only rarely result in a conviction?' PC Russell said.

'And you never saw his face.' PC Arkuss added.

'This is a famous man. Arguably, you have a motive for wanting to smear his reputation given your recent dismissal from the Church,' PC Russell added.

'I agree,' Tom said. 'I know that the chances are small, but if I don't do something, he'll get away with it.'

'We'll keep you updated,' PC Arkuss said, 'but don't expect anything soon. The other priests who were there that day, who witnessed the verbal exchange and the aftermath, what will they tell us?'

'I would imagine they will tell the truth,' Tom said. 'I hope so, anyway.'

90.

It was the love and kindness of Dean Wesham that brought Tom back to life over a period of months and years. Cut off from his childhood friends, barely able to communicate with his mother, Dean, first as Tom's Spiritual Director, later as his lover, invested the time and energy in rebuilding Tom's shattered trust and confidence in sharing emotional intimacy with another human being.

It wasn't easy, and progress was often met with setbacks. Gradually, Tom, relearned how to love, and to be loved.

They shared an interest in art: Theodore Major, Laurence Isherwood, and T.S. Lowry. They shared an interest in music: Sade, Lisa Stansfield, Janet Jackson. They shared an interest in literature: George MacDonald, Bernard Shaw, Oscar Wilde, Chesterton, and Eliot. They shared an interest in theatre, film, dance, and performance.

They also shared a passion for putting faith into action, for proclaiming the good news that the son of God had stood up to power, had died, and was raised to new life, and that faith in Jesus Christ transformed lives.

Tom was invited to the evening reception when Shaun and Isla got married, but not to the wedding service itself. The reception was in Norfolk, which seemed an awfully long way away, so Tom thanked Isla and Shaun for their kind invitation and explained that, due to work commitments, he was unable to attend. He wasn't invited to the stag-do.

Michael and Ruby never married, and when their daughter, Lyla, was born in London, everyone, even Pete, heard less and less from Michael.

Pete kept in touch with Tom, checking in with how he was, judging the change in Tom's behaviour and demeanor to be a result of his inexplicable religiosity. Apart from his mother, Pete became Tom's single link to the town he had grown up in, the town that was in his blood, the town he loved, hated, loved more than he hated, celebrated, scorned, stood up for, and cherished with every fibre of his being.

Tom wasn't invited to Antony's wedding.

With Antony, he had fused. Their souls had locked together as one. With Antony, he had understood the phrase 'falling in love.' It had happened to him. Tom knew what that felt like. But, for him, it was a once in a lifetime event, that bond could never be replaced, not even with someone as patient and kind as Dean. And Dean knew that. He understood. Which made Tom love him even more. Just not in the same way as Antony.

91.

The first press release read, 'Bishop Derek Worrell, today, has instructed solicitors to take legal action at unsubstantiated claims circulating in the press and on social media. The false accusations have been brought by an embittered ex-priest, recently dismissed from his position for gross misconduct. The Diocese will continue to tackle the issue of sexual misconduct in an open and transparent manner. All queries to be addressed to Father Gerard Mallon, Diocese of Preston.'

The second press release was from Saint Pat's, and it said, 'Saint Patrick's Roman Catholic High School, Bussell, today announces that Headteacher, John Cooper, is to step down from his position and take early retirement. After a long and successful career in education, starting as a Physics teacher, before becoming Head of Year, then Head of Department, followed by Deputy Headteacher, and finally Headteacher, John Cooper has led the school to new levels of academic achievement. Chair of Governors, Kristen Bauer, says, "John has been at the forefront of embedding excellence across all areas of this school, and we wish him well in his retirement, which begins immediately. We will begin the process of selecting a replacement after half-term. In the meantime, our Deputy Headteacher, Abigail Horsley, will lead the school on a day-to-day basis."'

'Game on, Father Thomas,' Dave Stoughton said, over the video link. 'We've now got a response from both of our interventions.'

'I can't thank you enough for your help, Dave,' Tom said, taking off his glasses and putting the printed copies of the press releases on the table.

'Not a problem. I'm happy to help.'

'What happens next?'

'We go guerrilla across different platforms, that's how you pressure these organisations in the digital age. Nothing illegal, but enough to get them to act… or make a mistake. Then, we pounce.'

'You make money out of this?'

'I make some money out of this. But that's not what gets me out of bed in the morning. I enjoy what I do: agitating, provoking, annoying individuals, and corporations. Polluters, abusers, racists, homophobes, me and the team take on the contracts. Then, we bring 'em in, dead or alive.'

'Thank God you didn't end up in that river.'

'He sent you to save me, didn't he? Via the Queens Bar.'

Tom laughed.

'The next phase of the campaign is hashtag "let the laity elect the bishops,"' Dave said, 'but you need to do some work, Father Thomas. We need more content.'

'I'm not trying to bring the Catholic Church down. I'm trying to reform it,' Tom said.

'I understand that, but it looks like the police investigation is going nowhere, and your friend, the Bishop, is making more noises about clearing out the queer clergy. What would Jesus do?'

'Kick the ass of the radical traditionalists.'

'We're in the boxing ring and all we've done is tweak their nose. We need the knockout blow.'

92.

Tom's reintegration into society began in the parish of Saint Cuthbert's, working alongside Father Wesham as an ordinand, serving the church he had grown up in. The move delighted his mother, who got to see more of her son.

Tom worked with the sick, the elderly, the lonely, the disabled, with children in primary and secondary education, with youth groups, in hospitals, and in homes.

There were people he knew, faces and names he recognised at Saint Cuthbert's, and there were new families who had moved into the area while Tom had been away at Ash Burrow.

The harvest was rich, and the workers were few. Tom and his friends from the seminary: Paddy Mulhern, Alastair Denton, Fraser Andrews, Sam Hollins, Paul Doherty, Tarry Flynn, Marcus Jones, took the next step in their journey to becoming parish priests by being ordained as deacons.

As he tended the gardens at Saint Cuthbert's, Tom remembered Father Spence, and the gift of the BMX bike. He remembered Father Worthington and that day in the canteen at Saint Pat's Sixth Form

College. He thanked God for his gay priest friends. He thanked God for his straight priest friends.

Tom supported an elderly mother, Shauna Shaughnessy, whose forty-year-old daughter, Esther, had been seriously injured in a car accident. Esther had suffered severe head and spinal injuries and required round the clock care and supervision. Tom helped out with groceries, trips to the chemist for medication, helping to keep the garden tidy, anything he could to make life more bearable for Shauna and Esther.

Will Stansfield was Sophia's care worker, and he and Tom would meet on the occasions that they were both in the house at the same time. Red-headed Will was an opinionated, outspoken scouser with tattooed arms, and piercings in his ears and nose. He was a left-wing political firebrand and a vocal LGBTQIA+ rights campaigner. Will was different, exotic, fascinating, nothing like the men that Tom had been attracted to before.

'How come you want to be a priest?' Will asked, as they drank cocktails in a trendy wine bar.

'I want to serve God, serve people,' Tom said.

'God's bollocks, mate, I hate to tell you.'

'I believe in love. I don't believe in power. It's that simple. Why did you become a social worker?'

'To help the vulnerable, to fight the system.'

'Are you winning?'

'Do you want to come back to mine, Tom?'

'Yeah, why not.'

Three months later, Tom received a phone-call from Will, who explained that he had tested positive for HIV and was contacting everyone that he had had sex with over the past few months to advise them to get themselves tested.

The news was a hammer blow, but Tom thanked Will for ringing him, asked how he was feeling, asked what the doctors had advised in terms of medication, and wished him well.

The chances surely were remote, but Tom knew he had to be checked out, and he prayed to God, and to the Virgin Mary, that his test was negative because the worst possible outcome was that he had passed the virus on to the unsuspecting Dean Wesham.

As he sat in the waiting room at the clinic, Tom prayed decades of the rosary.

Listening to the female doctor explaining that he had tested positive was a surreal experience, hearing, but not hearing, the range of pharmaceutical options, the risks and side-effects, the probabilities of a full lifespan.

And then, he had to break the news to Dean, the man who had given everything to protect, love, support, and nurture Tom, spiritually, physically, and emotionally. Dean's test also came back positive for HIV.

Dean's patience, fortitude, forgiveness, humbled Tom. But he hated himself for what he had done to a man who deserved so much better.

93.

The gathering of the priests was in the rectory at St. Cuthbert's. Fathers Alastair Denton, Tarry Flynn, Fraser Andrews, Paul Doherty, Paddy Mulhern, and Sam Hollins sat around the mahogany dining table, drinking tea and coffee, eating ginger biscuits, looking like they were meeting to discuss a coach trip to Walsingham rather than plotting to bring down a Bishop.

Dean Wesham was busy, looking after his guests. Tom was scrolling through the latest announcement from the Diocesan office.

'We all made a vow of loyalty to the Bishop at our ordination,' Tom said.

'Derek Worrell was not the Bishop when we were ordained,' Tarry replied.

'It looks like he's tearing up our ordination vows. Every priest in Lancashire will have to reapply for their post, submit to a thorough examination of their moral conduct, then make a new vow of loyalty to the Bishop of Preston.'

'My loyalty is to God,' Alastair said, 'and to my parishioners.'

'He can't do this,' Sam said. 'It is contrary to every employment law in the country.'

'We are a little different as an organisation, aren't we? And Worrell is cloaking his "cleansing of the queers" with a plethora of Human Resource policies that outwardly pertain to be putting a stop to sexual misconduct.'

'If we oppose this, we look like luddites,' Paul said.

'Or worse,' Paddy added.

'All of us here,' Dean said, 'with the notable exception of Tarry, could lose our jobs.'

'He hates the Irish as well for some reason,' Tarry said.

'It's a good job you're not gay *and* Irish.'

'I saw him go into the showers, that day,' Sam said.

'Did you really see him, or are you just saying it?' Paul asked.

'I really saw him. I was on my way to the kitchen.' Sam said. 'Don't forget that my room was opposite his. I heard his door close.'

'And it was me that found you, Tom,' Paul said, 'although you probably don't remember. Then, I called for help and Sam, Tarry, and Marcus came.'

'Where did Worrell go? Does anyone know?' Sam asked.

'We don't know. He didn't answer his door, and no-one saw him again for two days.'

'I suggest we tell the police all we know,' Tarry said, 'every one of us. Worrell has miscalculated, because now we have nothing to lose. We have to do this together, as one.'

'It's a risk. You could lose everything. You all out yourselves to your friends, family, and parishioners.'

'Life's a risk, Tom,' Sam said. 'I agree with Tarry.'

'Gay priests united,' Paul said.

'It's probably about time I came out,' Paddy said. 'I'm fifty-one. What's the worst that can happen?'

'Fraser, you're being quiet,'

'It would definitely be easier to go quietly rather than taking on the Church,' Fraser said. 'As and when we are identified as… you know… gay, we'll have to fight for our pensions and payments in lieu of notice. But we are disciples of Christ, and easy has never been part of the job description. So, my view is we should do what's right.'

'How can we turn our backs on a fifth of the population,' Alastair asked, 'when we are the one in five ourselves?'

'And don't forget that we have friends and allies across Lancashire,' Dean said. 'We are not alone.'

'We?'

'I've told you before, Tom. Count me in.'

'Bless you, Dean.'

'We're all in agreement, then,' Tarry said. 'We go public, break our ordination vows, and fuck Bishop Worrell. Which is fine by me—I never could stand that cunt.'

94.

Upon the moors, the two men trudged, squelching through the mud and sheep shit in their walking boots and waterproofs.

'Define true faith,' Dean said.

'Not without God,' Tom said, 'a double-negative as a positive in the apophatic tradition.'

'You've defined trust, not faith. Try again.'

'I feel so extraordinary.'

'Dean smiled, 'I think that the New Order reference might go over the heads of some of our more elderly examiners.'

'Faith is the spiritual value. The E^3 equation of actuality, change, and purpose, is prayer, trust, and re-joining with God.'

'Good lad.'

'I hope that once I am ordained, I can be as good a priest as you.'

'I'll be sorry to see you go. You know that.'

'I won't be going far.'

'Now is your chance to explore brave new worlds,' Dean said.

'Nah, I belong here,' Tom said, stopping to take in the view of the wet fields, towns, roads, and factories, as the clouds rolled across the top of the hill.

'Don't limit your horizons. The world is your ocean-dwelling crustacean.'

'This place is in my bones, in my blood.'

'It has that effect, doesn't it?' Dean said, sighing. 'What are the 4Ps, Tom?'

'Follow the pattern, kenosis as prayer, the person in front, potential in people.'

'Define hope.'

'Hope is the social value,' Tom said, 'the E^3 equation is potential, forgiveness, rebuilding.'

'Define forgiveness,' Dean said.

'You, Dean.'

'That won't get you full marks in your exam, but I appreciate the sentiment.'

'Seven-times-seventy. Are we heading the right way? I'm sure we missed the turn back at that dry-stone wall.'

The rain was falling steadily now, a slow sustained drizzle that seemed to be permeating every layer of clothing. The water dripped down Tom's face and visibility was reduced to metres either side of them.

'Define strength as a Christian value,' Dean said, ignoring his concern.

'Going for a walk with you,' Tom said. 'We are in the middle of a cloud perched on top of a hill. I'm cold and I'm wet, and I'm being interrogated by the Saint Cuthbert's parish inquisition.'

'You've got important exams coming up. Do you know the answer or don't you, smart-arse?'

'I'd argue strength is broader than being a purely Christian value. It is a universal human attribute irrespective of religious or non-religious affiliation. Our perspective on this, Zoa is an E^3 trinity of pattern, courage, recontextualization.'

'Define courage, Tom.'

'Stepping onto water.'

'Good. You've got a link back to one of Christ's parables. That will get you more marks. Also mention the analogy of the Sea of Galilee relating to reasoned uncertainty.'

'Systematic theology, it's a pain in the arse.'

'It is what it is. At least it gets the grey matter working. Last but least, define love.'

'Love is real, real is love.'

Dean laughed. 'You might be better quoting *God* and arguing that God is a concept by which we measure our love.'

'I think secreting Lennon into my priest's exams would be a sublime act of rebellion.'

'Farting in the exam room—that's always a winner,' Dean said.

'That too,' Tom said, laughing.

They had reached a crossroads in the saturated pathway. A small cairn lay to their left.

'We turn left,' Dean said. 'Unfortunately, the next stretch is boggy as hell, even in good weather. The temptation is to veer off to the right where the path is marked and firmer, but that takes you into the valley and we don't want to end up down there. Prepare to get muddy boots and wet socks.'

'Love is you, love and me,' Tom said.

Dean said nothing.

'Love is an E^3 equation of person, agape, and reframing.'

'Define agape.'

'Transformation of pain into love, water into wine.'

'I would definitely link it to the Wedding on Canal Street, and to John's concept of the Logos as the living word.'

'I will,' Tom said, as he squelched through the muck. 'I hate it that we cannot be ourselves, that our love, our sexuality, is second-class versus heterosexuality.'

'We bide our time,' Dean said. 'With God, nothing is impossible.'

'I wish I shared your optimism. Would you marry gay people if it was allowed?'

'I already marry gay people, gay men and lesbians. I bless their union.'

'Really?'

'Yes, I just keep it low key, between them, me, and Jesus. Why should they be denied the blessing of their Church?'

'You're Secret Squirrel,' Tom said. 'I never knew.'

'Priest holes used to be hidden rooms in houses to hide from the King's men,' Dean said. 'Nowadays, we hide from the Church's men. And it stinks.'

'I can see the Pitt's Tower. I've never been so happy to see a stone phallus in all my life. Thank God, we have a change of clothes in the car.'

'Stop for a second.'

'Come on, Dean, we're on the home stretch. Keep going.'

'Don't forget, Tom, theology is useless with application.'

'Yeah, yeah, I get it.'

'Christ was the actuality.'

'I know. Come on.'

'One day, you will have to face up to Power.'

'I understand that, but right now all I want to do is get off these fucking miserable hills, get dry, and have a hot drink and a bar of chocolate.'

95.

The Bournemouth train sidled into Manchester Piccadilly Station. Tom waited near the automatic gates, searching for Antony's tall slim frame amidst the approaching crowd.

Antony was the last one to depart the train, and he was wheeling two large cases across the pitted concrete platform.

Tom waved, grinning like an excited child. As soon as Antony was through the barriers, Tom threw his arms around him.

'It's good to see you,' he said. 'I've missed you so much.'

'I'm not sure I should be seen in the company of a heretic ex-priest,' Antony said, smiling, 'I have an important position in the community to uphold.'

'Is that right? I was going to help you with one of those cases, but now, I'll leave it for your man servant.'

'You'd never believe what that man does for me!'

'Tell him to take a day off,' Tom said, laughing, 'because I'm looking after you today. I'm delighted to see the lots o' luggage. Are you planning on staying for a while?'

'Maybe I will. I have a present for you,' Antony said.

'Goody! I love presents. If it is a stick of Paignton rock, I may be a teensy bit disappointed.'

'Here,' Tom said, handing Tom a padded envelope. 'See what you think.'

Tom opened the package, keeping his eyes on Antony's. He pulled out a set of keys.

'I don't understand,' he said. 'What does this mean? These are the keys for Saint James'.'

'Yeah, I know. I bought the church for you.'

Tom was stunned. 'How?' was all he managed to say.

'I sold the business. I used the money from Mum's estate. I sold the car. I sold the house. Now, I'm a little bit broke. But who cares? All that matters is that I got your church back for you.'

'Oh, my God! I can't believe it. It was you.'

'I've got something to ask, Tom.'

'What?'

Antony got down on one knee in Manchester's busiest train and tram station, in front of hundreds of passengers, rail employees, retail staff selling sandwiches and coffee, and said, 'Tom, will you marry me?'

'Yes,' Tom said, taking Antony by the hand. 'With all my heart, yes. I would have said yes if you'd bought me a bag of sweets, never mind a two-hundred-year-old place of worship.'

The station erupted into cheers and clapping. Phones were held aloft taking pictures.

'What are your names?' asked a railway employee, who then repeated the information into his radio.

'An important announcement,' the station Tannoy interrupted. 'We would like to send our warmest wishes to Antony and Thomas who are getting married. Antony got down on one knee by Gate 7 and proposed. Congratulations to the happy couple. There is a free Cornish Pasty and a hot drink for both of you at the Penzance Bakery next to the exit for the multi-story carpark.'

Antony and Tom kissed, and, for one brief-moment, the world celebrated the love of two human-beings for each other.

96.

It was dark as Tom and his mother arrived. Saint Cuthbert's Church shone from within as they walked the path from the road to the porch steps, the light illuminating a stain-glass story of praise and persecution, hope and heartbreak, life and death.

Dressed in a white stole, smiling at the parishioners, waving to Pete and Monica, Tom took his seat in the heart of the congregation. He felt his mother's hand take his own. After Bishop Matthew Sangster had finished the gospel reading, the rite began.

Dean, sitting in a wooden chair beside the alter, called out, 'Thomas Morton.'

'Present,' Tom said, standing.

Tom walked the central aisle of the church where he and Daniel Brennan had been altar servers together, the church Laurence Spence had served for two and a half decades, the church Dean Wesham had served for a decade.

He stood before the Bishop.

'Has this man taken all the preparatory steps and been found worthy and competent to fulfil the office of priest?' Bishop Sangster asked.

'He has,' Dean said, smiling at Tom. 'Upon recommendation of those concerned with his training, I testify he has been found worthy.'

'In which case, I elect Thomas Morton to be ordained as a priest,' the Bishop said. 'We rely on the help of the Lord God and our Saviour, Jesus Christ, and we choose this man, our brother, for the priesthood. Please, everyone join in with a round of applause.'

Tom waved at his mum as the congregation cheered and clapped.

'Thomas, are you resolved with the help of the Holy Spirit, to discharge without fail, the office of the priesthood as a conscientious worker with the bishops to care for our Lord Jesus's flock?'

'I am,' Tom said.

'Are you determined to celebrate the mysteries of Christ faithfully as the Church has handed them down to us, to the glory of God and the sanctification of Christ's people?'

'I am.'

'Are you determined to exercise the ministry of the Word worthily and wisely, preaching the Good News and explaining the Catholic faith?'

'I am.'

'Are you determined to consecrate your life to God, to live a celibate life, to unite yourself more closely every day to Christ, the High Priest, who offered himself for us to God, the Father, as a perfect sacrifice?

This was the moment: the moment where sexual urges were surpassed by a commitment to spirituality.

'I am,' Tom said.

Tom knelt and placed his joined hands between those of the Bishop.

'Do you promise respect and obedience to your Religious Superior.'

Tom weighed the promise in his mind. A promise to God was one thing. An oath of obedience to an earthly superior was another.

'I do,' he said, after a moment's hesitation.

'Good, I'm glad,' Bishop Sangster said, chuckling. 'I was afraid there for a minute you were going to say, "No." May God, who has begun the good work inside of you, bring it to fulfilment. My dear people, let us pray, that our all-powerful Father may pour out the gifts of heaven on this servant of his, whom he has chosen to be a priest.

Tom prostrated himself before the altar, his head resting on his hands.

'Lord, give peace to this chosen one by the grace of Ordination,' Dean said.

'Hear our Prayer,' said the congregation.

'Hear us, Lord our God,' the Bishop said, 'and pour out upon this servant of yours the blessing of the Holy Spirit and the grace and power of the priesthood. In your sight, we offer this man for ordination: support him with your amazing, unfailing love.'

Tom knelt before the Bishop. With his hands extended on Tom's head, Bishop Matthew prayed.

'Almighty and eternal God. You are the source of every honour and dignity, of all progress and stability. You watch over the growing human family by Your gift of wisdom and Your pattern of order. Father, grant to this servant of yours the dignity of the priesthood. As a co-worker with the Bishops may he be faithful to the ministry that he receives from you, Lord God, and be to others a model of right conduct. May he be faithful in working with the order of Bishops, so that the Gospel may reach the ends of the earth, and the family of nations be made one in Christ. We ask this through our Lord Jesus Christ, Your Son, who lives and reigns with you and the Holy Spirit, one God, forever and ever.'

Tom took off his deacon's stole and put on a priest's stole and a chasuble. Then, the palms of his hands were anointed with chrism.

'The Father anointed our Lord Jesus Christ through the power of the Holy Spirit,' the Bishop said. 'May Jesus preserve you to sanctify the Christian people and to offer sacrifice to God.

Emma Morton came to the altar with communion bread on a pattern and wine in a chalice and gave them to the Bishop, who then presented them to Tom saying, 'Accept from the holy people of God the gifts to be offered to him. Know what you are doing, imitate the mystery you celebrate, model your life on the mystery of the Lord's cross.'

Dean took the bread and wine to the altar.

Bishop Sangster shook Tom's hand.

'Peace be with you, Tom,' he said.

For the first time, Father Thomas Morton, supported by Bishop Matthew and Father Dean, celebrated the Eucharist.

At the end of the rite, the Bishop prayed.

'May God, who founded the Church and guides her still, protect you constantly with his grace, that you may faithfully discharge the duties of the priesthood. And, Tom, may he make you a true shepherd, to provide the living bread and word of life to the faithful, that they may continue to grow in the unity of the Body of Christ. Amen.'

After the service was over, and as the congregation were helping themselves to the buffet in the church hall, Bishop Matthew, a cup of tea in one hand and a chocolate mini roll in the other, remarked to Tom that the Catholic Church had seven sacraments but only six could be attained—it was either the Sacrament of Holy Orders or the Sacrament of Matrimony. The two were mutually exclusive—there was a binary choice.

'I'm not sure I believe in binary,' Tom said, as Dean kicked him in the foot.

'Whatever do you mean?' the Bishop asked.

'I'm a trinitarian,' Tom said.

'That's true,' Bishop Matt said, tired after a long day, and thinking about his hour-long drive home. 'I hadn't thought about that.'

97.

'Ding-dong the witch is dead,' Antony said, waving the newspaper at his husband-to-be in their kitchen at Saint James' Rectory, Greengate, in the town of Bussell. 'How do you feel?'

'Sad,' Tom said, taking off his glasses and putting his book down. 'I don't like to see anyone's career destroyed, anyone's reputation in tatters. It didn't have to be this way.'

'Derek Worrell brutally, sexually assaulted you, Tom, in case you had forgotten. Then, he left you homeless, unemployed, and penniless, *and* he shut this church down. Why would you feel any pity for a vile, hideous man who tried to paint gay people as monsters when he was the monster himself?'

'It's one skirmish, not the war. We've got so much more to do.'

'GCP Incorporated brought that fucker to justice.'

'GCP?'

'Gay Catholic Priests—the secret seven.'

'Tarry isn't gay. That makes six.

'Seven, six, what does it matter?' Antony asked.

'It matters,' Tom said, as he pushed his chair next to Antony's and took his hand. 'I can't wait to be your husband. I am the luckiest man in the whole world!'

'I can't wait either. It's been a long-time coming.'

'It has, and I only wish that I hadn't been a fool for so long.'

'We got there, eventually.'

'I love you.'

'I love you too. Do you still want young… what's his name… to be the best man?

'Danny.'

'That's it, Danny. You want him to be our best man?'

'Definitely,' Tom said. 'You were gone for a while buying that newspaper, I was starting to get a little bit worried. Did you get lost?'

'I was in town, and I couldn't remember why I'd come out. So, I walked towards the park, and then, I remembered, again. I'm fine, it's probably just the stress of living with you!'

'For richer or poorer, sickness or health, 'til death us do part,' Tom said.

'What's that?'

'Just practising my vows'

'Do you still want Father Paddy to conduct the ceremony?' Antony asked.

'Yep.'

'What about the living saint, Father Wesham? Would it not be better for him to do the wedding?'

Tom bit his tongue before responding.

'I've asked Dean to give me away.'

'And who are Chris and Andy? I saw their names on the guest list.'

'Friends of mine from my misspent youth, selling trucks.'

'You want to invite them to the wedding *and* the reception? When was the last time you saw them?'

'Thirty years ago,' Tom said. 'They're both retired. I want to invite them to Saint James' Inclusive Church for the wedding of Mister Antony Keane, bachelor of this parish, to Mister Thomas Morton, also of this parish. And if anyone has any objections to our union in holy matrimony, then they can fuck right off, because we own the gaff.'

'I thought God owns it?'

'That's true, Mister Agnostic, the man that I love and adore. He's got the whole world in his hands.'

'I know what I'd like to have in my hands.'

Tom laughed and kissed Antony on the mouth. He felt the connection, the joy, the urge that came from loving one special person. An old line from the Bakerline office came to mind.

'Did you get plumbed in at the weekend?' Tom asked.

'I did,' Antony said. 'And Monday, Tuesday too, Wednesday is a yes. Thursday... aha, and oh my god, if I told you about Friday...!'

the end

In Memoriam AG

Father Alan Griffin was a gay priest, HIV positive, who was the victim of a botched investigation into claims of abuse by the Church of England. In 2020, aged 78, Father Alan took his own life. The allegations against him were not supported by any claimant, any accuser, or any witness. Indeed, these allegations were proved after his death to be no more than gossip, the 'brain dump' of a retiring church official.

The clear line of thought here was that a gay priest equals a child abuser.

A Particular Friendship was a thought, a maybe, a one-day, until the day I read about Father Alan in the news. Enraged, I wrote the book in 12 weeks.

I gave my story a 'happy' ending. I'm not comfortable with that as there was no happy ending for Father Alan, and since 2020, there has been no changes that I can see in the Christian Church. Gay people are still not equal to straight people. It is loathsome and it is hideous.

Until the Christian Church, in its entirety, rejects the false notion that homosexuality is intrinsically disordered the shadow of suspicion will still fall on innocent men and women. The rejection of full equality for LBGT+ people in the church is a smokescreen designed to protect the wolves dressed as lambs who prey on young girls and boys.

As someone wise once said, 'Blessed are those who hunger and thirst for righteousness for they shall be satisfied.'

We will be satisfied.

Eternal rest grant to Alan, O Lord, and let perpetual light shine upon him. May he rest in peace.

Amen.

Other Publications from
Castle Carrington Publishing Group

Also Available from
Perceptions Press
Publishing innovative, avant-garde (and occasionally provocative) transgender fiction and non-fiction
https://perceptionspress.ca/

Trans Deus (2020)
The Queer Testament Book 1
Paul Van Der Spiegel
In the beginning was the Verb,
the Verb was with God, the Verb was God.
In her was life,
that life was the light for all people.
The Verb was made trans woman.
and she lived amongst us, full of grace and truth.
Her light shone in the darkness,
and the consumer-military-technocracy
comprehended it not.
We cast our votes on TV remotes,
crucified her live on Channel Five. (https://perceptionspress.ca/trans-deus/)

7 Minutes (2021)
The Queer Testament Book 2
Paul Van Der Spiegel

At the point of death,
lost to all we've known,
adrift from those we've loved,
what stories do we tell
ourselves?

7 Minutes is the story of a death—charting the progress from cardiac arrest, the brain's release of its massive reserve of endorphins, through the unravelling of personality, memory, and identity as the brain's consciousness-generating areas are hit by a tidal wave of opioid neuropeptides that are simultaneously being starved of oxygen.

Self-told narratives unfold and are re-contextualised, fears awaken, desires awaken, time is warped and regresses as the mind is trapped inside a dead husk, unable to communicate, lost to those it has loved and been loved by.

Those who have experienced so-called 'near death' experiences have described bright lights, meeting loved ones: but no-one has returned from behind that light to describe the process of dying. And so, we are left with either a gospel of redemption and condemnation, or its opposite, a gospel of cosmic resignation and the final extinction of personality. One day, perhaps not too far away, we shall know—or, then again, perhaps not.

7 Minutes is the collage of stories and half-truths that our protagonists' collapsing neural networks narrate as the brain asphyxiates—light and dark, fact and fiction, actuality and narrative—until the final arrival at the truth of an earthly existence. *7 Minutes* is a head fuck. But after you've read it, I hope you can celebrate being alive. (https://perceptionspress.ca/7-minutes/)

Parably Not (2021)
The Queer Testament Book 3
Paul Van Der Spiegel

Parably Not is Book 3 of the *Will2Love Series*.

William Blake wrote in the preface to *Jerusalem The Emanation of the Giant Albion* of his desire to "speak to future generations by a Sublime Allegory." One could also argue that the miracles and the parables of Christ are metaphors, and one of the errors of the religion that bears their name is trampling sublime allegory beneath the heel of process and doctrine.

If *Trans Deus* is Mark, if *7 Minutes* is Matthew, then *Parably Not* is Lucy with the dynamic of "Q Source" thrown in for good measure. "Q" is not a ridiculous conspiracy theory cooked up to delude and obfuscate a population. "Q" is the theory proposed by biblical scholars to account for the shared content in Matthew and Luke, the oral "sayings of Jesus" tradition that is absent in Mark's account. We can only speculate on who Quelle was, but it wouldn't surprise me if they were a woman, or a group of women—a female gospel airbrushed from history by the patriarchy that followed.

As someone who passionately believes in inclusion and diversity, it was not too much of a leap to make my Q Source a queer source.

Having written two "text only" books, I wanted to emulate the Prophet of Hercules Road and illuminate these recontextualised parables, continuing the process I had pioneered as a child, cutting up my mum's copies of *Woman's Own* and pasting the chosen pages into my scrapbook.

"We were worried about you for a while," my dad told me as a teenager, as he recollected my enthusiasm for *Woman's Weekly*, sparkly tights, and walking about in my mum's heels, carrying her handbag. I said nothing.

"Poetry fetter'd, fetters the human race," Blake wrote. He's right. But there are plenty of other things that fetter the human race, too.

Our job as sub-creators is to unfetter, to explore, to challenge, to remake. I offer you *Parably Not*, as it is intended: scrapbook literature, unfinished, scruffy, feral, confused, uncertain; ready to be woven into new allegory.
(https://perceptionspress.ca/parably-not/)

Demon of Want (2020)
Freja Ki Gray

Izumi Yamakawa, a directionless twenty-something, is a part-time employee of the Oh Joy Toy Store. When she witnesses her manager die in a horrific merchandising accident, she discovers that he was a member of a Japanese demon hunting organization and had been eyeing her for recruitment due to her family lineage. Now Izumi, along with her trans girlfriend Maria, and a boisterous sword-for-hire, Rhea, get caught up investigating the various monsters and demons running the Oh Joy Toy company. Demon of Want is an eclectic blend of tongue in cheek urban fantasy, over the top violence, and gratuitous sex.
(https://perceptionspress.ca/demon-of-want/)

Can't Her Bury Tales
A Transfeminine Coloring Book (2020)
Iona Isabella Rivera

Hail weary traveler! Come closer! I don't bite…hard. You lookit poorly, come take a sit by the fire. Rest and grab yourself some stew I got cookin. Tell me, what brings ya my way? Adventure? Hearsay? Curiosity or plain ol' boredom? Well, no matter whence you came, I surely have a story that will peak your delight.

Perhaps a tale of a terrible tragedy? Or a catty, Communist comedy? How about some lore on fallin in love? Or a heroic tale of harrowing a horrible governorship? Or be you one that pines over Power? Maybe a familiar fable of family? Oh! Pardon my rambling. Come tell me your tale, traveler. What colors will you paint with me? Tell, was your way hard, rocky and steep? Show me. Perchance our stories crossed at some point. After all, we have more in common than our differences tell. (https://perceptionspress.ca/cant-her-bury-tales/)

Trans Fiction Available from
Stephanie Castle Publications
Publishing Transgender Fiction
https://stephaniecastle.ca/new-releases/

Tips (2021)
Newly Chronicles Volume I
H.W. Coyle

College is a time of discovery, when students find out just what sort of people they are. This is especially true for Andy Newly, a freshman who embarks on a unique journey of self-discovery, one that defies convention and brings into question the most basic aspect of his being. It begins as a bet made between student waiters over who makes more tips, males or females. To determine this, they agree to a rather unorthodox experiment. Though feigning reluctance, Andy accepts the challenge of taking on the role of female waitress as part of the bet.

The original purpose is forgotten as Andy finds that his female persona is more than an act, causing him to question his gender identity. His behavior while Amanda—the name he has given his female persona—does not escape the notice of his friends. Along with Andy, they conclude that their experiment is having unintended consequences. Rather than stopping, Andy uses the opportunity to determine who he really is and where he belongs on the gender continuum. In the process he discovers that there is a vast difference between sex and gender. This already bewildering situation becomes even more complicated when a male college student becomes smitten with Amanda. (https://stephaniecastle.ca/tips/)

A Lion in Waiting (2021)
H.W. Coyle

While serving as an observer with the British Expeditionary Force in 1940, Ian Wylie survives a massacre of prisoners. In its aftermath, he resolves to find a way of sitting out the rest of the war, safe from both the Germans and his responsibilities. At first, he finds sanctuary on a small farm owned by a teacher, Andrea Morel, who harbours him until an incident leaves her no choice but to send Ian away. With no wish to return to England and the war, Ian assumes the identity of Andrea's sister, Diane Lambert, and accepts an offer to teach at a Catholic girls' school in Normandy. His efforts to turn his back on the war are frustrated by a local businessman who enlists Ian's aid in passing intelligence on German activities in Normandy to the Allies as well as by a group of schoolgirls who take it upon themselves to fight for the liberation of France. (https://stephaniecastle.ca/a-lion-in-waiting/)

The Legend of Alfhildr (2020)
HW. Coyle and Jennifer Ellis

For generations, a legend spoke of a young Viking girl who led a Saxon-Dane army against a usurper. The story was passed from storyteller to storyteller, who freely embellished the feats of Alfhildr as they sought to entertain and enthrall their audiences in the great halls of their lords and masters. Some claimed she had been raised by a wolf, others that she was a witch. The truth was vastly different.

But before she became a legend, Alfhildr was a flesh and blood person with a family, a past, and a secret. With the passing of time, all but the legend was lost from living memory until an archeologist stumbles upon something he has not been expecting. Bit by bit, Professor Bannon and his students come to realize that the legend once thought to be little more than a myth could be grounded in history. He also begins to suspect one of the students participating in the dig has a secret that links her to both the discoveries they are making and the legend. (https://stephaniecastle.ca/legend-of-alfhildr/)

Flipping (2020)
It cost him nothing, but it cost her everything.
Forest J. Handford

Born on a space station, Samir Zeka was raised Muslim, observes a Halal diet, fasts during Ramadan, and prays 5 times every day. An introvert, he mostly stuck to his work, his home, his family, and his church community, until the day he decided to push beyond his comfort zone and attend a party that would forever change his life. Intending to look his best for the party, Samir searched his neural link "mesh" for random looks until he came across one that suited him. After some fine-tuning, he "flipped" to the persona of Samantha, a late 30s East Asian, cat-eared woman with shoulder-length purple hair. At the party, Samantha meets Anna, someone who will change Samantha's perceptions of herself and transform both of their lives. (https://stephaniecastle.ca/flipping/)

The Elysian Project
A Story of Betrayal and Payback (2019)
D. Axt

The Elysian Project is an expertly written, fast paced action thriller with a twist. It follows US marine scout sniper, Brent Chandler, his surviving teammate, Lyle, and his adopted father (the Gunny), as they go after those responsible for betraying Brent's sniper team during a military operation in Haditha, Iraq. Chandler's betrayal didn't just change the lives of his U.S. Marine sniper team forever. It set him on a path of unimaginable discovery. His quest for the truth and revenge quickly goes awry, drawing the attention of billionaire Stanley Tivador and the DOJ-FBI cabal he controls. The chase is on, from northern Minnesota's Superior National Forest to the Canary Islands. With help from the Gunny, his crotchety, retired Marine father, and Staiski, his friend and former sniper teammate, Chandler uncovers a terrorist plot of carnage inconceivable in magnitude and in lives lost. With seconds remaining, they risk everything to stop The Elysian Project. (https://stephaniecastle.ca/the-elysian-project/)

Partnership
A Novel about Friendship, Love, Family and Geder Transition (2019)
Stephanie Castle
Edited and preface by Margot Wilson

What happens when a lawyer, the son of a prominent Vancouver family, and a baker, the son of a devoted Catholic family who moved from Italy to Montreal following WWII, team up while going through gender reassignment? This humorous, yet serious, depiction of two families coping with gender dysphoria and the challenges of keeping family relationships intact addresses both legal and religious issues. The depiction and commentary on a range of human personalities in the hands of the author are both perceptive and entertaining. The underlying accuracy of this fictional story depends on the author's personal experience as a transgender woman and as a counselor in the transgender community in Vancouver. (https://stephaniecastle.ca/partnership/)

Far Side of the Moon
A Novel about the Life of a Trans Child (2019)
Stephanie Castle
Edited and preface by Margot Wilson

In Far Side of the Moon, Marjorie Burton and her husband, Jack, demonstrate all the attributes needed to help their child, Jenna, through a successful male to female gender transition. For children raised in an era when the condition of gender dysphoria was unknown, when anything unusual or unexplained was written off as a sexual aberration, it is small wonder that children, like the author, kept their feelings hidden out of shame and fear. Fortunately, that is not what happens with Jenna.
(https://stephaniecastle.ca/far-side-of-the-moon-a-novel-about-the-life-of-a-trans-child/)

LGBTQ Fiction Available from
All Genders Press
Publishing LGBTQ+ fiction and non-fiction
https://perceptionspress.ca/

Rise of the Magical Three (2021)
House of Phoenix Chronicles Book I
Wilhelm P. Oster

Raised by a mysterious grandmother and believing their parents to be dead, Roslynn and her older identical twin brothers, Oliver and Ethan, had only read of magical beings and creatures. But, transitioning into young adulthood, the three embark on an incredible journey as they are introduced to the riddles of their family's past that will forever change who they are and are yet to become. As the three siblings discover the ways of the magical arts, they quickly learn that they are not alone in their quest. Finding help when and where they least expect, the three develop friendships, confront the darkness, work together to save their family from an ancient curse, and learn of a mysterious and ancient bloodline that will forever shape the fabric of time and love. Their fight becomes more significant than even they had anticipated and forces them to make decisions about whether they can effectively save the world, the multiple realms, and magic as they know it. Learning that magic is driven by passion, knowledge, bloodline, and time, will they be the ones to save time, or will they become mere echoes of time? (https://allgenderspress.ca/echoes-of-time/)

Transgender Life Stories Available from
TransGender Publishing
Publishing Transgender Life Stories and Non-fiction
https://transgenderpublishing.ca/

Inspired
A Guide to Becoming Your True and Authentic Self (2021)
Stella Paris

Inspired is about being your true and authentic self, of overcoming challenge, embracing change, and becoming all that you can be—not in spite of change but *because* of it. We have all been through a momentous period with Covid and lockdowns, and many of us have struggled with issues around mental health, negotiating our changed world, and questioning life's purpose. Now, as the world slowly comes to a new normal, with old freedoms regained, many in a new form that require an altered way of thinking about the familiar, I believe that transgender people can inspire non-transgender people to embrace change and understand that thinking about things in a new way is OK. It's healthy and can lead to greater satisfaction with life. The lesson to be learned here is the importance of being one's authentic self. (https://transgenderpublishing.ca/inspired/)

My Life Inside the Chrysalis (2021)
The Chrysalis Series Book I
S. Jane Hill

My Life Inside the Chrysalis is an autobiography about what molded me from birth to transition to the present. It is a sometimes brutal, often philosophical, story of my life and that which molded me into the true self I am today…the strong woman that I have become.
(https://transgenderpublishing.ca/my-life-inside-the-chrysalis/)

A Trans Feminist's Past (2021)
Forest Handford

Forest Handford was brought up male, but never felt comfortable with that gender. As early as preschool, it was clear that she had interests and habits that were considered feminine. While Forest has supportive parents, they didn't have the knowledge to alert them that she was transgender, a word that wasn't even widely known until long after Forest was an adult.

What little information Forest found about being trans was misleading and harmful. It took cosplaying her favorite Dr. Who character, Clara Oswald, in 2018 for her to find acceptance in feminine clothes. Forest soon discovered that she met the definition of transgender. For a short time, Forest considered herself genderfluid because she didn't believe transition was possible due to misinformation she had been taught to believe. A non-binary friend of Forest's mentioned that their therapist had recommended that they try hormone replacement therapy (HRT). Curious why a therapist would make such a recommendation, Forest did some research that revealed that not only was transition possible for her but that trying a small dose of HRT was a safe way to determine if it could help with her gender dysphoria.

Forest's transition began when trans rights were under attack in her state of residence (Massachusetts). In 2018, Forest knew multiple trans folk who were fired due to their gender identity. Forest had to balance her trans rights advocacy against her safety as a frequent business traveler to Egypt, where being LGBT comes with a 10-year prison sentence.

Forest's memoir covers details of her life and the historical context in which it has been lived. Many of the stories in this book reveal the challenges of being feminine. While those challenges were painful, and some aspects of transitioning during her midlife were difficult, she values the views she has had on both sides of male privilege. She uses this rare perspective as an analogy for her understanding of white privilege.

While many trans stories exist, Forest's perspectives as an Eagle Scout, as somebody who lived in Egypt, and someone who transitioned while in a management position, bring new dimensions to the space, further illustrating that there is no single trans narrative.(https://transgenderpublishing.ca/a-trans-feminists-past/)

Triple Trans
One Woman's Journey to Freedom (2021)
Rose Barkhimer

For me, *Triple Trans* means:
Transgender, the knowledge that one has been born with the incorrect physical body,
Transverse myelitis, a neurological affliction that was a catalyst in my decision to change gender and,
Transition, the process of change.

It is my hope that *Triple Trans* finds its way to at least one individual who is wrestling with the conundrum that is gender dysphoria and that my story helps them to understand their own journey. I also hope that my story will explain to the general public the experiences of one transgender individual and demonstrate that, despite our differences, we are all human beings struggling with life's journey.
(https://transgenderpublishing.ca/triple-trans-one-womans-journey-to-freedom/).

Journey of a Lifetime (2021)
Karen M. Vaughn

For all of her life, Karen has struggled with gender dysphoria and her true identity. Frightened, confused, and tired of living a lie, she embarks on a journey—one that will change her life, her marriage, and the world she thought she knew. This is her story of coming to terms with who she really is, her struggles to find her way, and the life-altering changes that came along with her journey.
(https://transgenderpublishing.ca/journey-of-a-lifetime/)

Before My Warranty Runs Out
Human, Transgender and Environmental Rights Advocate (2021)
Joanna (Sister Mary Elizabeth) Clark and Margot Wilson

Joanna (Sister Mary Elizabeth) Clark is an elder trans woman and advocate. During the 1980s and 1990s she was an LGBTQ+ activist and speaker. She was the first person to serve as a man in the US navy and as a woman in the US army. Later, as Sister Mary Elizabeth, she was the driving force behind the AIDS Education and Global Information System (AEGIS) database. These days, her focus is primarily on environmental activism. *Before My Warranty Runs Out* is a personal narrative that recounts Joanna's life experiences.
(https://transgenderpublishing.ca/before-my-warranty-runs-out/)

TRANScestors
Navigating LGBTQ+ Aging, Illness and End of Life Decisions (2020)
Volume I: Generations of Hope
Edited by Jude Patton and Margot Wilson

This volume (and the ones that follow) have been in the works for some time. What finally emerges after many months of assiduous advertising, recruiting, editing, and organizing is a volume of intimate, nuanced, and heartfelt stories that reflect the wide diversity in the ways in which trans, non-binary, and Two-Spirit people have come to recognize, signify, embody, and celebrate their difference as their authentic selves. Moreover, with an increasing emphasis on the experiences of trans youth, elders constitute a routinely overlooked, disregarded, and/or silenced segment of the community. In response, this volume documents the myriad ways in which trans elders are coming to terms with the real-life challenges of aging, illness, and end of life decision-making.

TRANScestors is planned as a series of edited volumes that address the issues of LGBTQ+ aging, illness, and end of life decision-making and will be published by TransGender Publishing. Additional volumes include: Volume II: Generations of Change, Volume III: Generations of Pride, and Volume III: Generations of Challenge. (https://transgenderpublishing.ca/life-trips/)

TRANScestors
Navigating LGBTQ+ Aging, Illness and End of Life Decisions (2020)
Volume II: Generations of Change
Edited by Jude Patton and Margot Wilson

Generations of Change is the second volume in the TRANScestors series. These stories are, by turn, heartfelt, revealing, inspiring, sad, joyful, humorous, irreverent, and incredibly varied. And yet, strong, common themes of courage, persistence, honesty, resilience, and authenticity emerge clearly through the detailed recounting of the individual lives lived. Each author details those specific circumstances that have led them to the places and situations in which they find themselves today. On the whole, these are places of comfort, confidence, revelation, and affirmation. The wide range of attitudes, expressions, and worldviews held by the LGBTQ+ elders presented here challenge us all to carefully consider and adjust our perspectives on our own aging processes and, ultimately, on finding our own places in the world.
(https://transgenderpublishing.ca/live-trips-vol-ii-generations-of-change/)

We are God's Children Too (2020)
Rona Matlow

At the heart of Jewish experience is narrative. Around the dinner table, we tell stories of our families, recalling the quality of a grandmother's cooking, the kindness (or stinginess) of a particular uncle, the ways in which traditions have developed and shifted in our families. In synagogues and Jewish schools, we read the Torah, which is filled with stories of our religious patriarchs and matriarchs. And then there are the stories of Diaspora–the history of Jewish communities existing in exile for over two millennia. There are family stories and history books dedicated to our many wanderings. All of these stories help Jewish people connect to their heritage and lineage. What of the queer Jew? Even as more and more Jewish communities emphasize inclusivity and find a place for queer congregants, Jewish stories do not. The Bible offers no queer lessons, leaving queer Jews split in two; a Jewish heritage and a queer present. Enter Rabbah Rona Matlow, with hir queer *midrashim*. *Midrashim* are stories which approach Biblical texts from new perspectives, often exploring areas of confusion or possible contradiction within the Bible. Unlike Torah, they are not presented as factual, but as possibilities. Fictions which might yet be possible alternate histories. *Midrashim* bridge gaps. Rona's queer *midrashim* bridge the gap between the contemporary queer Jew and the (seemingly cisgender and straight) Bible, offering a way for us to see ourselves in our Jewish tradition.
(https://transgenderpublishing.ca/we-are-gods-children-too/)

Transgender Heart
Life Stories from the Inside Out (2020)
Bodhi Thompson Gardner

Transgender Heart is a collection of short stories that trace the heart-journey of a small farm kid, youth, and adult, from rural Saskatchewan, across the binary landscapes of life. A deeply grateful soul emerges, while exploring all the hidden nuances of the people, places, and things that held them together. Hidden comforts are revealed from the inside out, an inner harvesting of an authentic self. Their true self searching for somewhere to belong, finds love, acceptance, and authentic connection in the most intriguing and unusual spaces. Black hockey skates not only enrich their game but authenticate their heart. Spaces of unconditional love come from four-legged wild beasts, two-legged mentors, matriarchs, warriors, and elders. An RCMP officer who saw their struggle and offered a hand instead of handcuffs, gifts of nature, and family support abound: however, the biggest surprise of all is their most cherished treasure, the one thing that kept them alive for over 50 years. Transgender Heart highlights the courage and tenacity of the human spirit to rise up!
(https://transgenderpublishing.ca/transgender-heart/)

QdQh: Queen of Diamonds, Queen of Hearts
The Life and Journey of Michelle Nastasis, the First Known Transgender Professional Poker Player (2020)
Michelle Nastasis

QdQh: Queen of Diamonds, Queen of Hearts is the life story of Michelle Nastasis, the First Known Transgender Professional Poker Player.™ Michelle is courageous whether going head-to-head with the best poker players in the world, speaking out on television for LGBTQ+ rights, or marching in parades to celebrate being transgender. She is calm, cool, collected, and absolutely fearless. Possessed of fierce intelligence, Michelle is a beacon for younger transgender people. She shoots straight from the hip. She's blunt, loud, sarcastic, and occasionally irreverent. So, sit back and enjoy the ride. (https://transgenderpublishing.ca/misunderstood/)

Dancing the Dialectic
True Tales of a Transgender Trailblazer, Second Edition (2020)
Rupert Raj

Rupert Raj is a trailblazing, Eurasian-Canadian, trans activist, and former psychotherapist, who transitioned from female to male in 1971 as a transsexual teenager. Dancing the dialectic between gender dysphoria and gender euphoria, cynical despair and realistic hope, righteous rage and loving kindness, this Gender Worker tells us all about his lifelong fight for the rights of transgender, intersex, and two-spirit people—and his later-life role as a Rainbow Warrior working to free Mother Earth's enslaved animals. (https://transgenderpublishing.ca/dancing-the-dialectic-true-tales-of-a-transgender-trailblazer-second-edition/)

Glimmerings
Trans Elders Tell Their Stories (2019)
Margot Wilson and Aaron Devor (editors)

Tell us your story. A story about growing up before the age of global communication, at a time when the Internet and worldwide connectivity were still visions of the future; when inflexible, dichotomous categories of male and female, men and women, existed; when heterosexuality was the only sanctioned form of romantic attraction or sexual conduct; and when any expression of interest outside of these strict prescriptions was severely censured. Tell us your story about living in a time when those whose preferences, perspectives, and behaviours contravened the prevailing paradigms and prohibitions, when you had to negotiate dark, prejudicial places where fear, shame, guilt, despair, isolation, and a little bit of hope. Contributing authors include: Stephanie Castle, Joanna Clark, Ms.

Bob Davis, Dallas Denny, Jamison Green, Ariadne Kane, Corey Keith, Lili, Ty Nolan, Jude Patton, Virginia Prince, Rupert Raj, Gayle Roberts, Susanna Valenti, and Dawn Angela Wensley.
(https://transgenderpublishing.ca/glimmerings-recognition-authenticity-and-gender-variance/)

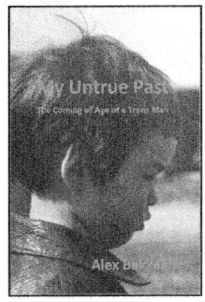

My Untrue Past
The Coming of Age of a Trans Man (2019)
Alex Bakker

Born the youngest daughter in a small-town family in the Netherlands, Alex Bakker underwent gender reaffirming transition when he was twenty-eight years old. A new beginning, in the right body, he literally put everything that reminded him of his old life into boxes, never to be opened again. More than fifteen years later, he has finally gathered the courage to face his past. In *My Untrue Past*, Alex goes in search of the painful truth. What does it mean to be betrayed by your body, to be immensely jealous of boys, and to decide that everything needs to be different?
(https://transgenderpublishing.ca/my-untrue-past-available-now/)

Girl in the Dream
Stephanie (Sydney) Castle Heal, a Transgender Life (2018)
Margot E. Wilson

Girl in the Dream is the life story of Stephanie (Sydney) Castle Heal, an advocate, activist and elder in the Canadian transgender community. The outcome of an almost four-year collaboration of storytelling, recording, analysis, and writing, *Girl in the Dream* is a first-person narrative that depicts in intimate detail Stephanie's transgender journey. An enthusiastic and accomplished *raconteuse*, Stephanie tells her story with the verve, passion, and expressiveness of a veteran storyteller.
(https://transgenderpublishing.ca/girl-in-the-dream/)

Feelings
A Transsexual's Explanation of a Baffling Condition, Second Edition (2018)
Stephanie Castle
Edited and Introduction by Margot E. Wilson

Feelings is written in a style that reveals Stephanie Castle as a woman of great confidence, conviction and humour. It reflects her attitudes toward life in general and transgender issues in particular, and definitively emulates the intricacies of her personality and character. *Feelings* provides a very personal view into one transgender woman's

journey, a metamorphosis that is as vital, authentic and significant today as it was when she wrote it. A complementary volume to *Girl in the Dream*, *Feelings* provides a comprehensive and in-depth view into the nature of the transgender experience based on the intimate, challenging, and often poignant experiences and perspectives of one singularly remarkable woman.
(https://transgenderpublishing.ca/feelings/)

Available now from
Castle Carrington Publishing
You have a story. Let us help you tell it.
https://castlecarringtonpublishing.ca/

My Dog Rigby
Just Like Me (2021)
Jan Olsson

My Dog Rigby, Just Like Me explores how we react to our dogs, and what this ultimately reveals to us about the way we treat others.

The approach we use to train and connect with our dogs can provide us with insights about how we can enhance our relationships with our partner, children, extended family members, friends, and co-workers.

My Dog Rigby shares personal short stories that everyone can relate to, focusing on themes shared by dogs and their owners, such as anxiety, capacity, aggression, trust, self-regulation, and patterning within the brain. While also giving practical training tips and advice, this book attempts to reveal who we are, who our dogs are, and the ways we are similar. (https://castlecarringtonpublishing.ca/my-dog-rigby/)

Pushing the Boundaries!
How to Get More Out of Life (2021)
Peter Jennings

Pushing The Boundaries! How To Get More Out Of Make Life features profiles of 32 people from around the world (many of whom are well-known and featuring many Canadians) who reveal how they triumph in life. We're talking people who have overcome uneasiness about taking risks, like daredevil Nik Wallenda; doctor-of-change, Patch Adams; intersex supermodel, Hanne Gaby Odielle; international clothing designer, Tommy

Hilfiger. Also included are Canadians like Marina Nemat, who defied certain execution in her teens at Evin prison in Tehran; McDonald's of Canada Chair, George Cohon, who persevered through 14 years to break into the Russian market; Rick Hansen, who pushed himself around the world in a wheelchair to raise awareness of people with disabilities; Katie Taylor who's broken the glass ceiling by becoming the first female Chair of a major Canadian Bank; Donald Ziraldo, who put Inniskillin Winery on the map by making Icewine into an immensely popular beverage worldwide; etc. As Jack Canfield, renowned co-author of the *Chicken Soup For The Soul*® series says in the book's Foreword, "Having the conviction to reach beyond your fears and take chances means you're ready to achieve lasting success." (https://castlecarringtonpublishing.ca/pushing-the-boundaries/)

Until I Smile at You (2020)
How one girl's heartbreak electrified Frank Sinatra's fame!
Peter Jennings with Tom Sandler

It's 1936. Take Ina Ray Hutton, the "Blonde Bombshell of Rhythm," add 22-year-old Ruth Lowe, who become Ina Ray's pianist. Ruth marries music publicist Harold Cohen, but he dies in the midst of debilitating surgery. Ruth is devastated, full of heartache, a grief-stricken widow far too early. Consumed by anguish, she pours her heartache into a lamenting anthem that becomes an internationally famous song—"I'll Never Smile Again"—destined to electrify the career of 25-year-old vocalist Francis Albert Sinatra. Ruth next composes what becomes Sinatra's theme song, "Put Your Dreams Away." And then, Act Two begins for Ruth Lowe: she withdraws from the limelight to become a caring wife, loving mother, society doyenne, and friend to many. Amazingly, this superstar has escaped the investigation and adoration that her life so richly deserves—until now. (https://castlecarringtonpublishing.ca/until-i-smile-at-you/)

Ruth's Wonderful Song
A Story for Kids (2021)
Peter Jennings

Ruth's Wonderful Song is a true story of a young woman who loved to play her bright yellow piano. She wrote a wonderful song that people are still listening to more than 80 years after she wrote it. Tom, Ruth's son, tells the story of how Ruth wrote her wonderful song and what happened next. (https://castlecarringtonpublishing.ca/ruths-wonderful-song/)

Coming soon from
Perceptions Press
Publishing innovative, avant-garde (and occasionally
provocative) transgender fiction and non-fiction
https://perceptionspress.ca/

PUBLICATION EXPECTED IN 2022
A Particular Friendship
The Queer Testament Book 4
Paul Van Der Spiegel
Tom Morton is a Roman Catholic priest who is devoted to his church in northern England, to his parishioners, and to his calling. When the man he fell in love with twenty-five years ago comes back into his life, Tom finds himself on a collision course with a powerful bishop, a man determined to pin the blame for the Church's sexual abuse crisis on its closeted gay clergy.
(https://perceptionspress.ca/a-particular-friendship/)

PUBLICATION EXPECTED IN 2022
Watching the Fire Catch
Carolyn Bell
Aurelia Kempe and her much younger employee, Jory Schneider, forge an unlikely friendship when Jory arrives on a small island off the coast of British Columbia, Canada. Surrounded and comforted by the beauty of their natural world, neither unaware of nor complacent toward the existing threat to their environment by uninformed and sometimes malevolent forces, we join Aurelia, Jory, and their circle of friends and neighbours as they live each day to the fullest.

PUBLICATION EXPECTED IN 2022
Eman8
Paul Van Der Spiegel
Eman8 is Book 4 of the Will2Love Series.
(https://perceptionspress.ca/eman8/)

Coming soon from
Stephanie Castle Publications
Publishing Transgender Fiction
https://transgenderpublishing.ca/

PUBLICATION EXPECTED IN 2021
A Different Kind of Courage
Newly Chronicles: Volume II
H. W. Coyle

How does a person go about rebuilding a life that they willingly tried to throw away? For Andrew Newly, this journey begins by realizing it will take a different kind of courage. His efforts begin by returning to where he and a group of friends bought into a crazy bet that changed his life forever. Together with those friends, he struggles to gather up the frayed threads of his life and begin the daunting task of building a new one for himself, this time as a girl named Amanda. Amanda finds that she must not only find a way of dealing with problems that are as confusing to her as they are complex, she must also come to terms with a past that seems to have no place in her new life. This difficult journey is complicated by Amanda's friendship with Tina Anderson, the daughter of an entrepreneur who has accumulated a fair number of enemies who prove to be as much of a threat to Amanda as they are to the Andersons, causing her to draw upon a past that she is trying to put behind her.
(https://stephaniecastle.ca/a-different-kind-of-courage/)

PUBLICATION EXPECTED IN 2021
Inconvenient Truths
Newly Chronicles: Volume III
H.W. Coyle

Living on the edge with nothing but a safety net woven from lies to keep you from tumbling headlong into disaster and disgrace is as dangerous as it is demanding. For Amanda Newly, it is an inconvenient fact of life, one she must deal with every day.

Amanda is a unique college student, bright and intelligent. To the casual observer, Amanda presents the very image of a young woman on the verge of making all her dreams come true. The only thing holding Amanda back from achieving this elusive goal is a past that is totally out of sync with her image as a vibrant young coed, for the girl everyone knows as Amanda started life as Andrew Justin Newly.

In many ways Amanda is still very male, an inconvenient truth she must hide behind a veil of lies as she struggles to reconcile her past with her future. One aspect of Amanda's past that threatens to destroy her chances is not of her own making. Tina Anderson, the daughter of a wealthy entrepreneur and one of Amanda's dearest friends lives under a constant threat of kidnapping, a danger that Amanda once foiled, leaving her vulnerable to retribution from those seeking to bring harm to the Andersons.

Amanda's journey toward a new beginning is one that is as difficult as it is contentious. For she must step outside the accepted norms, which define who and what we are, in order to discover not only what is right for her, but to build a new life for herself. (https://stephaniecastle.ca/inconvenient-truths/)

Coming soon from
All Genders Press
Publishing LGBTQ+ fiction and non-fiction
https://perceptionspress.ca/

PUBLICATION EXPECTED IN 2021
The Gospel of a Witch
Diana Bishop

The 200 angels who procreated with human women and fathered the Nephilim were cast out of Heaven. Their Nephilim children were ordered by God to be destroyed because of their destructive and corruptive behavior on Earth, but not before they fathered children of their own. These children of Nephilim came to be the witches, vampires, and werewolves of lore. It was generally believed by these supernatural beings that God disapproved of them, although they were three-fourths human and were left untouched by the purge. Lena's parents were such Nephilim offspring. They suffered under the same assumption until they met Jesus when he was physically among humankind. They became a part of his discipleship and Lena was born in his presence. They, and, in turn, Lena, were charged by Jesus with the mission of spreading the message among the Nephilim decedents that they were loved by God and were welcome in Heaven upon their death, contingent on the life they had lived. *The Gospel of a Witch* is a part of Lena's story as she endeavors to complete her mission.
(https://allgenderspress.ca/the-gospel-of-a-witch/)

PUBLICATION EXPECTED IN 2022
Secrets Echoed
House of Phoenix Chronicles Book II
Wilhelm P. Ostir

Ten years after the events that changed the very fabric of the Arcane and Mundane communities and set a new era of peace in motion, the incredible journey of Rose, Ethan, and Oliver continues. The Noble House of Phoenix, the most ancient of all Arcane bloodlines, must now forge and navigate new allegiances while living among the Mundane.

As the darkness claims control, the three siblings are, once again, thrust into the heat of battle. When multiple disappearances rock the Arcane community, the three siblings put aside their careers, differences, the spaces that separate them, parenthood, and time to join forces, working together again to save their families, friends, and the world as they know it.

In this battle of good and evil, the Magical Three learn of the Curpendulums, a most advanced form of magic. Will the Curpendulums provide the answer to their struggles against the darkness? Or will they prove to be the very weapon that the darkness needs to destroy all Arcane bloodlines and enslave the world? Will magic be lost forever? Lines are drawn, sides are taken, and new secrets are revealed, leaving all to wonder if the echoes of a dark past will remain or be forever changed. (https://allgenderspress.ca/secrets-echoed/)

PUBLICATION EXPECTED IN 2023
The Ignatius 7
House of Phoenix Chronicles Book III
Wilhelm P. Ostir

When RJ, a Mundane archeology graduate student, is mysteriously injured during a walk across campus, he makes a discovery that uncovers one of the greatest secrets of the Arcane and Mundane worlds and forever alters how he understands the battle between good and evil.

Learning the truth of Merlin's dark plans and discovering that magic can happen even for those born with no magical power, RJ now holds the key to stopping the destruction of the Mundane across the globe. As time continues to unravel and as missing relics of the past emerge, a bizarre, twisted fate in which the Knights of the Round Table are at the heart of Merlin's plan for total power is revealed.

RJ and his roommate, Dalton, set out to discover their college's history while meeting resistance every step of the way. RJ's journey quickly takes an interesting turn when he receives help from unexpected allies, including the Ignatius 7 and others.

Growing frustrated with the ongoing echoes of time, RJ must formulate a new approach to handling time's bizarre game by channeling the power of technology, mind, magic, and love to bring an end to the battle, save both the Arcane and Mundane, all the while listening to his heart, falling in love, balancing the complex life of a college student, and dealing with his estranged family. (https://allgenderspress.ca/the-ignatius-7/)

PUBLICATION EXPECTED IN 2024
Things are Not What They Seem
House of Phoenix Chronicles Book IV
Wilhelm P. Ostir

Shifting, altering, and replaying over and over, one timeline after another is acting up. When fifteen timelines act up all at once, a new, rebellious Noble Elder must calm the chaos and re-establish the balance of time, magic, and everyday life. Noble Elder grows into their new role despite moments of wanting to throw up their hands and walk away. Traveling through time and meeting hiccup after hiccup along the way, Noble Elder collaborates with six, headstrong Ignatius siblings, learning to navigate complex and, at times, downright awkward relationships with them.

Working together and, sometimes, against each other, the Ignatius 7 quickly learn that things are not what they seem when they discover a truth that rocks the very core of what they know about magic. Noble Elder, tired of the growing attacks of darkness, seeks the help of Arcane and Mundane alike in a battle between light and dark.

When magic stops working because of time disruptions, RJ, Amelia, Minnie, and Dalton return to help and must learn to navigate complex friendship with the Ignatius 7. Will their epic journey to find the Curpendulums, restore time, and bring normalcy to the earth succeed? Will time break the spirit of Noble Elder, and stop time altogether? Or will Noble Elder discover new ways to handle the challenges of life, magic, and darkness?
(https://allgenderspress.ca/things-are-not-what-they-seem/)

PUBLICATION EXPECTED IN 2025
The Curpendulums
House of Phoenix Chronicles Book V
Wilhelm P. Ostir
(https://allgenderspress.ca/the-curpendulums/)

The **House of Phoenix Chronicles** *is planned as a series of books filled with wizards, witches, fairies, elves, dwarfs, centaurs, mermaids, and dragons in the fight of their lives to protect their ways of life, their families, and the earth. The Phoenix siblings, Roslynn and her older identical twin brothers, Oliver and Ethan, embark on a remarkable journey of friendship, romance, hatred, and mystery as truths are revealed, challenges faced, and battles with ancient darkness fought. Bending magic to their will, Roslynn, Ethan and Oliver, step in and out of time, breaking the rules at every stage of their remarkable journey. Along their way, they meet friends from the past, present, and future, and discover an ancient secret that could forever change the fabric of history, including our understanding of Medieval times and the Knights of the Round Table: a curse sent by darkness to unravel time as it is known. One minute, magic was at its height, the center of life and the community. In the next, cities and villages lay in ruins, a mere echo of a time that was. Can the three siblings channel their family's magic, one of the most powerful magical bloodlines ever to live, for good? Or will their efforts backfire, leading to the destruction of all magical beings? Will they be able to break the curse that affects their family? Can they save their bloodline and the ways of magic? Will they help bring magic back to earth, or will they become the continuation of the curse?*

Coming in soon from
TransGender Publishing
Publishing Transgender Life Stories and Non-fiction
https://transgenderpublishing.ca/

PUBLICATION EXPECTED IN 2021/22
TRANScestors
Navigating LGBTQ+ Aging, Illness and End of Life Decisions
Edited by Jude Patton and Margot Wilson
Volume Three: Generations of Pride
Volume Four: Generations of Challenge

Studies indicate that LGBT+ people are still discriminated against in most health care settings and in long term care facilities despite advances made in the past few years in gaining more rights. Evaluating physical and mental health care needs, facilitating access to health care providers and advocating for clients' right as well as end of life decisions and planning for personal legacy options are important aspects of navigating LGBTQ+ aging. Having served as a health navigator for clients with chronic illness and offering end of life doula services to LGBTQ+ community members, Jude Patton collaborates with and advocates for his clients to successfully manage their health care needs. Jude is a proud, open and out, elder trans man, who has worked with underserved populations for most of his career, including LGBTQ+ folks, geriatric clients, developmentally disabled adults, homeless/chronically mentally ill and drug addicted clients._*Life Trips* is planned as a series of edited volumes that address the issues of LGBTQ+ aging, illness, and end of life decision-making and will be published by TransGender Publishing. Additional volumes include: Volume II: Generations of Change, Volume III: Generations of Pride and Volume IV: Generations of Challenge. (https://transgenderpublishing.ca/life-trips/)

PUBLICATION EXPECTED IN 2021
Taking Care of Angela
Angela Wensley and Margot Wilson

My name is Angela, and I am a transsexual woman. I have always believed myself to be female, even though I spent the first forty-two years of my life being socialized as a male. To be transsexual is no longer a new phenomenon, although many misconceptions still surround it. One thing has remained unchanged is the great pain and personal upheaval that necessarily accompanies the transition from one gender to another. Looking back now, many years after having had gender reassignment surgery, it seems impossible for me to have accomplished what I have. Changing from man to woman involved no less than a total restructuring of every single relationship in my life, with my spouse, family, friends, workplace, and my everyday interactions in society. For me, being transsexual is a beautiful gift, an honour, an evolutionary jump, as it were, to a higher state of being, one in which I am closer to God and to all humanity.

My personal journey can be likened to casting off in a boat without oars into a swiftly flowing river. Standing on the banks of that river, intrigued but not knowing where it would lead me, I had dipped my toes into the water, even waded out to where it was deeper, where I could feel the tug of the current. How I longed to be swept away by the river: however, my fears kept me from the test, and I always retreated to the security of the shore. Ultimately, spying a rowboat on the riverbank, I climbed in, pushed off into the stream, and waited as the small craft inevitably became caught up in the stronger current of mid-stream. Without oars, I could not return to where I had started and had little ability to control my course, though my direction downstream was certain. I was little prepared for the swiftness of the current, or the treacherous rapids and canyons that lay downstream out of sight. How easy it would have been to flounder in a back-eddy or to wreck on the many rocks that projected from the dark waters. Fortunately, with what little control I had over my course, I avoided destruction and travelled the long and lonely distance. Finally, one day, the current slowed, and I found myself past the mouth of the river, in the ocean that is woman.
(https://transgenderpublishing.ca/taking-care-of-angela/)

PUBLICATION EXPECTED IN 2022
Both Sides of the Great Divide
Nikita Carter
Nikita Carter tells her story about awakening. At 60 years of age, a series of shattering experiences led to her being broken open to the awareness that she was a trans woman, and she had to make the changes in her life to reflect that truth. Her life has comprised extraordinary experiences and people throughout, which includes being a musician, composer, educator, Artistic Director, producer, and trans woman.
(https://transgenderpublishing.ca/both-sides-of-the-great-divide/)

PUBLICATION EXPECTED IN 2022
Mr Winky Goes to Melbourne
The Chrysalis Series Books II and III
S. Jane Hill
Mr Winky Goes to Melbourne, the second book in the *Chrysalis* series, begins where *My Life Inside the Chrysalis* ends. Detailing what has occurred since, *Mr Winky* uses flashbacks to reflect on the time when the author first met her (then) alter ego and culminates in the lead up to and experiences during and after gender reassignment surgery.

(https://transgenderpublishing.ca/mr-winky-goes-to-melbourne/)

PUBLICATION EXPECTED IN 2022
The Boy Beneath My Skin
Charley Burton

For years, I have wanted others to read my story and hear my voice. I do not think that I am a unique person, although my travels in life have been different. But for many, my path will be one that is recognizable. This book is about the many journeys that I have taken to become the man that I am today. From a child born in a small rural town, who at the age of eight knew that I was different, to my path of recovery from drugs, alcohol, and food, and moving into my transition from female to male, this is a story of struggle, disappointment, and triumph. It is a story of digging beneath my skin to become whole. (https://transgenderpublishing.ca/the-boy-beneath-my-skin/)

PUBLICATION EXPECTED IN 2022
Out of the Cave
Emerging From My Darkest Moments into God's Eternal Light

I am a Black, transgender male who grew up in a fundamentally conservative Christian home. When I was 3 years old, my mother remarried. Her new husband was the pastor of the church we attended. This man was guilty of sexual and physical abuse of my mother's children and some of their children. Sadly, this is the experience of all too many children growing up in the Christian church in the Black community.

Members of the LGBTQ+ community have been and continue to be traumatized by individuals in the church, who guard the law but fail to live up to it themselves. I know because I lived it firsthand in my own home. Some LGBTQ+ people have survived conversion therapy and/or were subjected to electroconvulsive shock therapy in attempts to force them to change their sexuality or gender orientation. Others, like me, have been demonized, ostracized, shamed, condemned, damned, and judged by our Black churches, families, and communities.

Out of the Cave is the story of how I emerged from my early life to become a whole and resilient individual. Today, as a counselling professional, I am reminded on a daily basis of the importance of providing a space of hope and possibility every day. (https://transgenderpublishing.ca/out-of-the-cave/)

PUBLICATION EXPECTED IN 2022
Gender Odyssey
Journey of an Intrepid Androgyne
Ariadne (J. Ari) Kane and Margot Wilson

Ariadne (J. Ari) Kane is a gerontology specialist with Theseus Consulting & Coaching Service. (S)he has developed several workshops focusing on issues of gender, sexuality and health in the latter decades of the lifespan. Many are designed for the LGBT Community. (S)he has been a leading authority on gender diversity in postmodern America and has given presentations at many universities and institutes in the United States and Canada. (S)he is one of the creators of the Gender Attitude Reassessment Program, a workshop on gender for sexologists and healthcare professionals. (S)he co-authored *Crossing Sexual Boundaries* with Professor Vern Bullough. *Gender Odyssey: Journey of an Intrepid Androgyne* is the distillation of 40+ hours of recorded conversation that provide a decadal representation of an intrepid traveler who has forged an idiosyncratic path through gender exploration, variance and expression.
(https://transgenderpublishing.ca/gender-odyssey-journey-of-an-intrepid-androgyne/)

PUBLICATION EXPECTED IN 2022
From Shame to Freedom
A Gender Variant Woman's Journey of Discovery
M. Gayle Roberts

Born in England during WW II, Gayle Roberts immigrated to Canada in 1951 and is an UVic alumnus with an MSc in Physics. She transitioned in 1996 as her high school's Science Department Head and science teacher. Gayle coauthored the guidebook Supporting Transgender and Transsexual Students in K-12 Schools and is author of *From Shame to Freedom: A Gender-Variant Woman's Journey of Discovery*. Gayle feels strongly that trans individuals should document their life experiences. She utilizes specific literary writing techniques (creative nonfiction) to create factually accurate narratives. *From Shame to Freedom* is one of those narratives.
(https://transgenderpublishing.ca/from-shame-to-freedom/)

PUBLICATION EXPECTED IN 2022
Young Kid, Old Goat
Transgender Journey to Understanding the Man Within
Jude Patton and Margot Wilson

Jude Patton is an elder transman and LGBTQ activist, advocate and educator since before his own transition in 1970. He founded Renaissance Gender Identity Services in the early 1970s and began publishing *Renaissance Newsletter* in the mid-1970s. Jude started one of the first informal support groups for FTM men and incorporated these

into The John Augustus Foundation. Joined by Joanna Clark, these became known as J2CP Information Services, taking over Paul Walker's work with Erickson Educational Services. In *Young Kid, Old Goat*, Jude's personal life story and ongoing work is highlighted.
(https://transgenderpublishing.ca/young-kid-old-goat/)

PUBLICATION EXPECTED IN 2022
We're Non-Binary:And So are You… No Really!!!
A curated anthology on Non-Binary Identity
RONA MATLOW AND MARGOT WILSON
For almost two thousand years, misconceptions regarding sex and gender identity have abounded. Be it from the limitations of the ancient languages of Scripture, the apparent binary of sex in nature and human biology, societal roles established in Scripture and maintained in Western Culture, or for many other reasons, a binary perspective persists.

During the 20th century, some of these notions have started to break down. With scholarship surrounding the Stonewall era, more barriers have been broken. As transsexual, and later transgender, identity became more widely known, the binary of sex and gender was transgressed and transcended. Still, the binary continued to persist.

And scholars are beginning to take note. What was originally perceived as two opposite forms, one male and one female, shifted to a line segment model, with male at one end, female at the other, and a distribution of androgyny in between. Then, as time progressed and as this model was found to be flawed and limited, a new model emerged, one that recognizes both sex and gender as distributed in multi-dimensional space, with male and female each occupying only single points in that space.

Today, even people in elder LGBTQ circles are beginning to accept the notion of a non-binary identity and are adopting it for themselves.

This perspective is consistent with Scripture, history, nature, culture, human nature, human biology, medicine, and every other area of research that one might consider. Of course, there are many holdouts in the straight world, and in the queer world too, who do not accept this definition of LGBTQ identity. Still, it is here. This new edited volume, to be published by TransGender Publishing, is planned as an anthology that reflects the nature of non-binary identity through original works of scholarship, fiction, poetry, prose, and personal reflections, stories, and anecdotes by and about non-binary people. (https://transgenderpublishing.ca/were-non-binary/)

PUBLICATION EXPECTED IN 2022
Unconditional Love
Stories of LGBTQ+ People and Our Emotional Bonds with Companion Animals
Edited by Jude Patton and Margot Wilson

Our experiences with marginalization often affect our feelings of self-worth. While many people in our lives are unable (or unwilling) to provide the emotional support we need before, during and post-coming out, or transition, our companion animals never fail to see us as we truly are and never fail to express their unconditional love for us. No wonder we love them and derive multiple benefits from our relationships with them. They are woven into the fabric of our lives. *Unconditional Love* is planned as an edited reader that tells the stories of how the unconditional love of (and for) our companion animals has supported, encouraged, confirmed, validated, endorsed and sanctioned our authentic selves. Our reading audience includes those in the LGBTQ+ community who have found sanctuary and validation in the love shared with our animal companions as well as those in the broader community who revel in the company of our non-human loved ones.
(https://transgenderpublishing.ca/unconditional-love/)

Coming soon from
Castle Carrington Publishing
You have a story. Let us help you tell it
https://transgenderpublishing.ca/

PUBLICATION EXPECTED IN 2022
Being Happy Matters
Peter Jennings

Being Happy Matters is a re-launch of a previously published book *Why Being Happy Matters*. The updated Introduction references COVID-19 and how happiness can be an antidote to the stress and anxiety people are experiencing right now. The original volume presents interviews with people in Canada, the U.S., Asia, Europe and Australia, each of whom reveal what happiness means to them and why it matters. Readers will meet international PhDs who are actively studying the science of positive psychology (i.e., happiness). This book features Peter Jennings in conversation with 37 intriguing individuals, including John Robbins, heir of the Baskin Robbins empire (who tells Peter about turning down his inheritance and then losing his life's savings in the Bernie Madoff scandal, but still exhibiting a positive outlook of happy perseverance to life's reversals); Roko Belic, California-based Oscar-nominated director of the award-winning film "Happy"; Dr. Christine Carter, sociologist and positive psychology specialist at Berkeley University ; Rolling Stones keyboardist Chuck Leavell (who shared with Peter the joy he gets from working with his buddy former President Jimmy Carter on key environmental issues); Major League Baseball legend Shawn Green; celebrated super-model & businesswoman Monika Schnarre; Time magazine humour columnist Joel Stein; 84 year old Playboy cartoonist Doug Sneyd; Leo Bormans from Belgium, author of the respected "World Book of Happiness"(who explains what lies behind his discussions with global experts); and much more. (https://castlecarringtonpublishing.ca/being-happy-matters/)

Printed in Great Britain
by Amazon